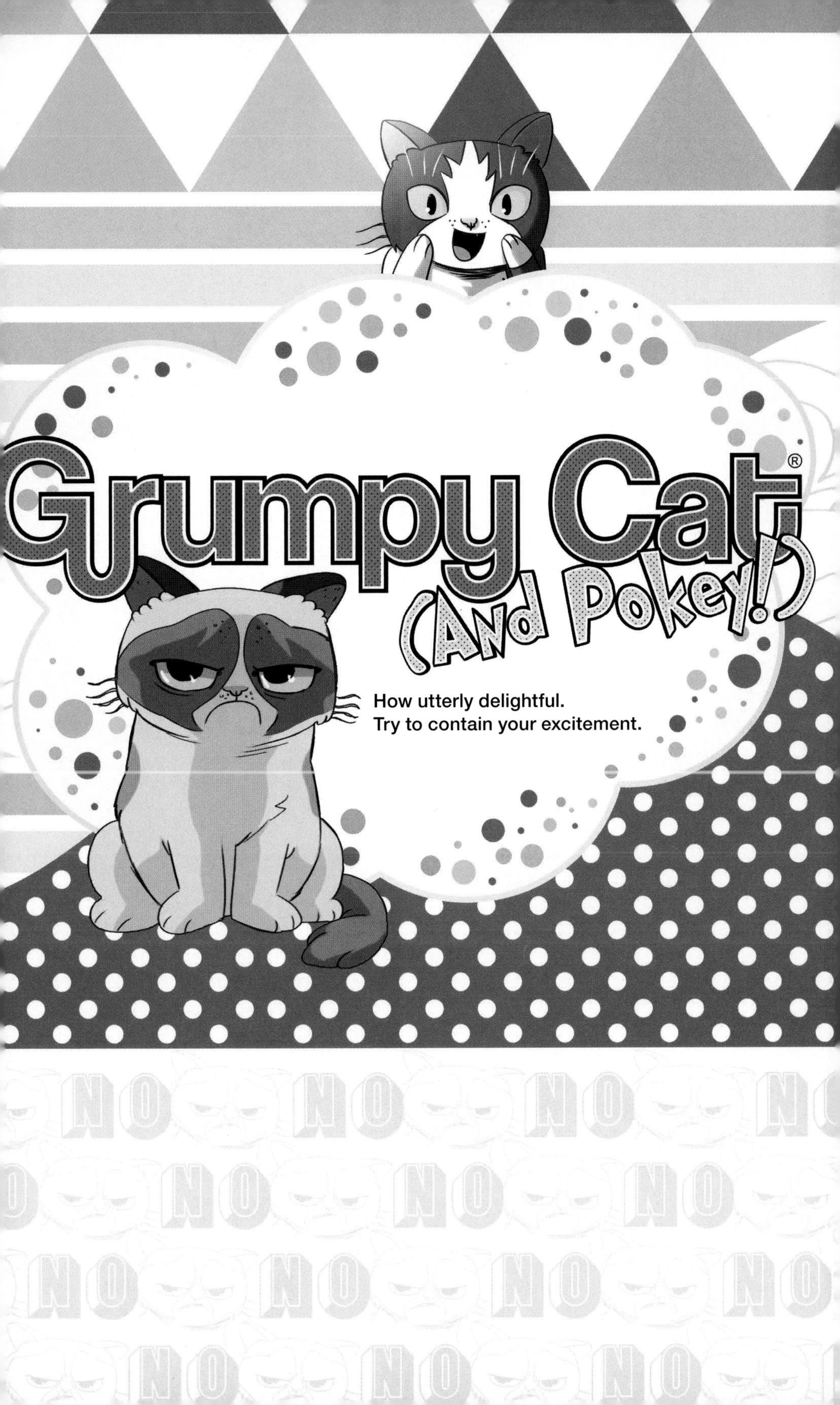
Grumpy Cat®
(And Pokey!)
How utterly delightful.
Try to contain your excitement.

# Grumpy Cat® (And Pokey!)

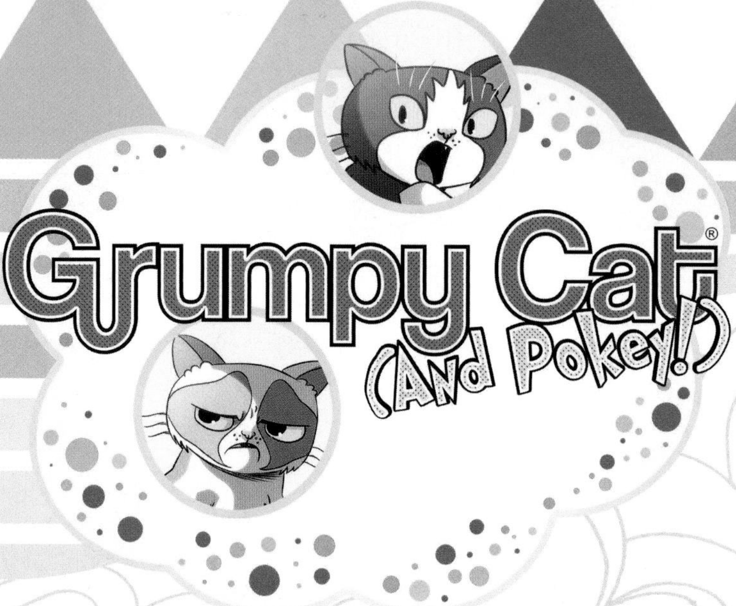

## GRUMPY CAT, HIDDEN DOGGIE

Written By Elliott Serrano
Art By Ken Haeser
Colors By Mohan
Letters By Bill Tortolini

## A GRUMP IN THE GRASS

Written By Ben Fisher
Art By Agnes Garbowska
Colors By Mohan
Letters By Bill Tortolini

## POKEY FALLS IN LOVE

Written By Royal McGraw
Art By Michelle Nguyen
Letters By Bill Tortolini

## THE TALLEST TREE

Written By Ben McCool
Art/Colors By Steve Uy
Letters By Bill Tortolini

## THE MAGICIAN'S UNPAID INTERN

Written By Ben Fisher
Art By Ken Haeser
Colors By Mohan
Letters By Bill Tortolini

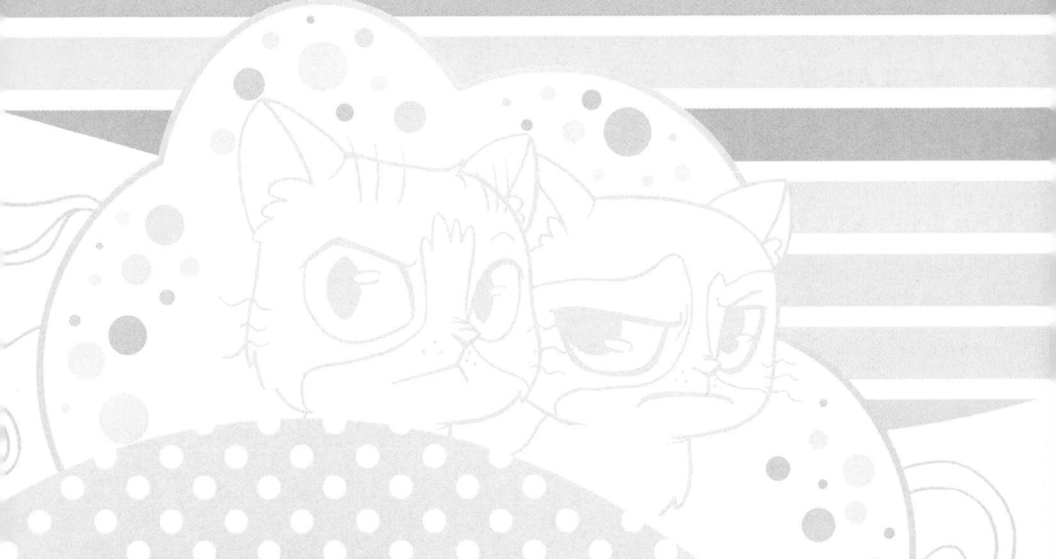

## THE VISITORS

Written By Ben McCool
Art/Colors By Steve Uy
Letters By Bill Tortolini

## THE GOOD, THE BAD & THE GRUMPY

Written By Elliott Serrano
Art By Ken Haeser
Colors By Mohan
Letters By Bill Tortolini

## DRONE ALONE

Written By Royal McGraw
Art & Colors By Steve Uy
Letters By Bill Tortolini

## ROAD TRIP!

Written By Ben McCool
Art By Mauro Vargas
Colors By Mohan
Letters By Bill Tortolini

Series Edited By
Rich Young & Anthony Marques

Collection Design By
Cathleen Heard

**DYNAMITE** f 🅘 t 🅨 YouTube

**For more Grumpy & Pokey, visit DYNAMITE.COM and GRUMPYCATS.COM!**

Nick Barrucci, CEO / Publisher
Juan Collado, President / COO

Joe Rybandt, Executive Editor
Matt Idelson, Senior Editor
Rachel Pinnelas, Associate Editor
Anthony Marques, Assistant Editor
Kevin Ketner, Editorial Assistant

Jason Ullmeyer, Art Director
Geoff Harkins, Senior Graphic Designer
Cathleen Heard, Graphic Designer
Alexis Persson, Production Artist

Chris Caniano, Digital Associate
Rachel Kilbury, Digital Assistant

Brandon Dante Primavera, V.P. of IT and Operations
Rich Young, Director of Business Development

Alan Payne, V.P. of Sales and Marketing
Keith Davidsen, Marketing Director
Pat O'Connell, Sales Manager

Online at **www.DYNAMITE.com**
On Facebook **/Dynamitecomics**
On Instagram **/Dynamitecomics**
On Tumblr **dynamitecomics.tumblr.com**
On Twitter **@dynamitecomics**
On YouTube **/Dynamitecomics**

Online at **www.GRUMPYCATS.com**
On Facebook **/TheOfficialGrumpyCat**
On Instagram **@RealGrumpyCat**
On Twitter **@RealGrumpyCat**

ISBN-10: 1-5241-0004-8
ISBN-13: 978-1-5241-0004

First Printing
10 9 8 7 6 5 4 3 2 1

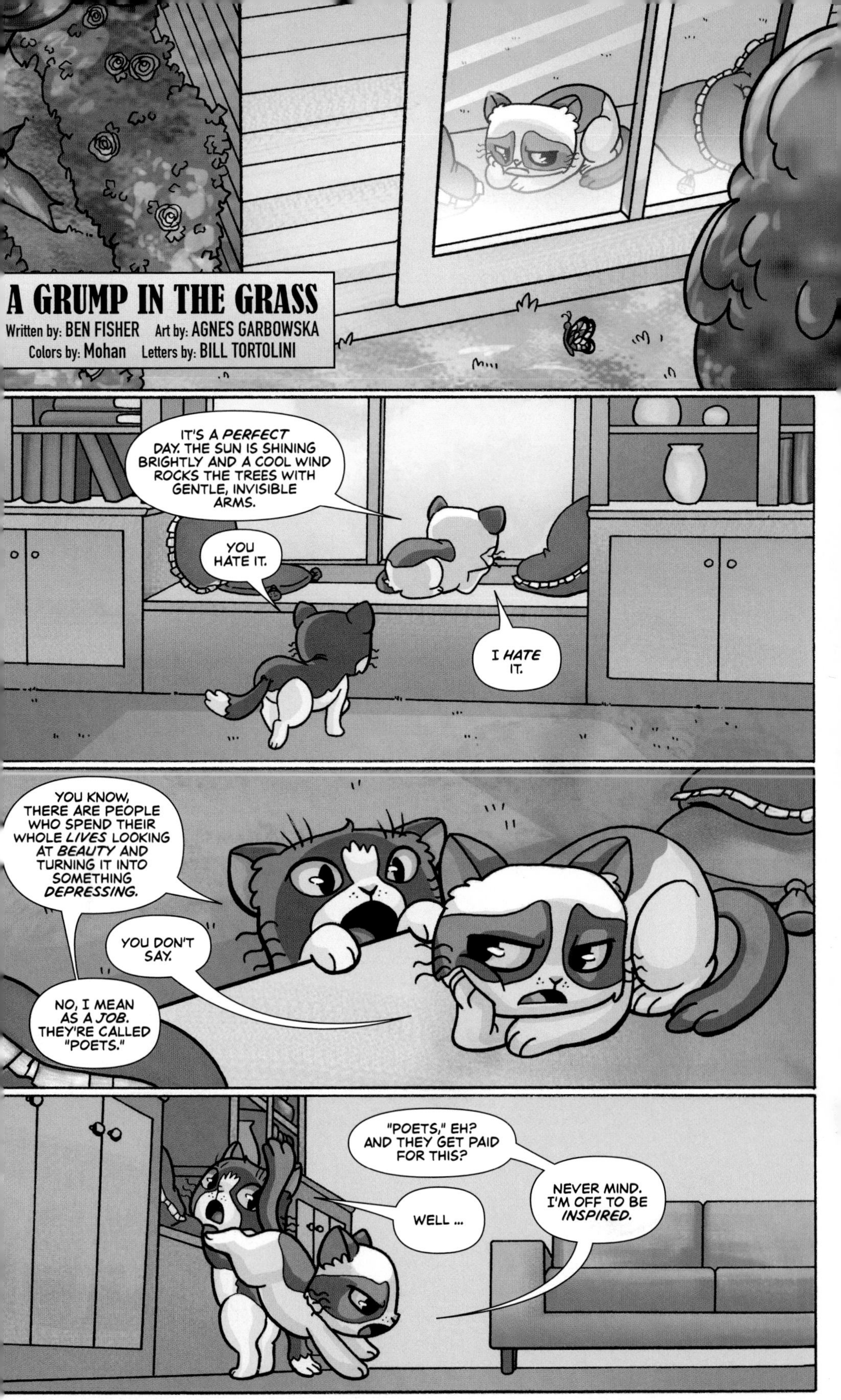
A GRUMP IN THE GRASS
Written by: BEN FISHER Art by: AGNES GARBOWSKA
Colors by: Mohan Letters by: BILL TORTOLINI
IT'S A PERFECT DAY. THE SUN IS SHINING BRIGHTLY AND A COOL WIND ROCKS THE TREES WITH GENTLE, INVISIBLE ARMS.
YOU HATE IT.
I HATE IT.
YOU KNOW, THERE ARE PEOPLE WHO SPEND THEIR WHOLE LIVES LOOKING AT BEAUTY AND TURNING IT INTO SOMETHING DEPRESSING.
YOU DON'T SAY.
NO, I MEAN AS A JOB. THEY'RE CALLED "POETS."
"POETS," EH? AND THEY GET PAID FOR THIS?
WELL ...
NEVER MIND. I'M OFF TO BE INSPIRED.

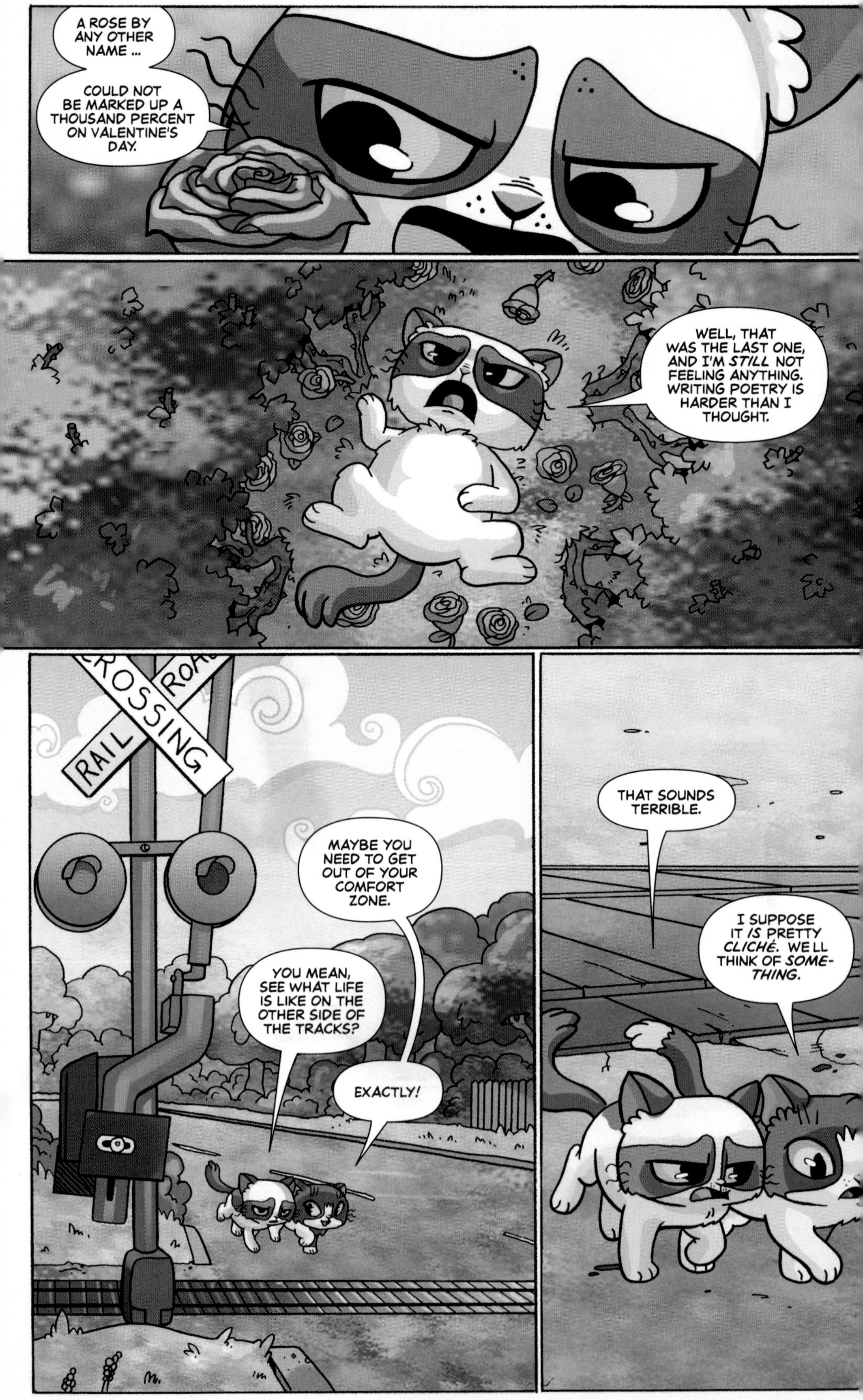
A ROSE BY ANY OTHER NAME ...
COULD NOT BE MARKED UP A THOUSAND PERCENT ON VALENTINE'S DAY.
WELL, THAT WAS THE LAST ONE, AND I'M *STILL* NOT FEELING ANYTHING. WRITING POETRY IS HARDER THAN I THOUGHT.
RAILROAD CROSSING
MAYBE YOU NEED TO GET OUT OF YOUR COMFORT ZONE.
YOU MEAN, SEE WHAT LIFE IS LIKE ON THE OTHER SIDE OF THE TRACKS?
EXACTLY!
THAT SOUNDS TERRIBLE.
I SUPPOSE IT *IS* PRETTY *CLICHÉ*. WE'LL THINK OF *SOMETHING*.

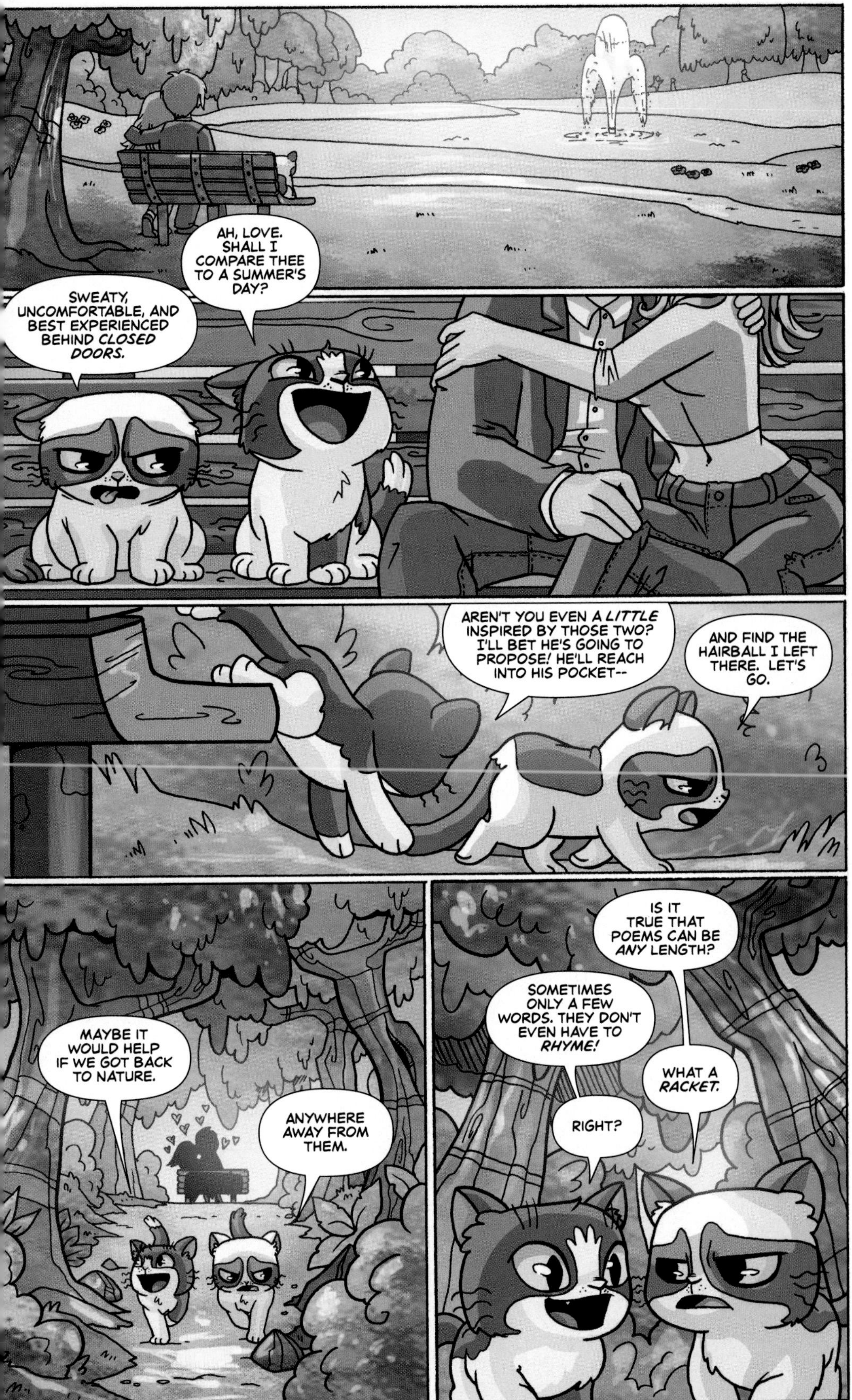

AH, LOVE. SHALL I COMPARE THEE TO A SUMMER'S DAY?
SWEATY, UNCOMFORTABLE, AND BEST EXPERIENCED BEHIND *CLOSED DOORS.*
AREN'T YOU EVEN A *LITTLE* INSPIRED BY THOSE TWO? I'LL BET HE'S GOING TO PROPOSE! HE'LL REACH INTO HIS POCKET--
AND FIND THE HAIRBALL I LEFT THERE. LET'S GO.
MAYBE IT WOULD HELP IF WE GOT BACK TO NATURE.
ANYWHERE AWAY FROM THEM.
IS IT TRUE THAT POEMS CAN BE *ANY* LENGTH?
SOMETIMES ONLY A FEW WORDS. THEY DON'T EVEN HAVE TO *RHYME!*
WHAT A *RACKET.*
RIGHT?

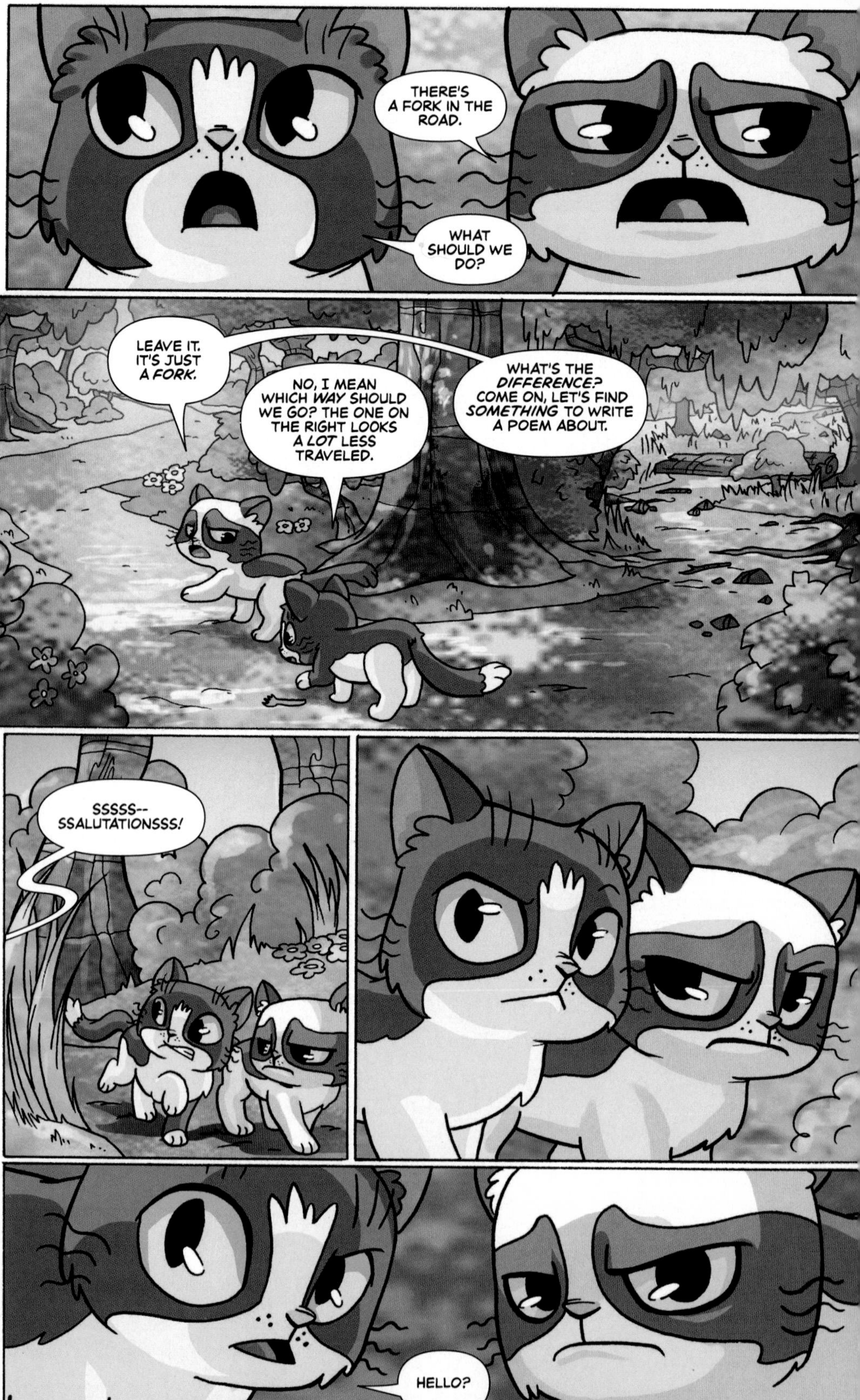

THERE'S A FORK IN THE ROAD.
WHAT SHOULD WE DO?
LEAVE IT. IT'S JUST A *FORK.*
NO, I MEAN WHICH *WAY* SHOULD WE GO? THE ONE ON THE RIGHT LOOKS A *LOT* LESS TRAVELED.
WHAT'S THE *DIFFERENCE?* COME ON, LET'S FIND *SOMETHING* TO WRITE A POEM ABOUT.
SSSSS--SSALUTATIONSSS!
HELLO?

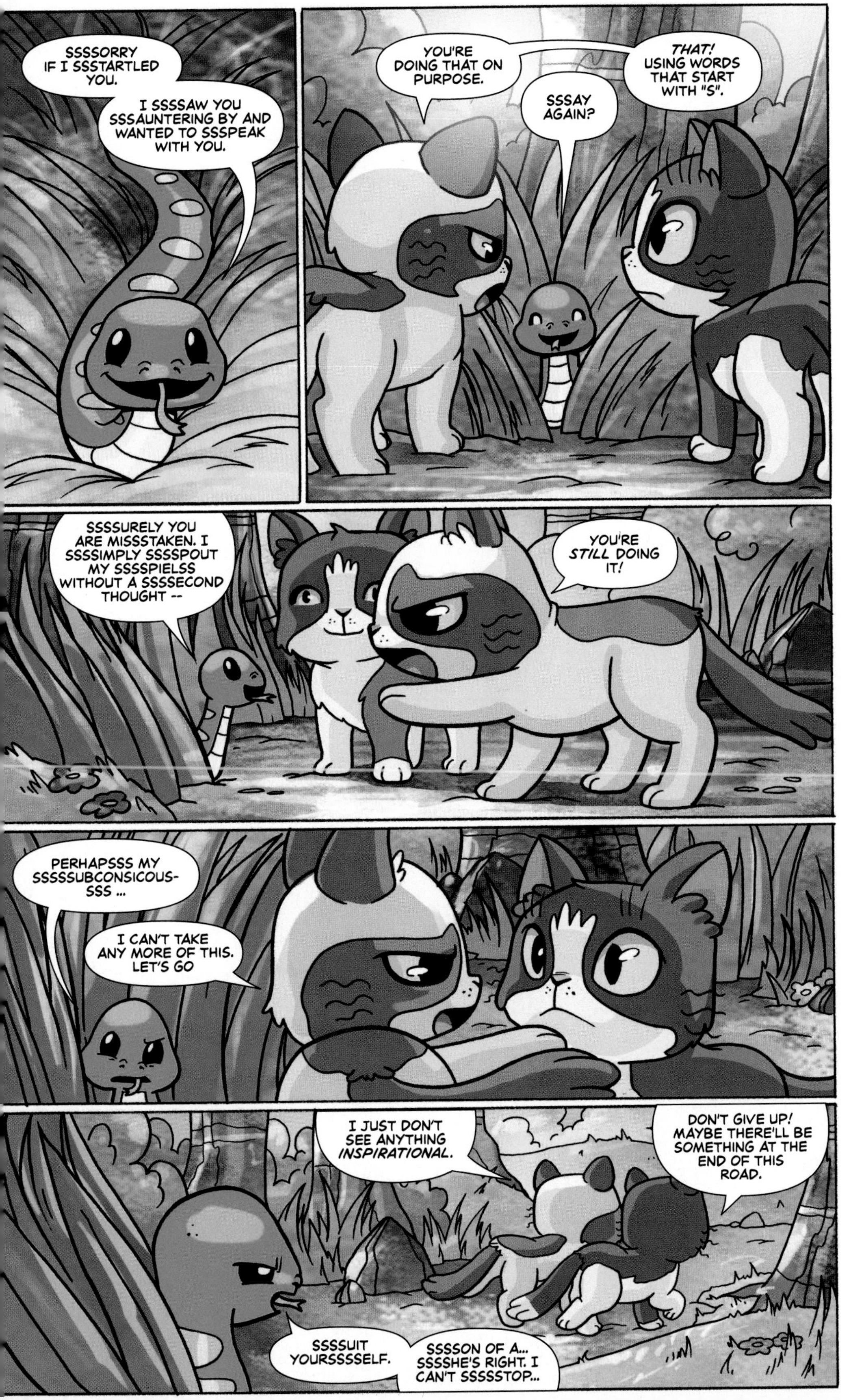

SSSSORRY IF I SSSTARTLED YOU.
I SSSSAW YOU SSSAUNTERING BY AND WANTED TO SSSPEAK WITH YOU.
YOU'RE DOING THAT ON PURPOSE.
SSSAY AGAIN?
*THAT!* USING WORDS THAT START WITH "S".
SSSSURELY YOU ARE MISSSTAKEN. I SSSSIMPLY SSSSPOUT MY SSSSPIELSS WITHOUT A SSSSECOND THOUGHT --
YOU'RE *STILL* DOING IT!
PERHAPSSS MY SSSSSUBCONSICOUS-SSS ...
I CAN'T TAKE ANY MORE OF THIS. LET'S GO
I JUST DON'T SEE ANYTHING *INSPIRATIONAL*.
DON'T GIVE UP! MAYBE THERE'LL BE SOMETHING AT THE END OF THIS ROAD.
SSSSUIT YOURSSSSELF.
SSSSON OF A... SSSSHE'S RIGHT. I CAN'T SSSSSTOP...

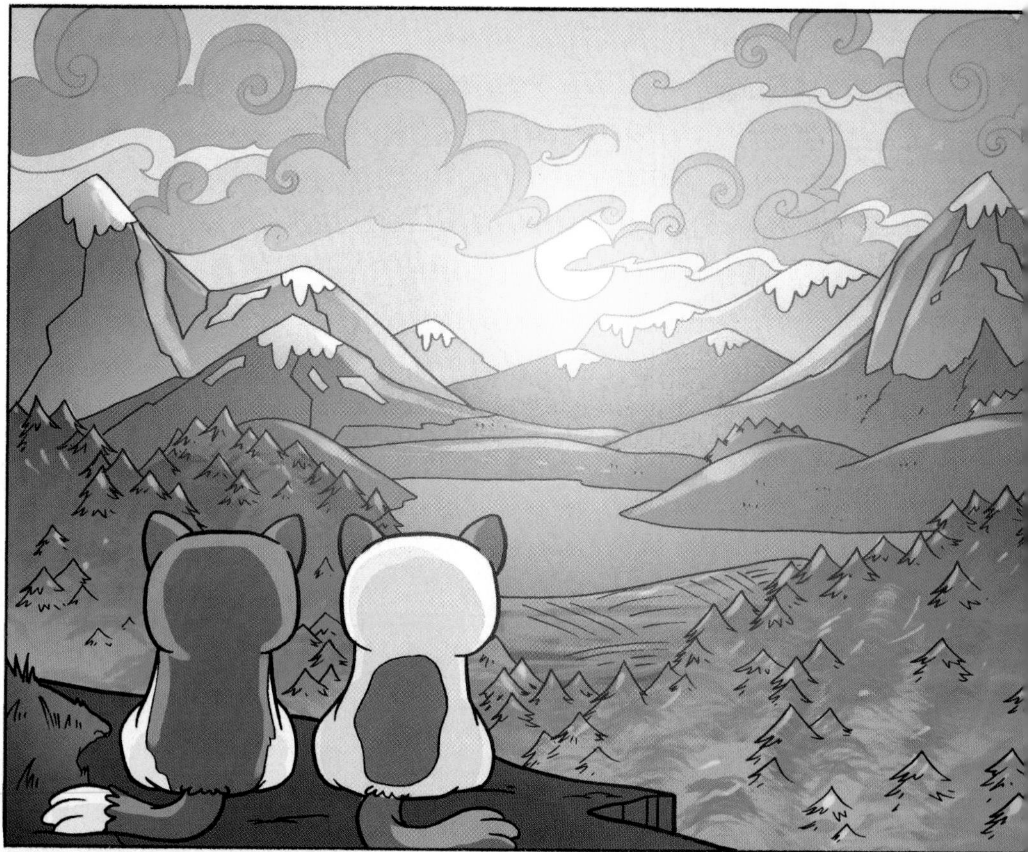

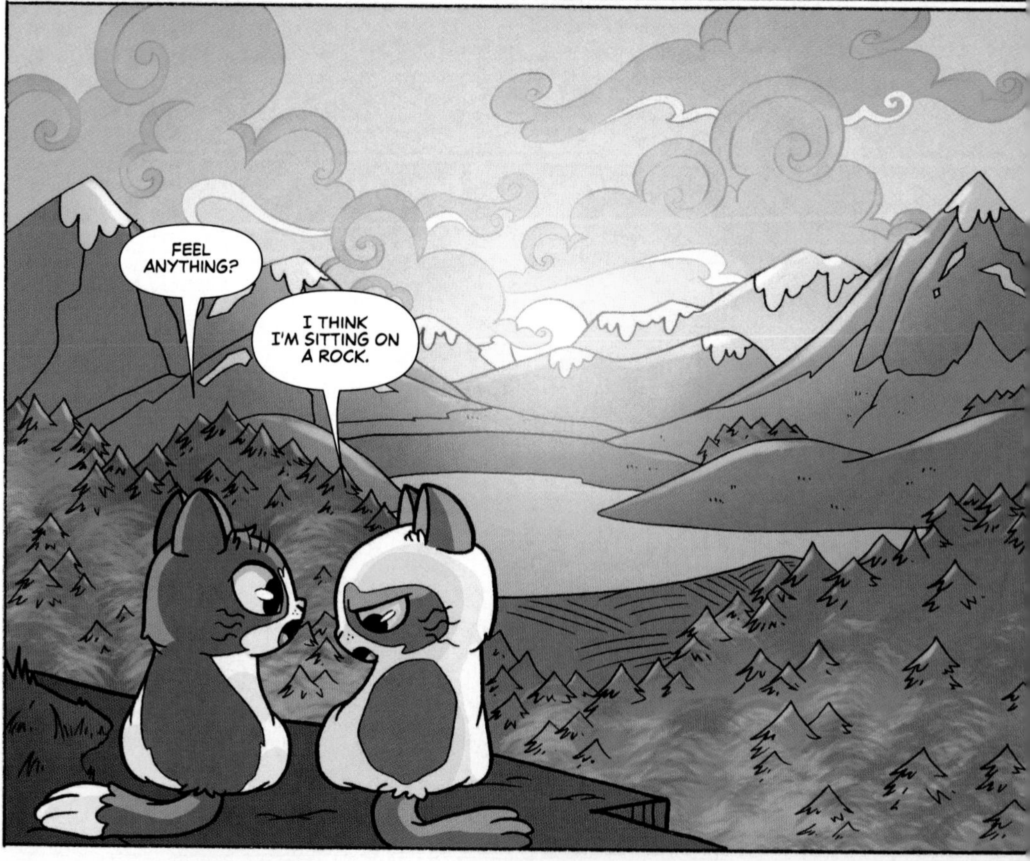
FEEL ANYTHING?
I THINK I'M SITTING ON A ROCK.

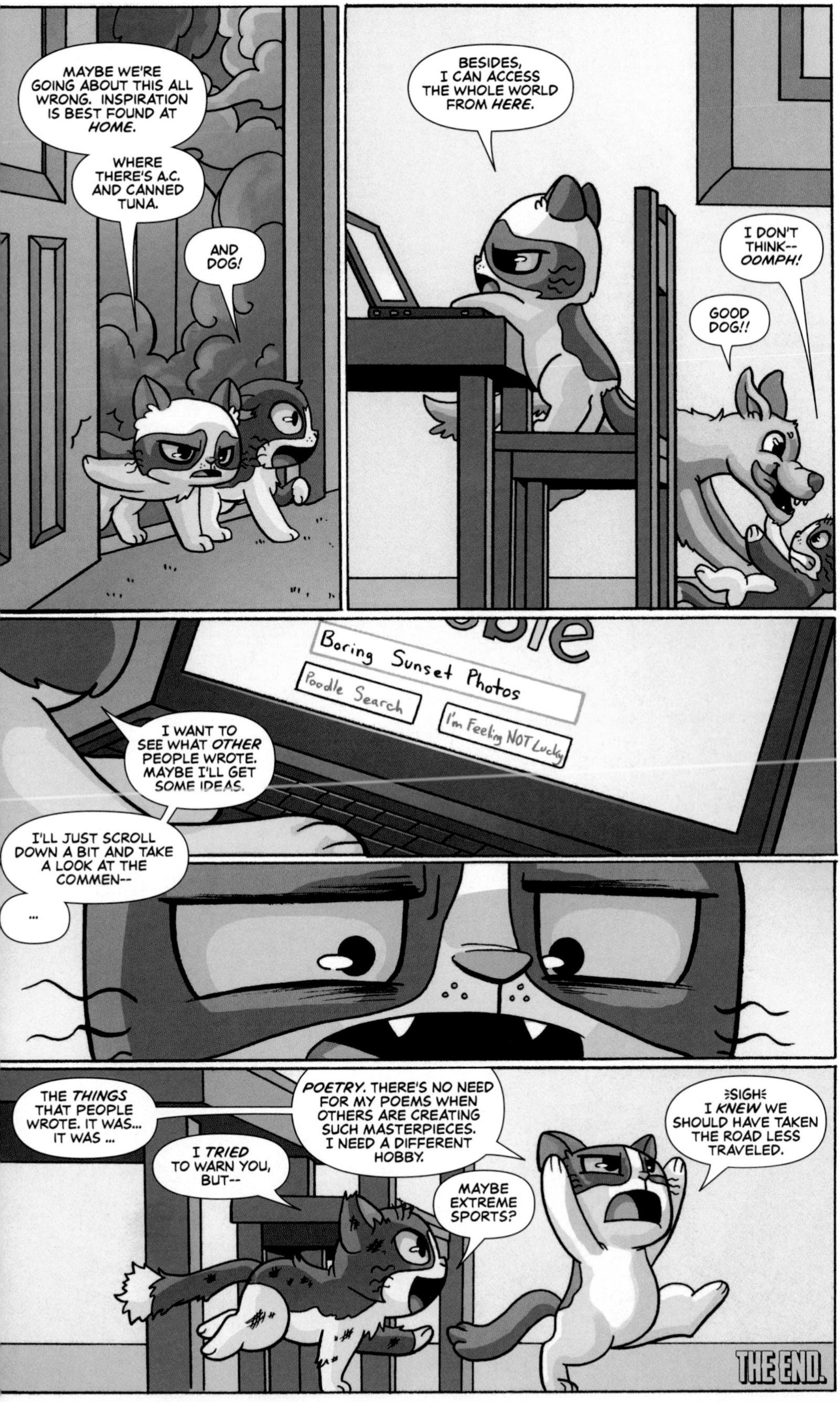
MAYBE WE'RE GOING ABOUT THIS ALL WRONG. INSPIRATION IS BEST FOUND AT *HOME*.
WHERE THERE'S A.C. AND CANNED TUNA.
AND DOG!
BESIDES, I CAN ACCESS THE WHOLE WORLD FROM *HERE*.
I DON'T THINK-- *OOMPH!*
GOOD DOG!!
Boring Sunset Photos
Poodle Search
I'm Feeling NOT Lucky
I WANT TO SEE WHAT *OTHER* PEOPLE WROTE. MAYBE I'LL GET SOME IDEAS.
I'LL JUST SCROLL DOWN A BIT AND TAKE A LOOK AT THE COMMEN--
...
THE *THINGS* THAT PEOPLE WROTE. IT WAS... IT WAS ...
I *TRIED* TO WARN YOU, BUT--
*POETRY*. THERE'S NO NEED FOR MY POEMS WHEN OTHERS ARE CREATING SUCH MASTERPIECES. I NEED A DIFFERENT HOBBY.
MAYBE EXTREME SPORTS?
SIGH I *KNEW* WE SHOULD HAVE TAKEN THE ROAD LESS TRAVELED.
THE END.

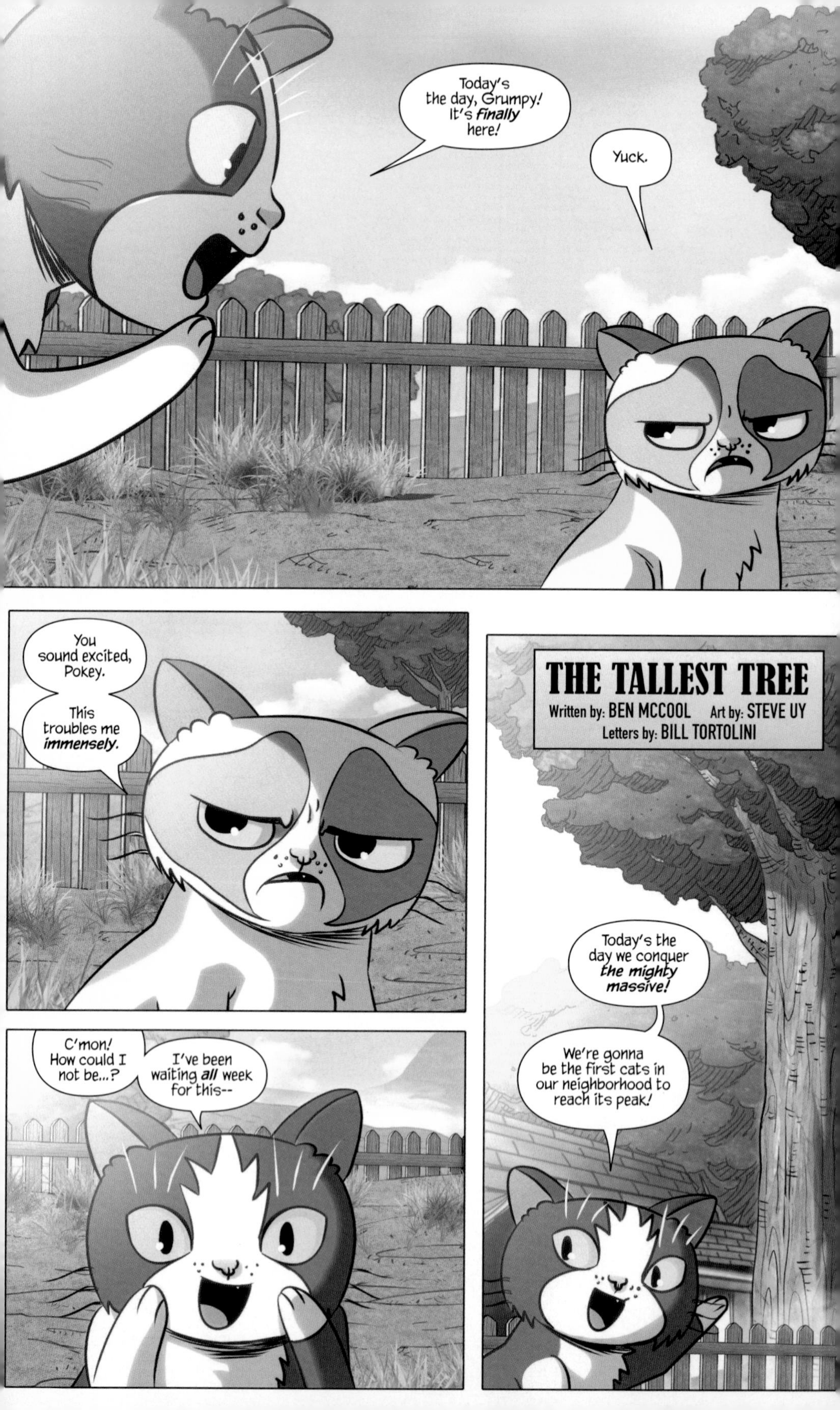
Today's the day, Grumpy! It's *finally* here!
Yuck.
You sound excited, Pokey.
This troubles me *immensely.*
THE TALLEST TREE
Written by: BEN MCCOOL Art by: STEVE UY
Letters by: BILL TORTOLINI
Today's the day we conquer *the mighty massive!*
We're gonna be the first cats in our neighborhood to reach its peak!
C'mon! How could I not be...?
I've been waiting *all* week for this--

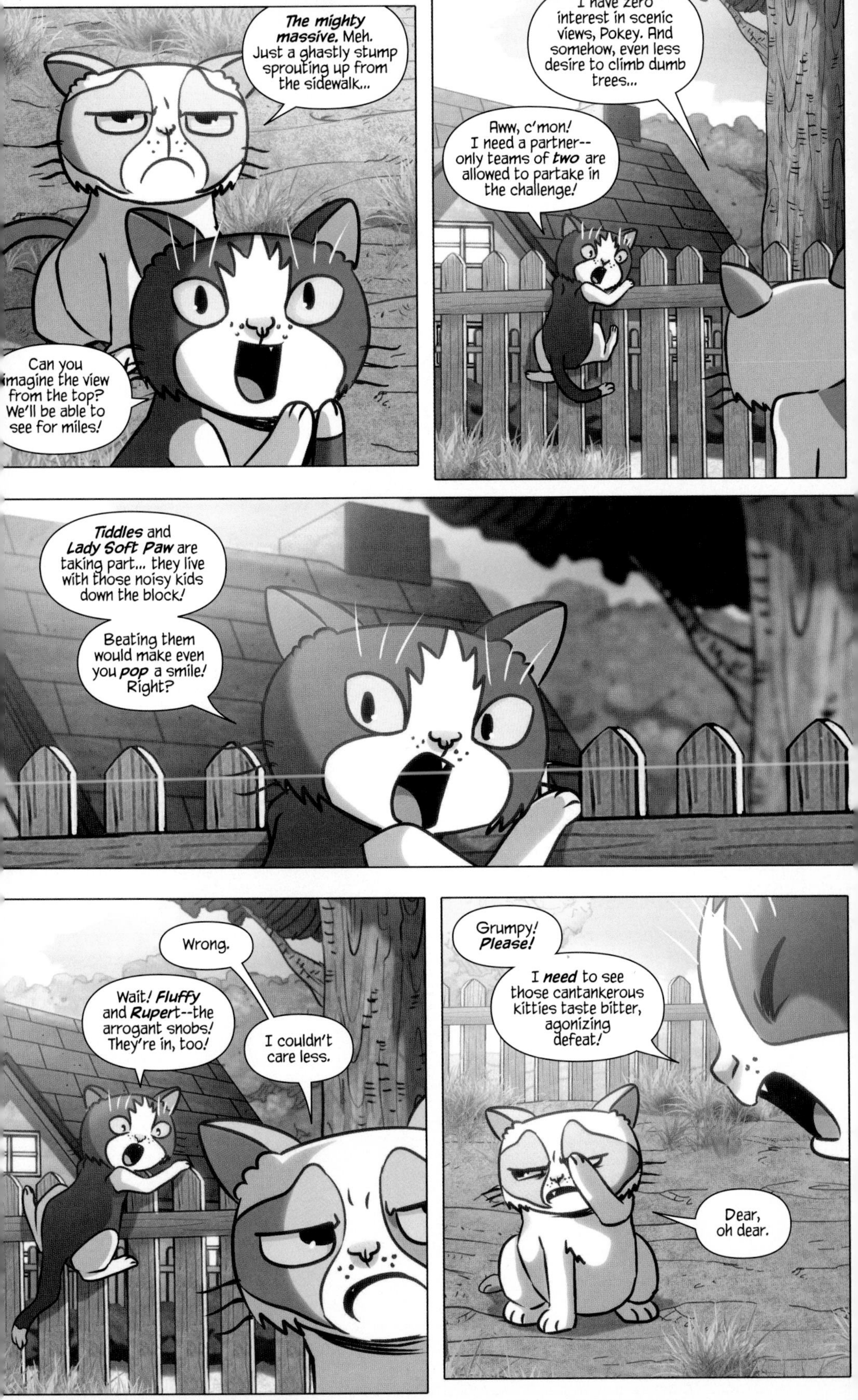
The mighty massive. Meh. Just a ghastly stump sprouting up from the sidewalk...
Can you imagine the view from the top? We'll be able to see for miles!
I have zero interest in scenic views, Pokey. And somehow, even less desire to climb dumb trees...
Aww, c'mon! I need a partner-- only teams of two are allowed to partake in the challenge!
Tiddles and Lady Soft Paw are taking part... they live with those noisy kids down the block!
Beating them would make even you pop a smile! Right?
Wrong.
Wait! Fluffy and Rupert--the arrogant snobs! They're in, too!
I couldn't care less.
Grumpy! Please!
I need to see those cantankerous kitties taste bitter, agonizing defeat!
Dear, oh dear.

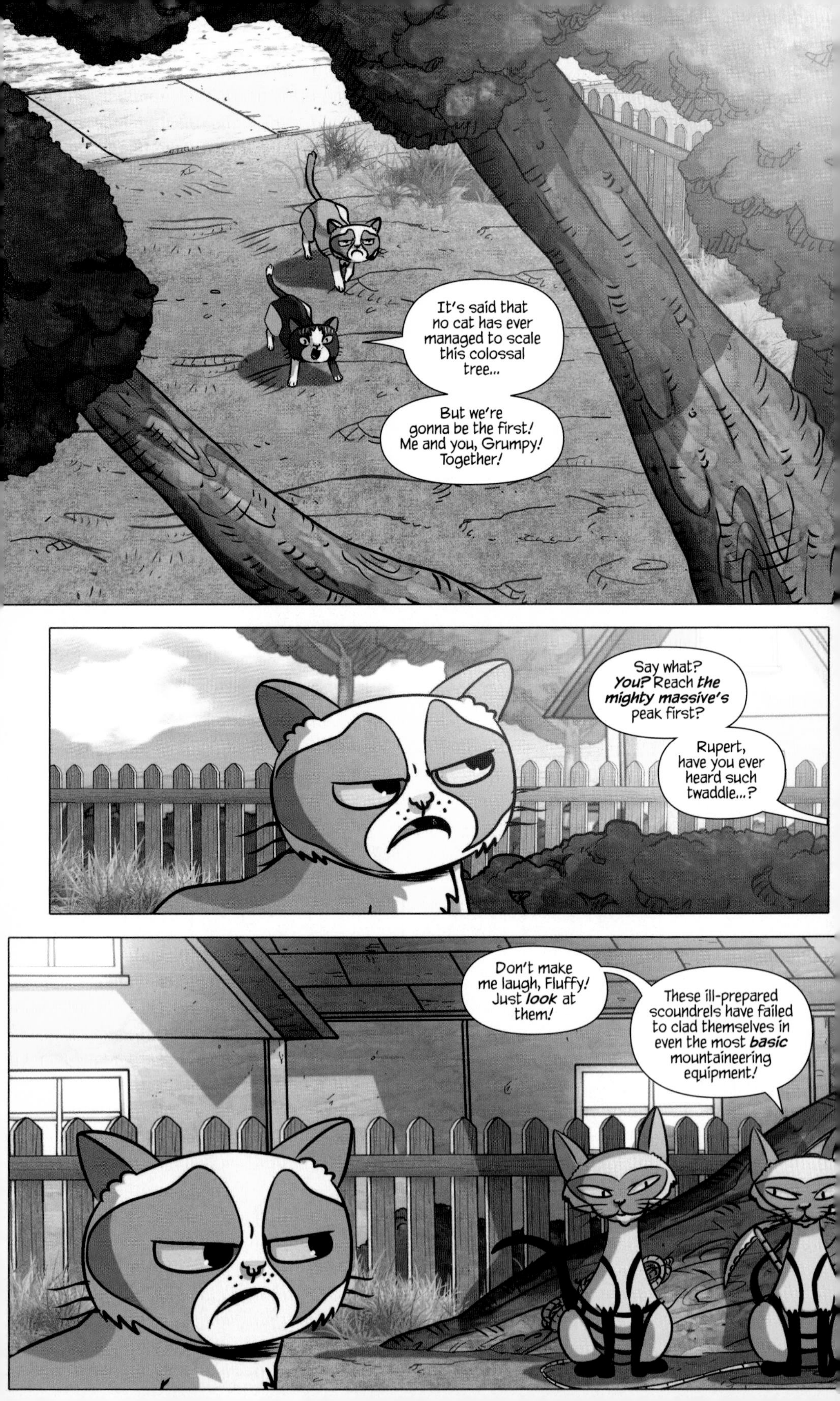
It's said that no cat has ever managed to scale this colossal tree...
But we're gonna be the first! Me and you, Grumpy! Together!
Say what? *You?* Reach *the mighty massive's* peak first?
Rupert, have you ever heard such twaddle...?
Don't make me laugh, Fluffy! Just *look* at them!
These ill-prepared scoundrels have failed to clad themselves in even the most *basic* mountaineering equipment!

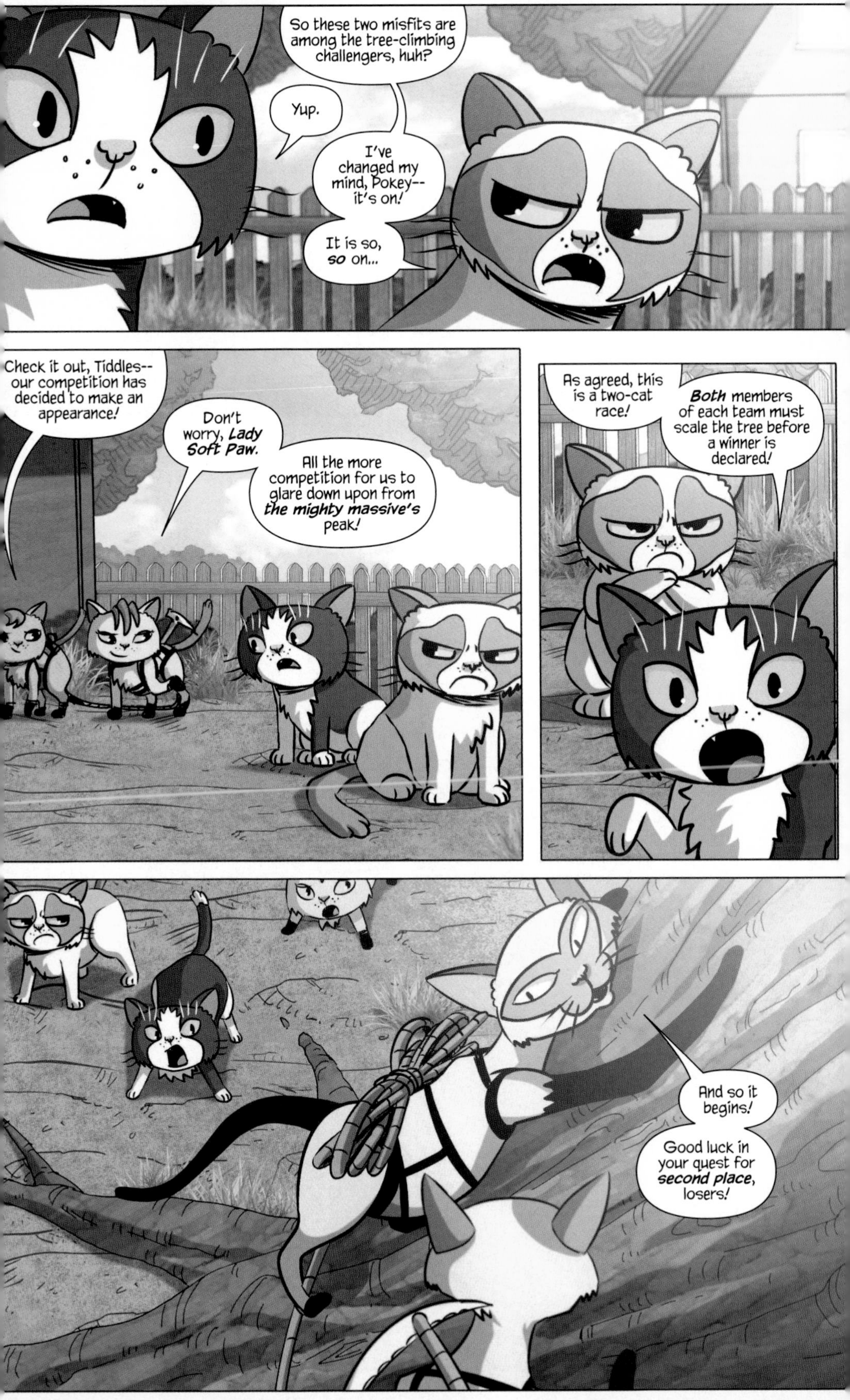
So these two misfits are among the tree-climbing challengers, huh?
Yup.
I've changed my mind, Pokey-- it's on!
It is so, *so* on...
Check it out, Tiddles-- our competition has decided to make an appearance!
Don't worry, ***Lady Soft Paw***.
All the more competition for us to glare down upon from ***the mighty massive's*** peak!
As agreed, this is a two-cat race!
***Both*** members of each team must scale the tree before a winner is declared!
And so it begins!
Good luck in your quest for ***second place***, losers!

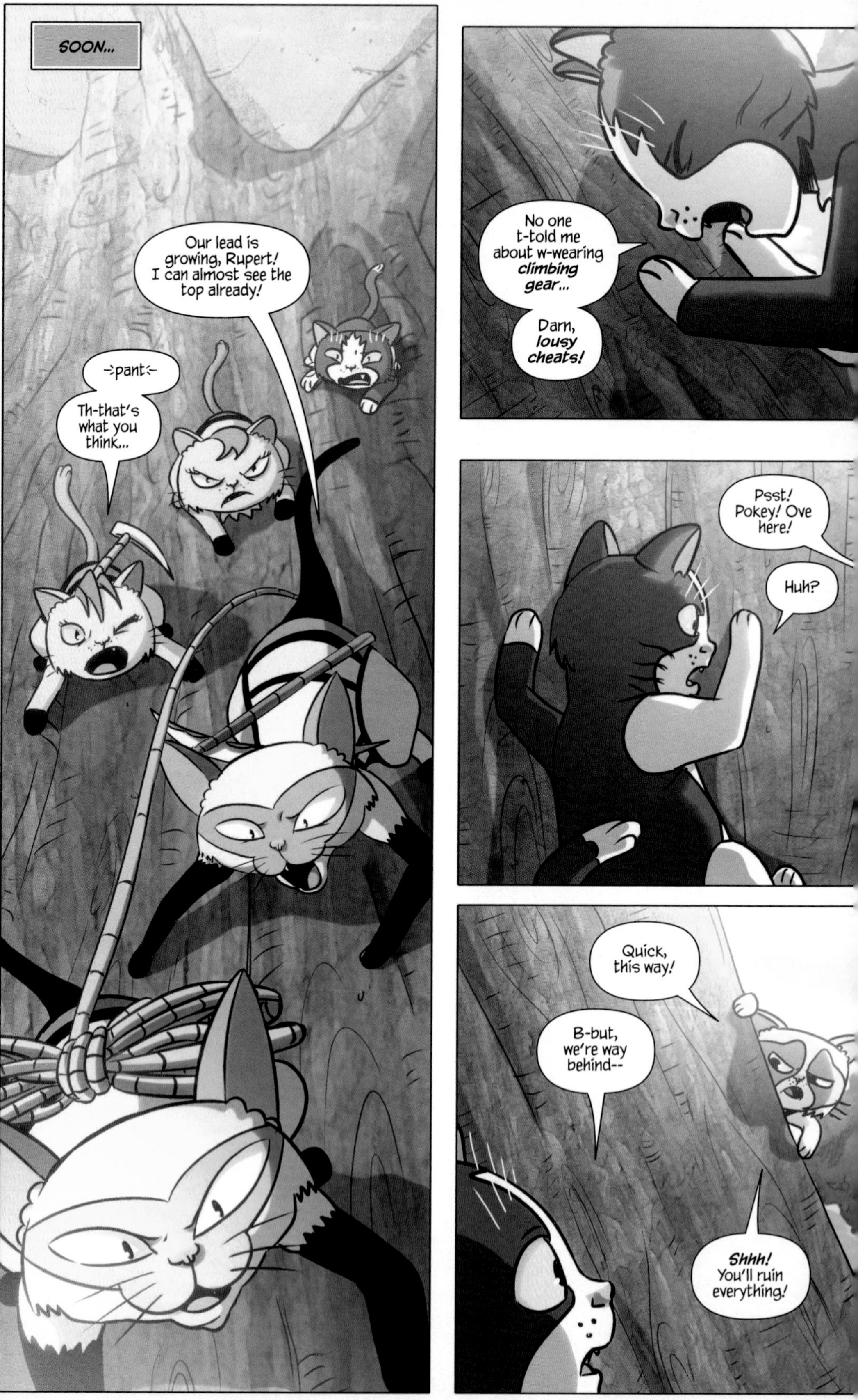
SOON...
Our lead is growing, Rupert! I can almost see the top already!
-pant-
Th-that's what you think...
No one t-told me about w-wearing climbing gear...
Darn, lousy cheats!
Psst! Pokey! Ove here!
Huh?
Quick, this way!
B-but, we're way behind--
Shhh! You'll ruin everything!

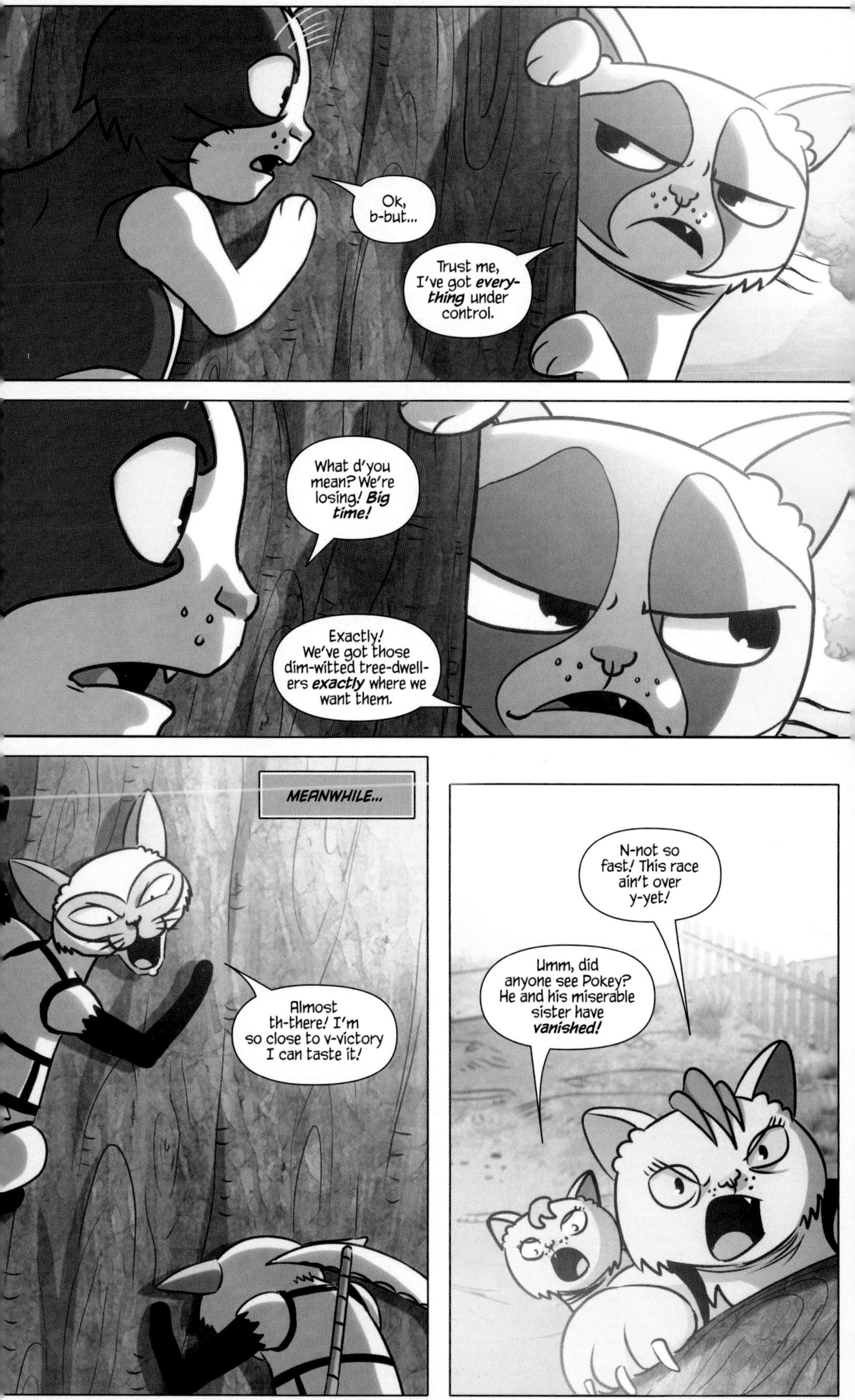

Ok, b-but...
Trust me, I've got *every-thing* under control.
What d'you mean? We're losing! ***Big time!***
Exactly! We've got those dim-witted tree-dwellers *exactly* where we want them.
MEANWHILE...
Almost th-there! I'm so close to v-victory I can taste it!
N-not so fast! This race ain't over y-yet!
Umm, did anyone see Pokey? He and his miserable sister have ***vanished!***

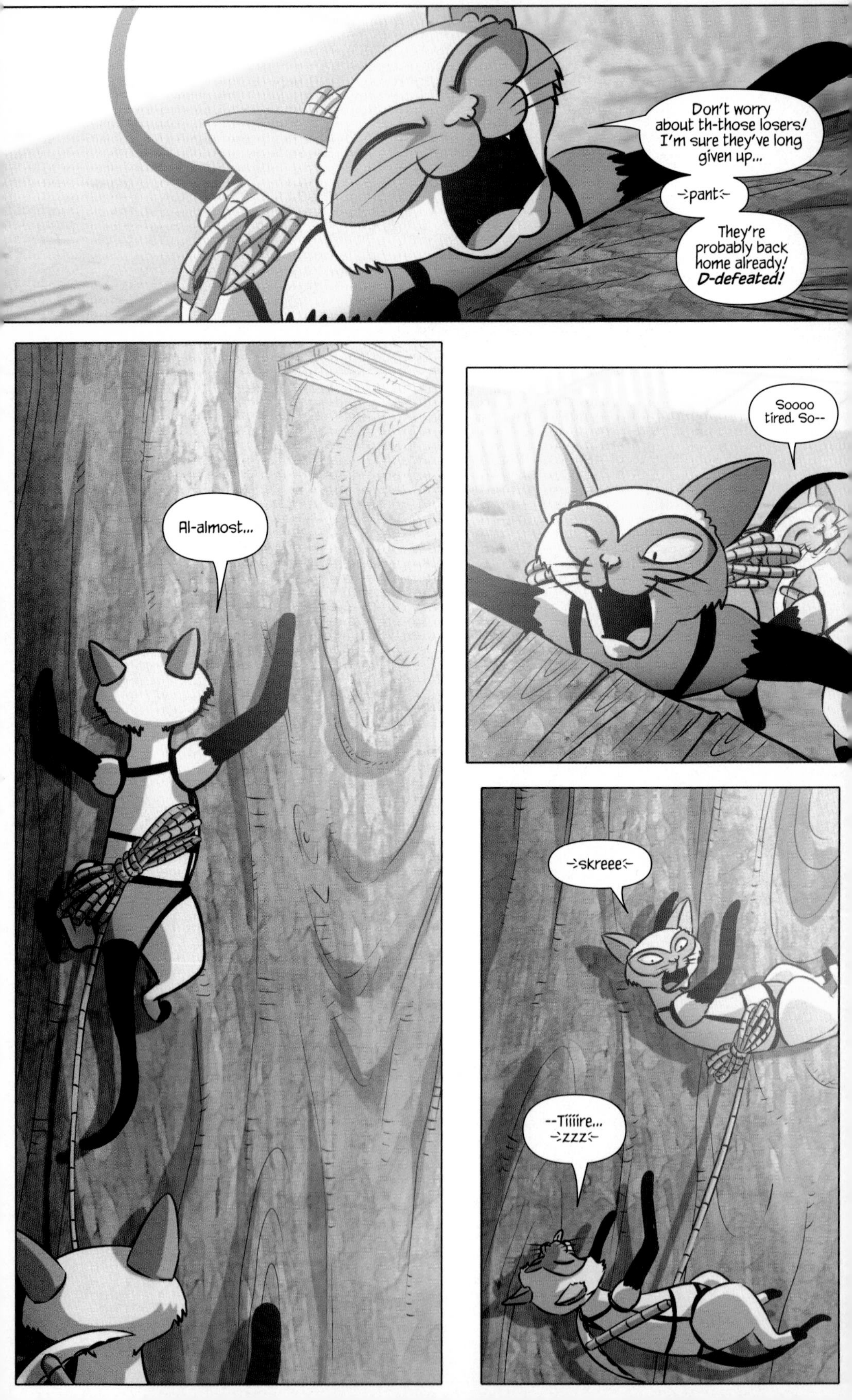

Don't worry about th-those losers! I'm sure they've long given up...
-pant-
They're probably back home already! D-defeated!
Al-almost...
Soooo tired. So--
-skreee-
--Tiiiire... -zzz-

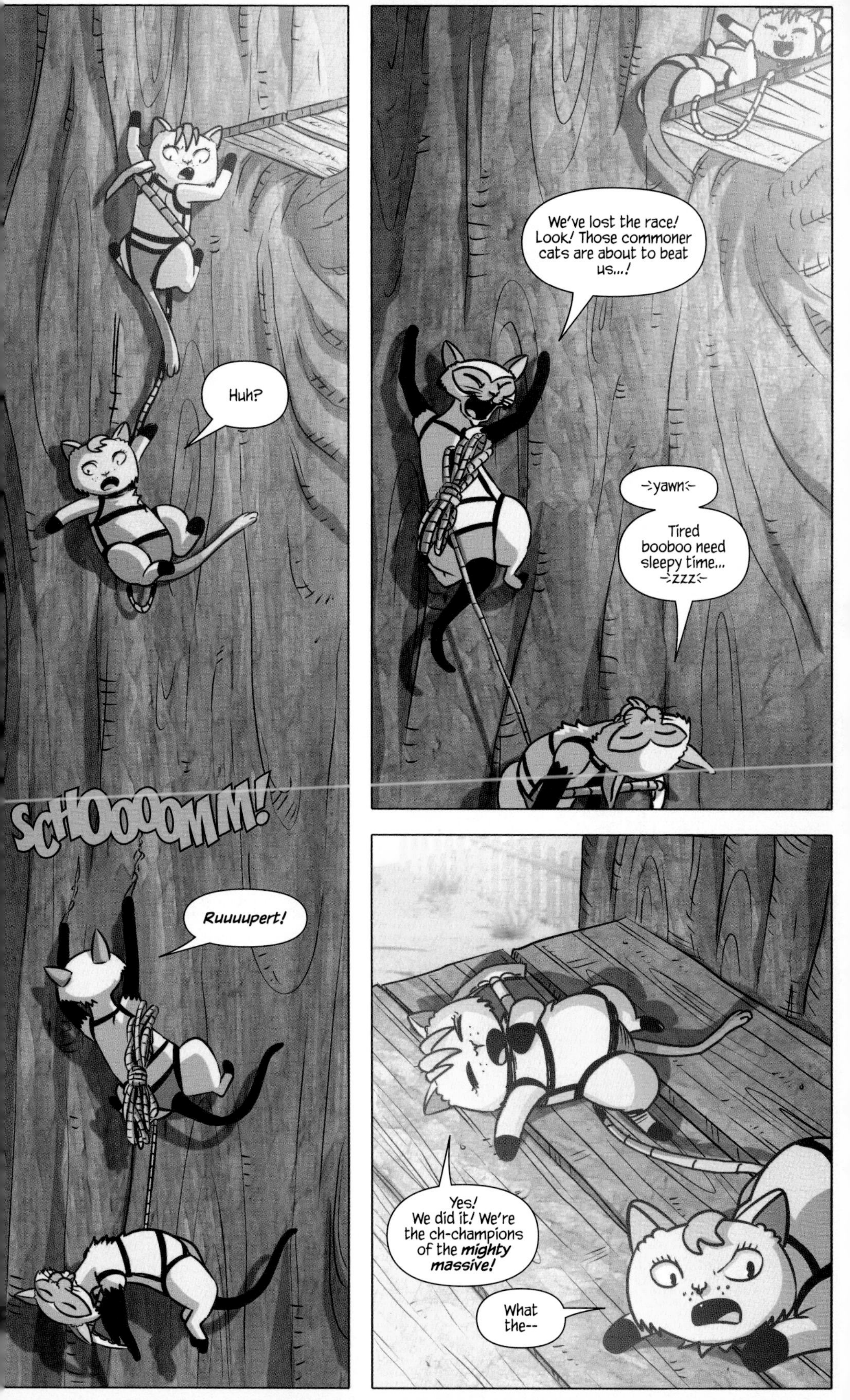
Huh?
We've lost the race! Look! Those commoner cats are about to beat us...!
-yawn-
Tired booboo need sleepy time... -zzz-
SCHOOOOMM!
Ruuuupert!
Yes! We did it! We're the ch-champions of the mighty massive!
What the--

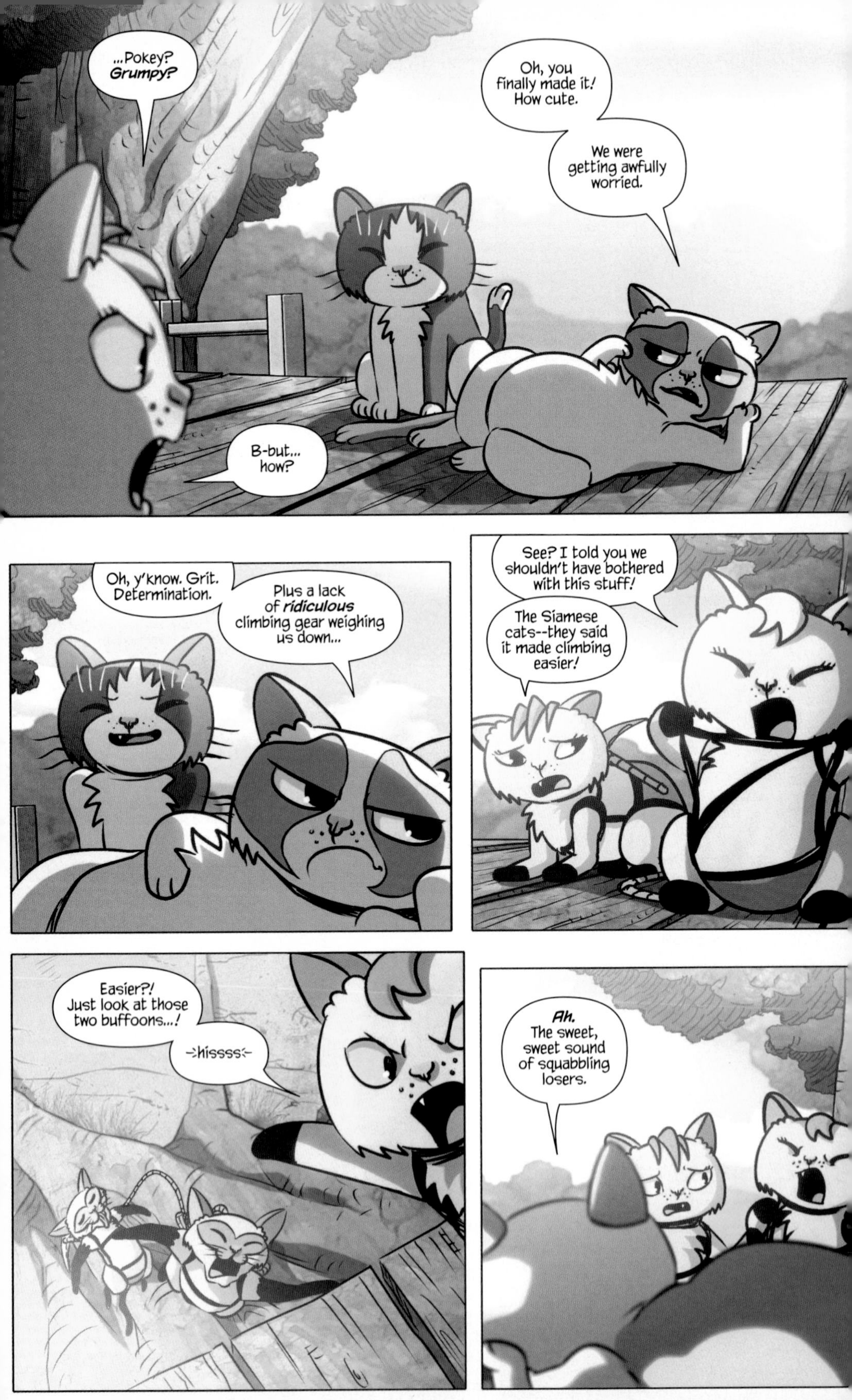
...Pokey? Grumpy?
Oh, you finally made it! How cute.
We were getting awfully worried.
B-but... how?
Oh, y'know. Grit. Determination.
Plus a lack of *ridiculous* climbing gear weighing us down...
See? I told you we shouldn't have bothered with this stuff!
The Siamese cats--they said it made climbing easier!
Easier?! Just look at those two buffoons...!
~hissss~
*Ah.* The sweet, sweet sound of squabbling losers.

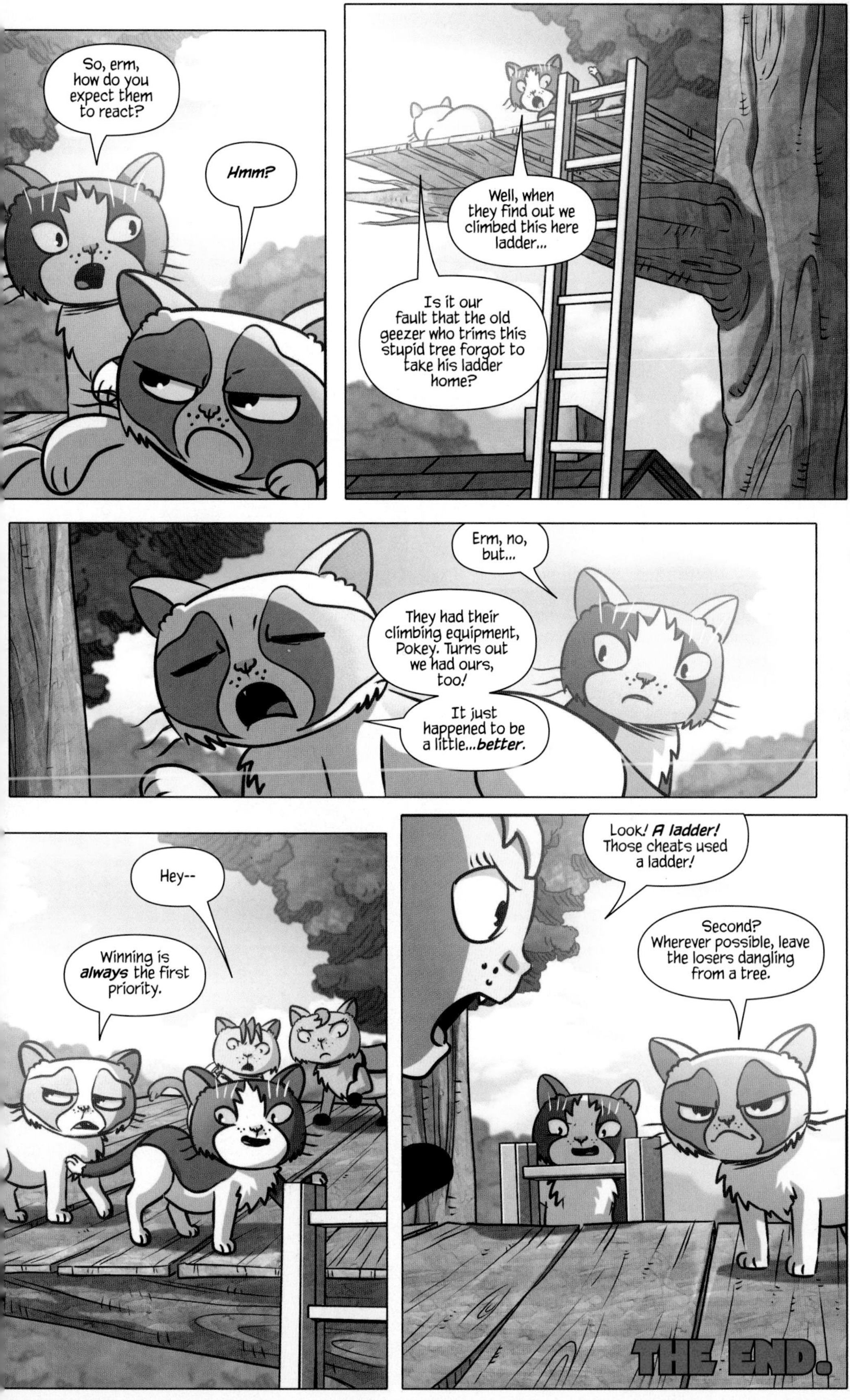
So, erm, how do you expect them to react?
*Hmm?*
Well, when they find out we climbed this here ladder...
Is it our fault that the old geezer who trims this stupid tree forgot to take his ladder home?
Erm, no, but...
They had their climbing equipment, Pokey. Turns out we had ours, too!
It just happened to be a little...***better***.
Hey--
Winning is ***always*** the first priority.
Look! ***A ladder!*** Those cheats used a ladder!
Second? Wherever possible, leave the losers dangling from a tree.
THE END.

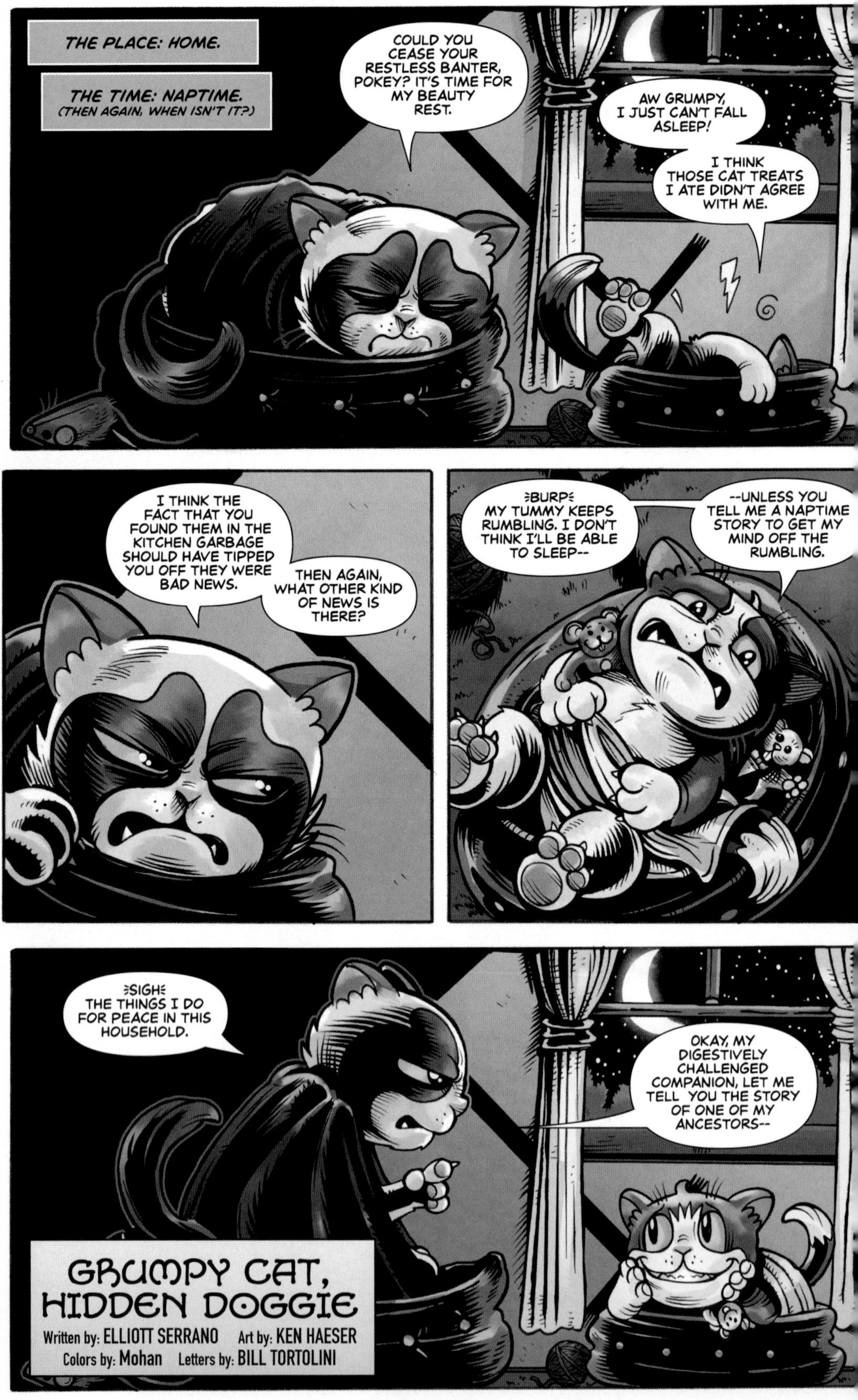
THE PLACE: HOME.
THE TIME: NAPTIME. (THEN AGAIN, WHEN ISN'T IT?)
COULD YOU CEASE YOUR RESTLESS BANTER, POKEY? IT'S TIME FOR MY BEAUTY REST.
AW GRUMPY, I JUST CAN'T FALL ASLEEP!
I THINK THOSE CAT TREATS I ATE DIDN'T AGREE WITH ME.
I THINK THE FACT THAT YOU FOUND THEM IN THE KITCHEN GARBAGE SHOULD HAVE TIPPED YOU OFF THEY WERE BAD NEWS.
THEN AGAIN, WHAT OTHER KIND OF NEWS IS THERE?
BURP MY TUMMY KEEPS RUMBLING. I DON'T THINK I'LL BE ABLE TO SLEEP--
--UNLESS YOU TELL ME A NAPTIME STORY TO GET MY MIND OFF THE RUMBLING.
SIGH THE THINGS I DO FOR PEACE IN THIS HOUSEHOLD.
OKAY, MY DIGESTIVELY CHALLENGED COMPANION, LET ME TELL YOU THE STORY OF ONE OF MY ANCESTORS--
GRUMPY CAT, HIDDEN DOGGIE
Written by: ELLIOTT SERRANO Art by: KEN HAESER
Colors by: Mohan Letters by: BILL TORTOLINI

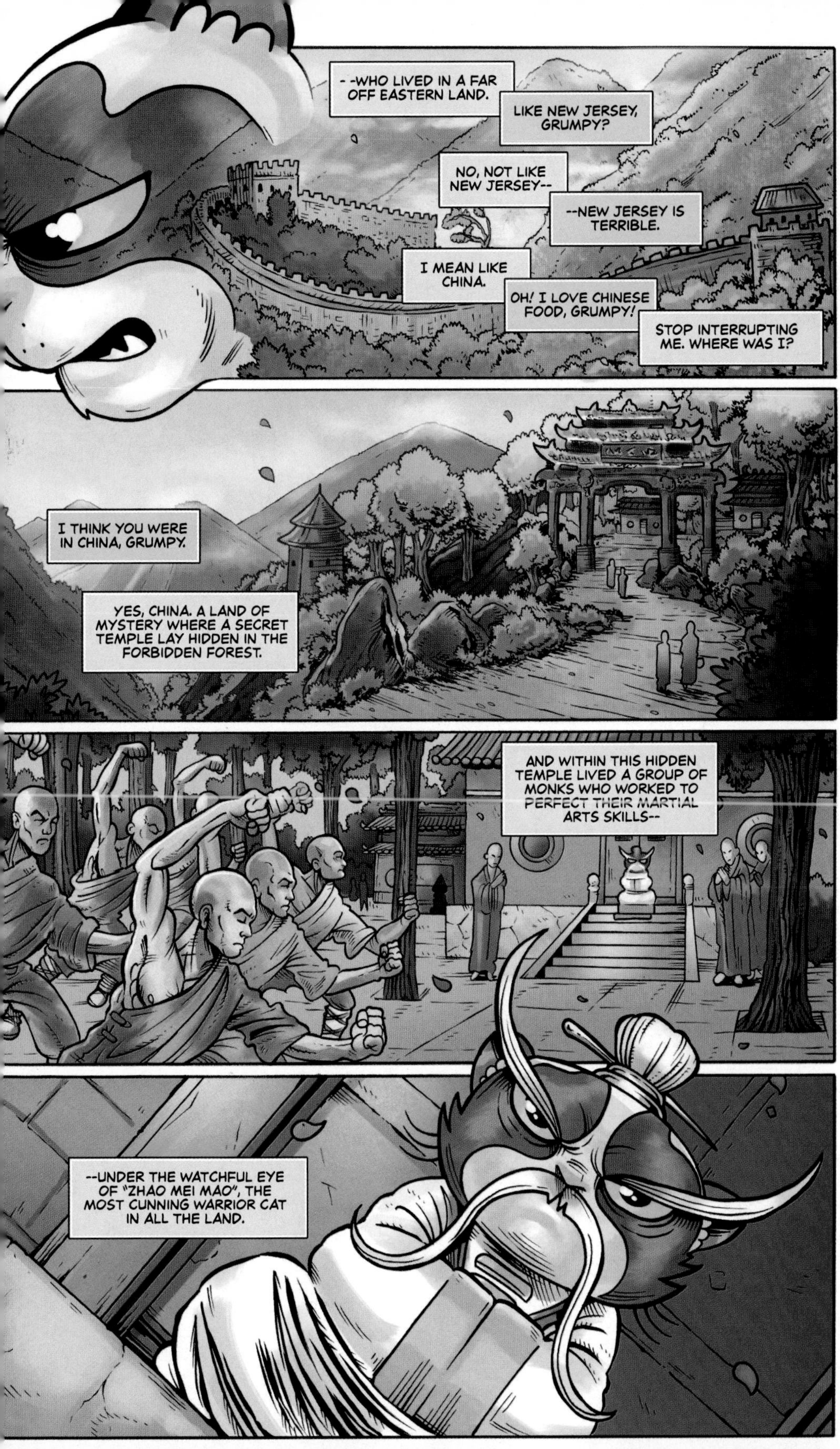
--WHO LIVED IN A FAR OFF EASTERN LAND.
LIKE NEW JERSEY, GRUMPY?
NO, NOT LIKE NEW JERSEY--
--NEW JERSEY IS TERRIBLE.
I MEAN LIKE CHINA.
OH! I LOVE CHINESE FOOD, GRUMPY!
STOP INTERRUPTING ME. WHERE WAS I?
I THINK YOU WERE IN CHINA, GRUMPY.
YES, CHINA. A LAND OF MYSTERY WHERE A SECRET TEMPLE LAY HIDDEN IN THE FORBIDDEN FOREST.
AND WITHIN THIS HIDDEN TEMPLE LIVED A GROUP OF MONKS WHO WORKED TO PERFECT THEIR MARTIAL ARTS SKILLS--
--UNDER THE WATCHFUL EYE OF "ZHAO MEI MAO", THE MOST CUNNING WARRIOR CAT IN ALL THE LAND.

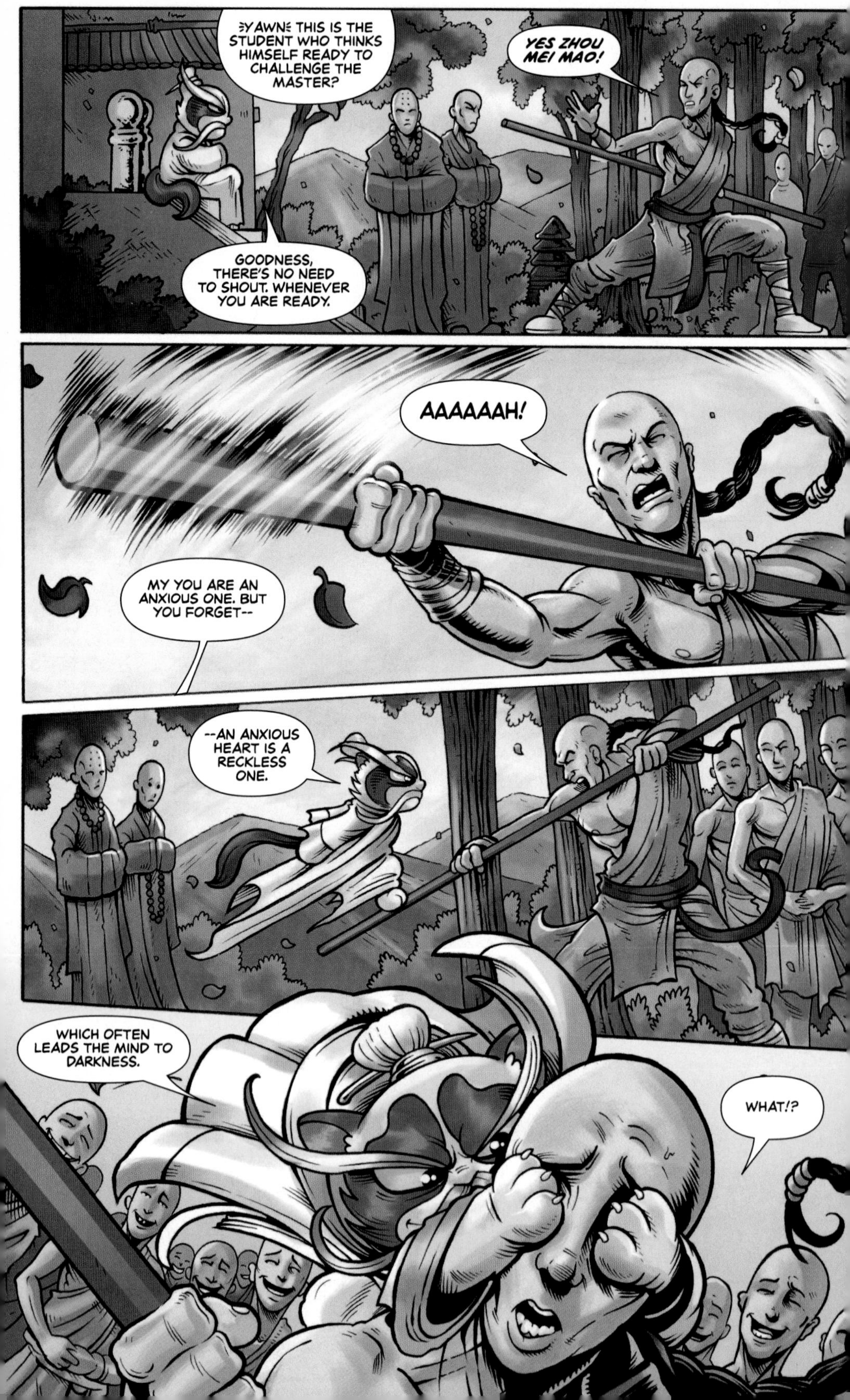

=YAWN= THIS IS THE STUDENT WHO THINKS HIMSELF READY TO CHALLENGE THE MASTER?
YES ZHOU MEI MAO!
GOODNESS, THERE'S NO NEED TO SHOUT. WHENEVER YOU ARE READY.
AAAAAAH!
MY YOU ARE AN ANXIOUS ONE. BUT YOU FORGET--
--AN ANXIOUS HEART IS A RECKLESS ONE.
WHICH OFTEN LEADS THE MIND TO DARKNESS.
WHAT!?

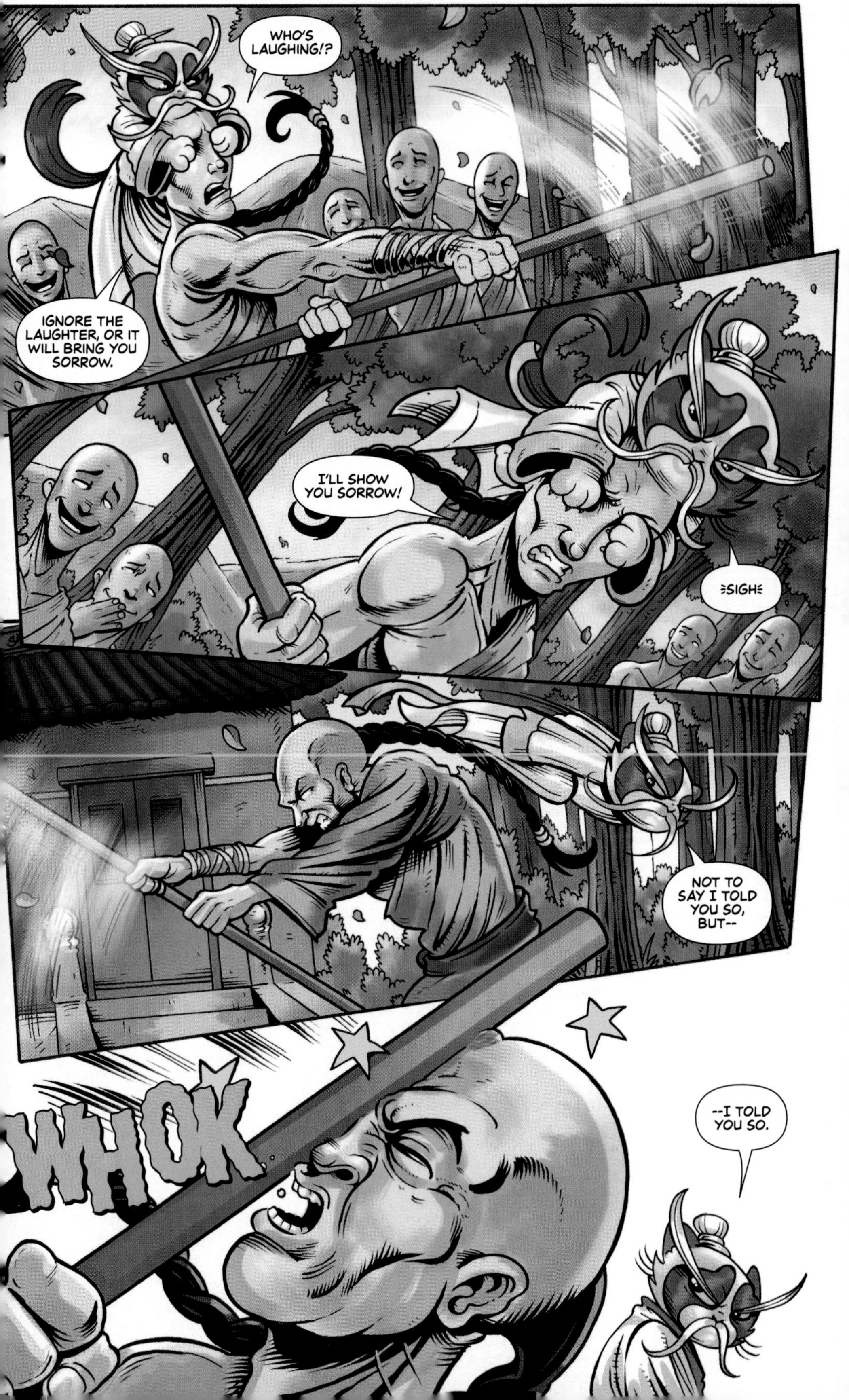
WHO'S LAUGHING!?
IGNORE THE LAUGHTER, OR IT WILL BRING YOU SORROW.
I'LL SHOW YOU SORROW!
SIGH
NOT TO SAY I TOLD YOU SO, BUT--
WHOK
--I TOLD YOU SO.

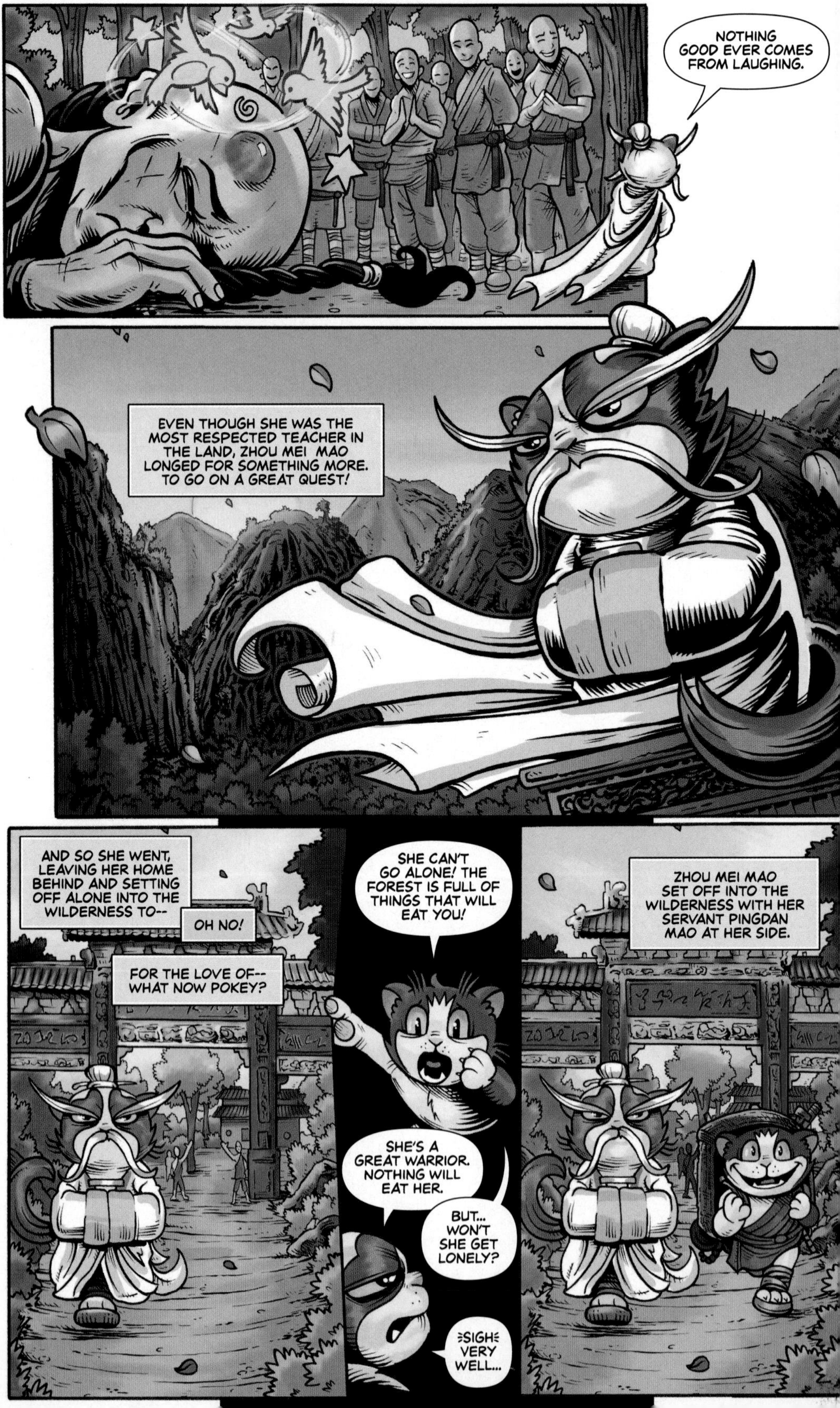
NOTHING GOOD EVER COMES FROM LAUGHING.
EVEN THOUGH SHE WAS THE MOST RESPECTED TEACHER IN THE LAND, ZHOU MEI MAO LONGED FOR SOMETHING MORE. TO GO ON A GREAT QUEST!
AND SO SHE WENT, LEAVING HER HOME BEHIND AND SETTING OFF ALONE INTO THE WILDERNESS TO--
OH NO!
FOR THE LOVE OF-- WHAT NOW POKEY?
SHE CAN'T GO ALONE! THE FOREST IS FULL OF THINGS THAT WILL EAT YOU!
SHE'S A GREAT WARRIOR. NOTHING WILL EAT HER.
BUT... WON'T SHE GET LONELY?
SIGH VERY WELL...
ZHOU MEI MAO SET OFF INTO THE WILDERNESS WITH HER SERVANT PINGDAN MAO AT HER SIDE.

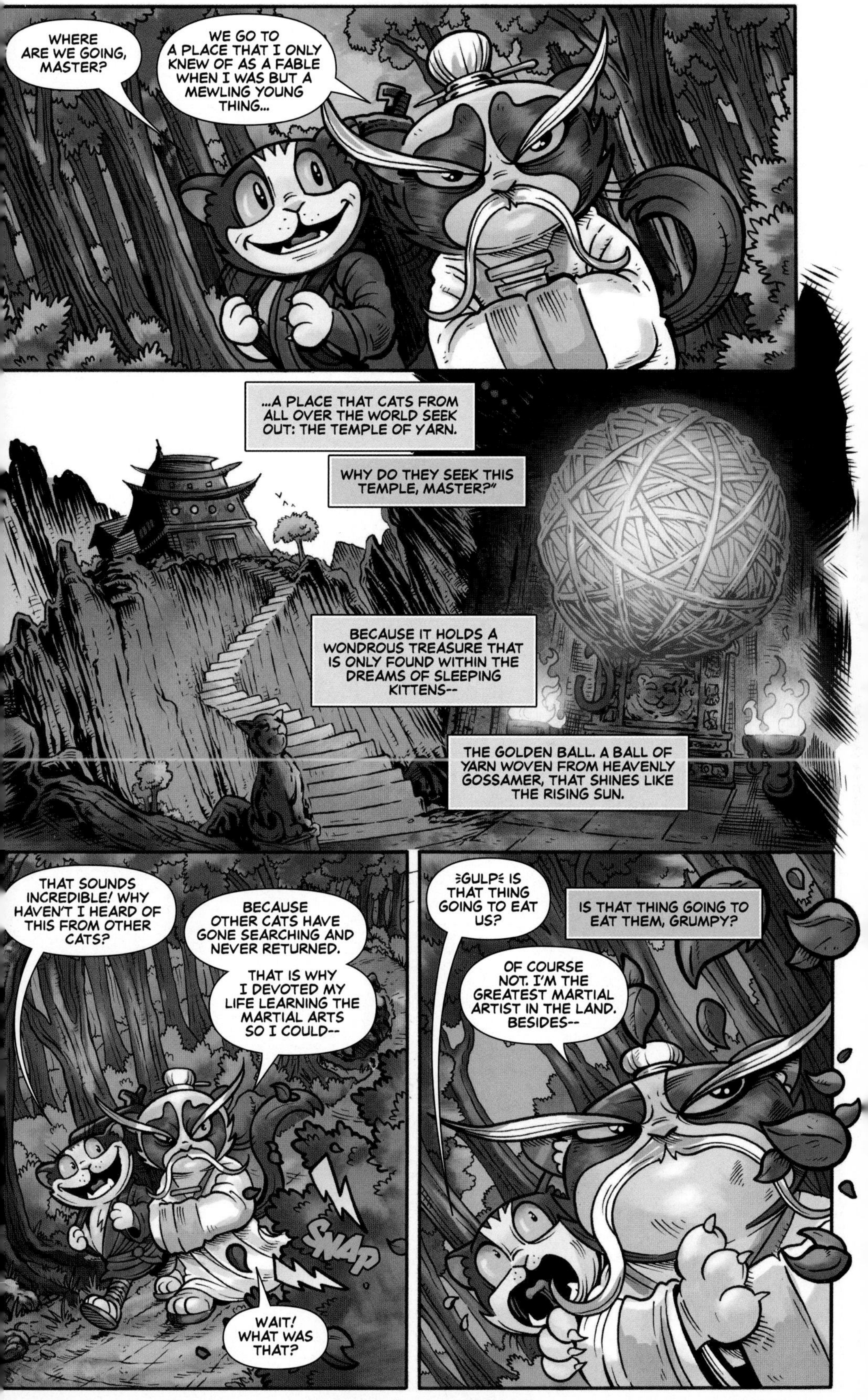

WHERE ARE WE GOING, MASTER?
WE GO TO A PLACE THAT I ONLY KNEW OF AS A FABLE WHEN I WAS BUT A MEWLING YOUNG THING...
...A PLACE THAT CATS FROM ALL OVER THE WORLD SEEK OUT: THE TEMPLE OF YARN.
WHY DO THEY SEEK THIS TEMPLE, MASTER?"
BECAUSE IT HOLDS A WONDROUS TREASURE THAT IS ONLY FOUND WITHIN THE DREAMS OF SLEEPING KITTENS--
THE GOLDEN BALL. A BALL OF YARN WOVEN FROM HEAVENLY GOSSAMER, THAT SHINES LIKE THE RISING SUN.
THAT SOUNDS INCREDIBLE! WHY HAVEN'T I HEARD OF THIS FROM OTHER CATS?
BECAUSE OTHER CATS HAVE GONE SEARCHING AND NEVER RETURNED.
THAT IS WHY I DEVOTED MY LIFE LEARNING THE MARTIAL ARTS SO I COULD--
SNAP
WAIT! WHAT WAS THAT?
GULP IS THAT THING GOING TO EAT US?
IS THAT THING GOING TO EAT THEM, GRUMPY?
OF COURSE NOT. I'M THE GREATEST MARTIAL ARTIST IN THE LAND. BESIDES--

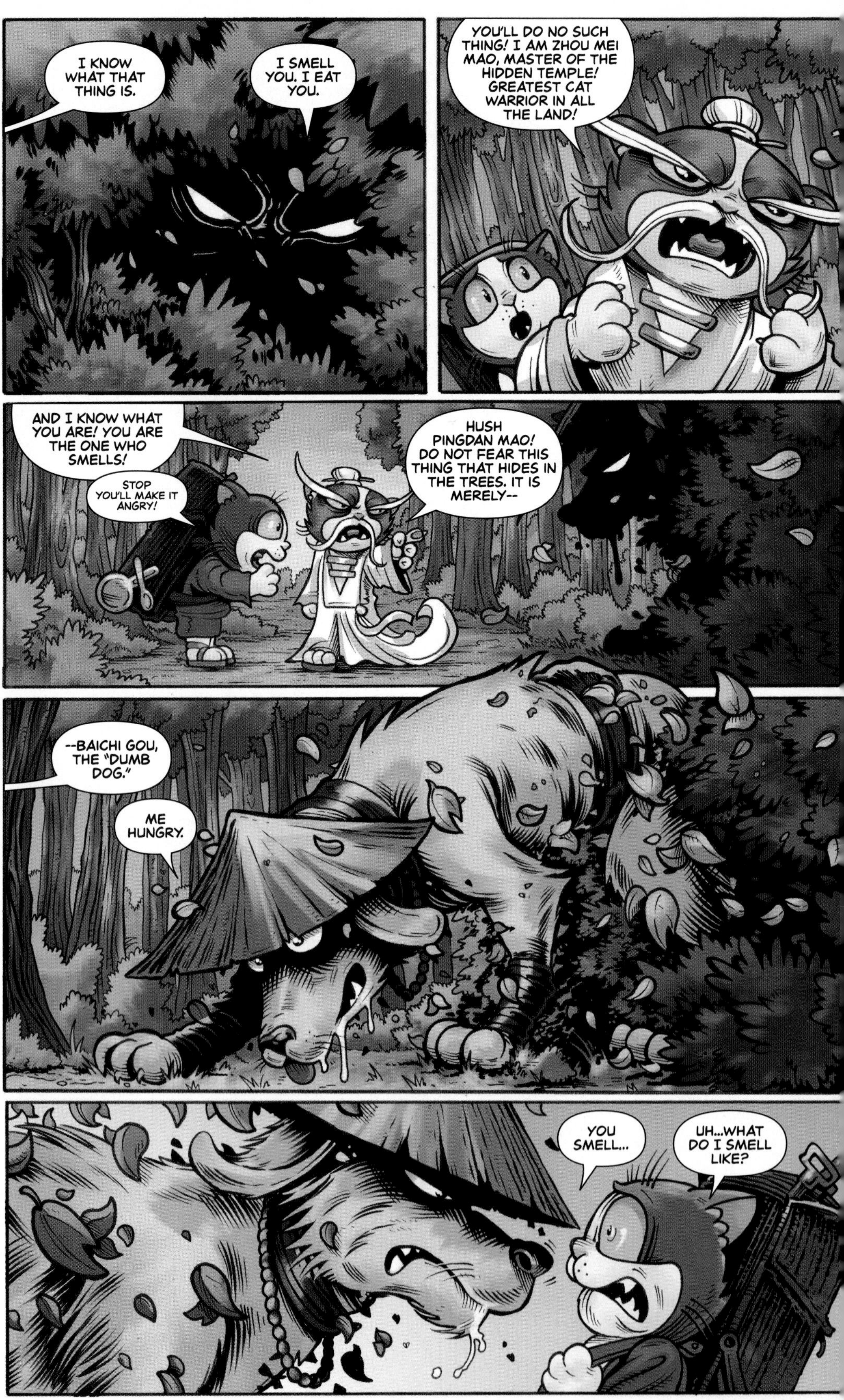
I KNOW WHAT THAT THING IS.
I SMELL YOU. I EAT YOU.
YOU'LL DO NO SUCH THING! I AM ZHOU MEI MAO, MASTER OF THE HIDDEN TEMPLE! GREATEST CAT WARRIOR IN ALL THE LAND!
AND I KNOW WHAT YOU ARE! YOU ARE THE ONE WHO SMELLS!
STOP YOU'LL MAKE IT ANGRY!
HUSH PINGDAN MAO! DO NOT FEAR THIS THING THAT HIDES IN THE TREES. IT IS MERELY--
--BAICHI GOU, THE "DUMB DOG."
ME HUNGRY.
YOU SMELL...
UH...WHAT DO I SMELL LIKE?

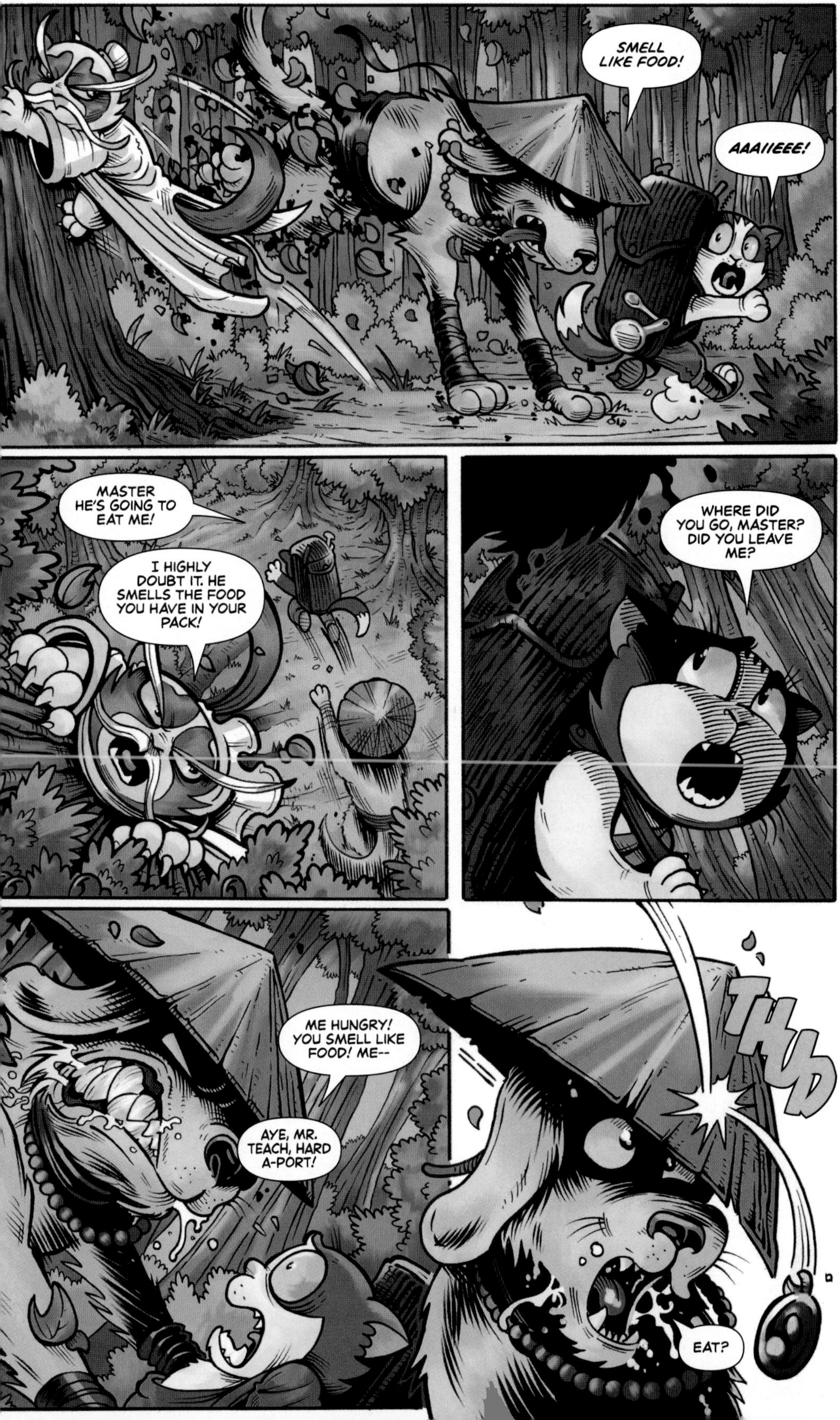
SMELL LIKE FOOD!
AAAIIEEE!
MASTER HE'S GOING TO EAT ME!
I HIGHLY DOUBT IT. HE SMELLS THE FOOD YOU HAVE IN YOUR PACK!
WHERE DID YOU GO, MASTER? DID YOU LEAVE ME?
ME HUNGRY! YOU SMELL LIKE FOOD! ME--
AYE, MR. TEACH, HARD A-PORT!
THUD
EAT?

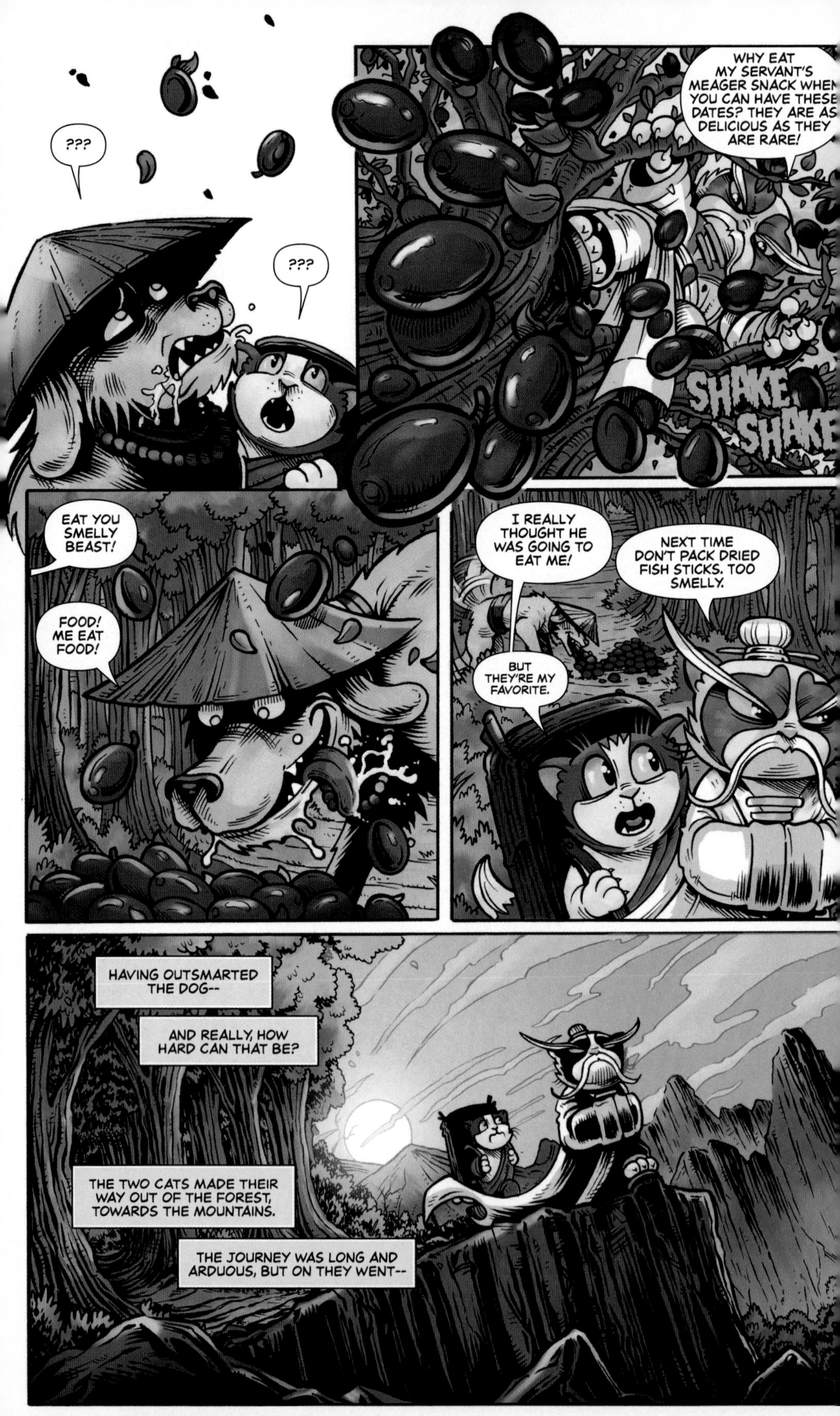
???
???
WHY EAT MY SERVANT'S MEAGER SNACK WHEN YOU CAN HAVE THESE DATES? THEY ARE AS DELICIOUS AS THEY ARE RARE!
SHAKE
SHAKE
EAT YOU SMELLY BEAST!
FOOD! ME EAT FOOD!
I REALLY THOUGHT HE WAS GOING TO EAT ME!
NEXT TIME DON'T PACK DRIED FISH STICKS. TOO SMELLY.
BUT THEY'RE MY FAVORITE.
HAVING OUTSMARTED THE DOG--
AND REALLY, HOW HARD CAN THAT BE?
THE TWO CATS MADE THEIR WAY OUT OF THE FOREST, TOWARDS THE MOUNTAINS.
THE JOURNEY WAS LONG AND ARDUOUS, BUT ON THEY WENT--

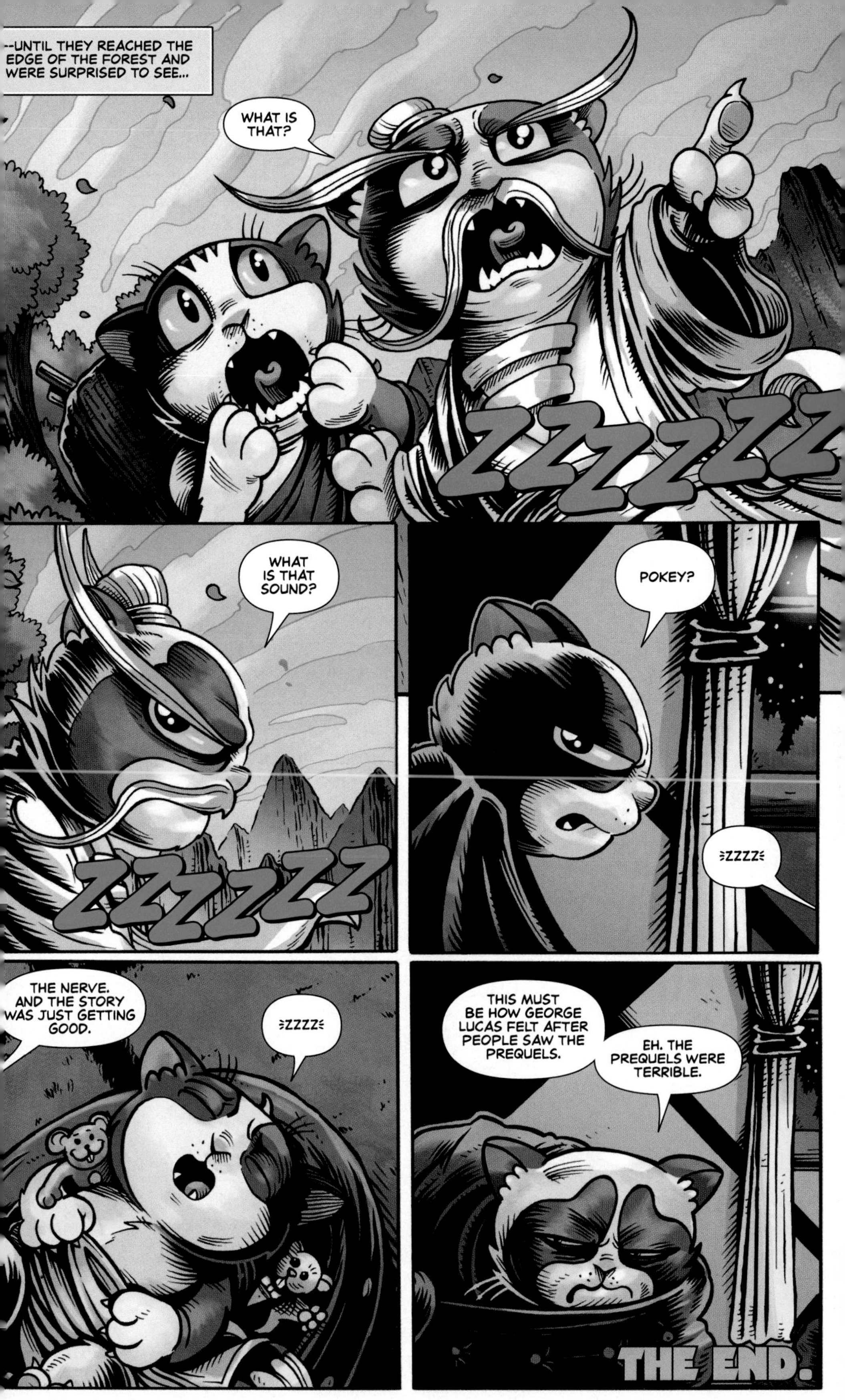
--UNTIL THEY REACHED THE EDGE OF THE FOREST AND WERE SURPRISED TO SEE...
WHAT IS THAT?
ZZZZZZ
WHAT IS THAT SOUND?
ZZZZZZ
POKEY?
ZZZZ
THE NERVE. AND THE STORY WAS JUST GETTING GOOD.
ZZZZ
THIS MUST BE HOW GEORGE LUCAS FELT AFTER PEOPLE SAW THE PREQUELS.
EH. THE PREQUELS WERE TERRIBLE.
THE END.

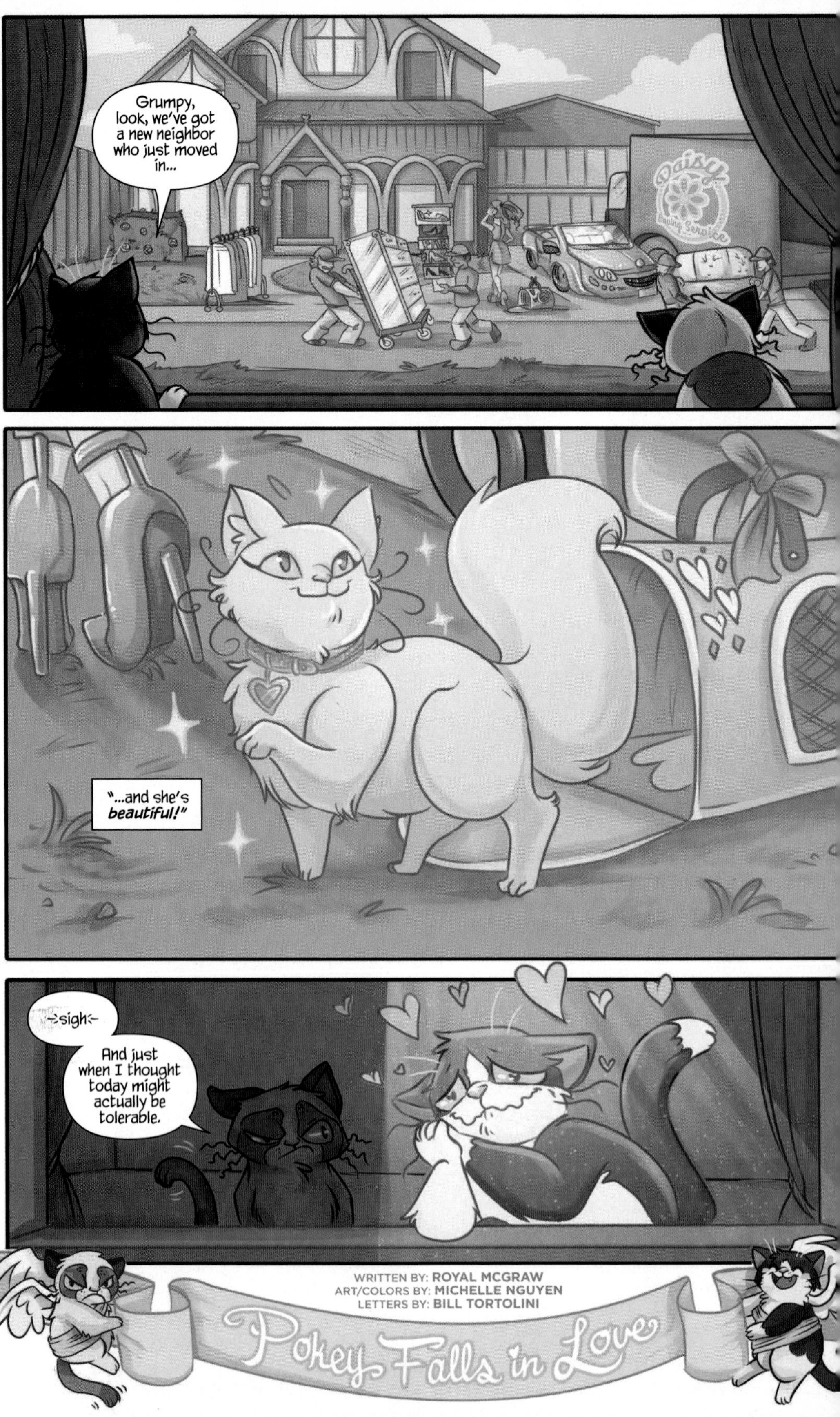

Grumpy, look, we've got a new neighbor who just moved in...
"...and she's *beautiful!*"
>sigh<
And just when I thought today might actually be tolerable.
WRITTEN BY: ROYAL MCGRAW
ART/COLORS BY: MICHELLE NGUYEN
LETTERS BY: BILL TORTOLINI
Pokey Falls in Love

Psst, Grumpy, wake up!

Yes, my minions, soon our triumph will be complete--

Grumpy!

Whut-- whuzzah--

Oh, Pokey, it's *you.*

Grumpy, I need your help.

My heart's beating fast, I'm sweating all over, and I can't sleep. I'm completely miserable!

What's wrong with me? Do I have the bubonic plague again?

You never had the bubonic plague, Pokey. I made that up.

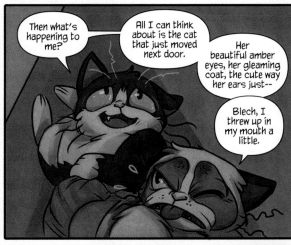

Then what's happening to me?

All I can think about is the cat that just moved next door.

Her beautiful amber eyes, her gleaming coat, the cute way her ears just--

Blech, I threw up in my mouth a little.

Pokey, you've done something very dumb. You've *fallen in love.*

...in love?

But I don't know the first thing about love, Grumpy!

Clearly.

Oh no! I don't even know her name.

What if I introduce myself and she rejects me?

Then you'll learn an important lesson, Pokey.

The world is a cruel, heartless place, and you were a fool to ever get your hopes up.

*Sweet dreams.*

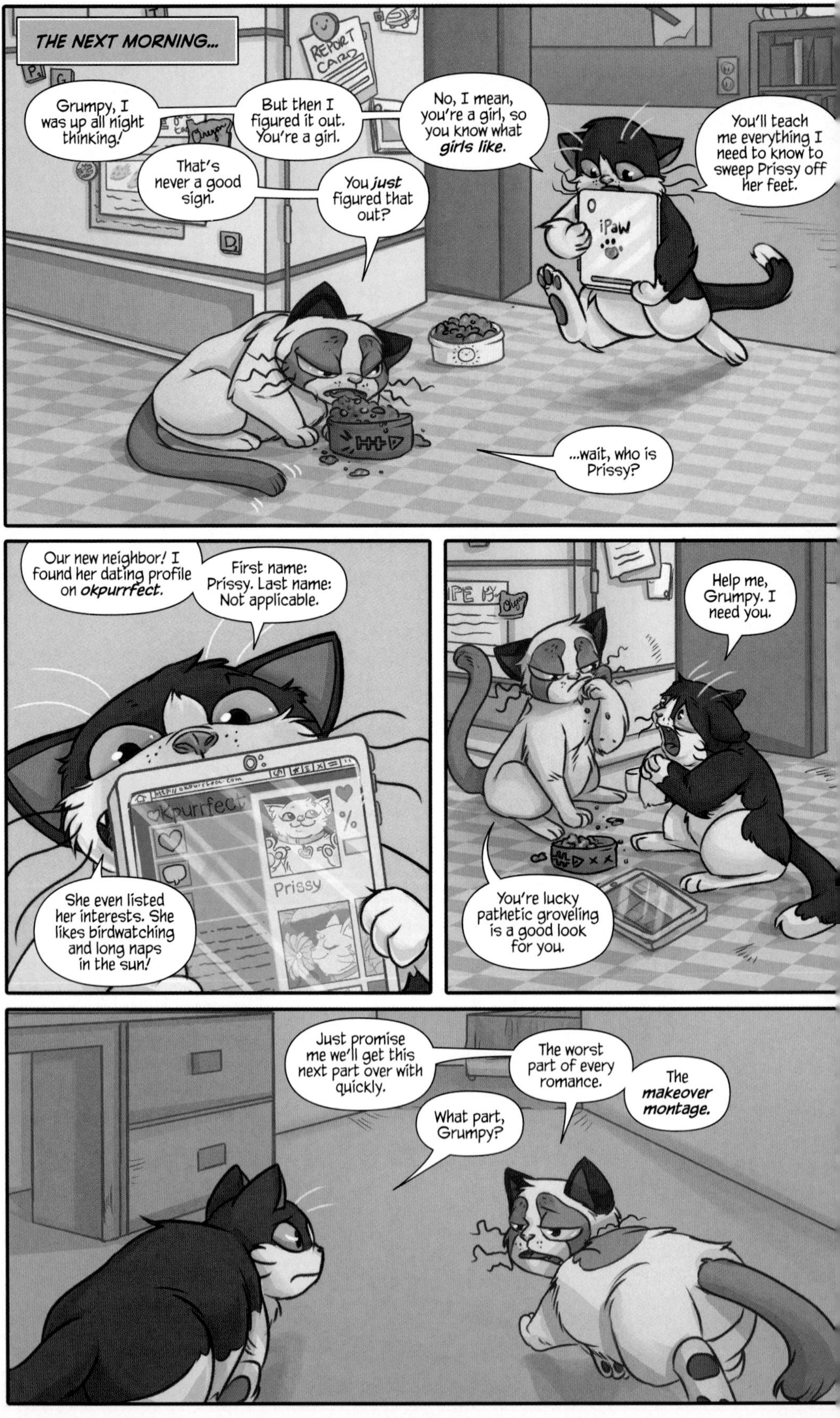
THE NEXT MORNING...
Grumpy, I was up all night thinking!
That's never a good sign.
But then I figured it out. You're a girl.
You *just* figured that out?
No, I mean, you're a girl, so you know what ***girls like***.
You'll teach me everything I need to know to sweep Prissy off her feet.
iPaw
...wait, who is Prissy?
Our new neighbor! I found her dating profile on ***okpurrfect***.
First name: Prissy. Last name: Not applicable.
okpurrfect
Prissy
She even listed her interests. She likes birdwatching and long naps in the sun!
Help me, Grumpy. I need you.
You're lucky pathetic groveling is a good look for you.
Just promise me we'll get this next part over with quickly.
What part, Grumpy?
The worst part of every romance.
The ***makeover montage.***

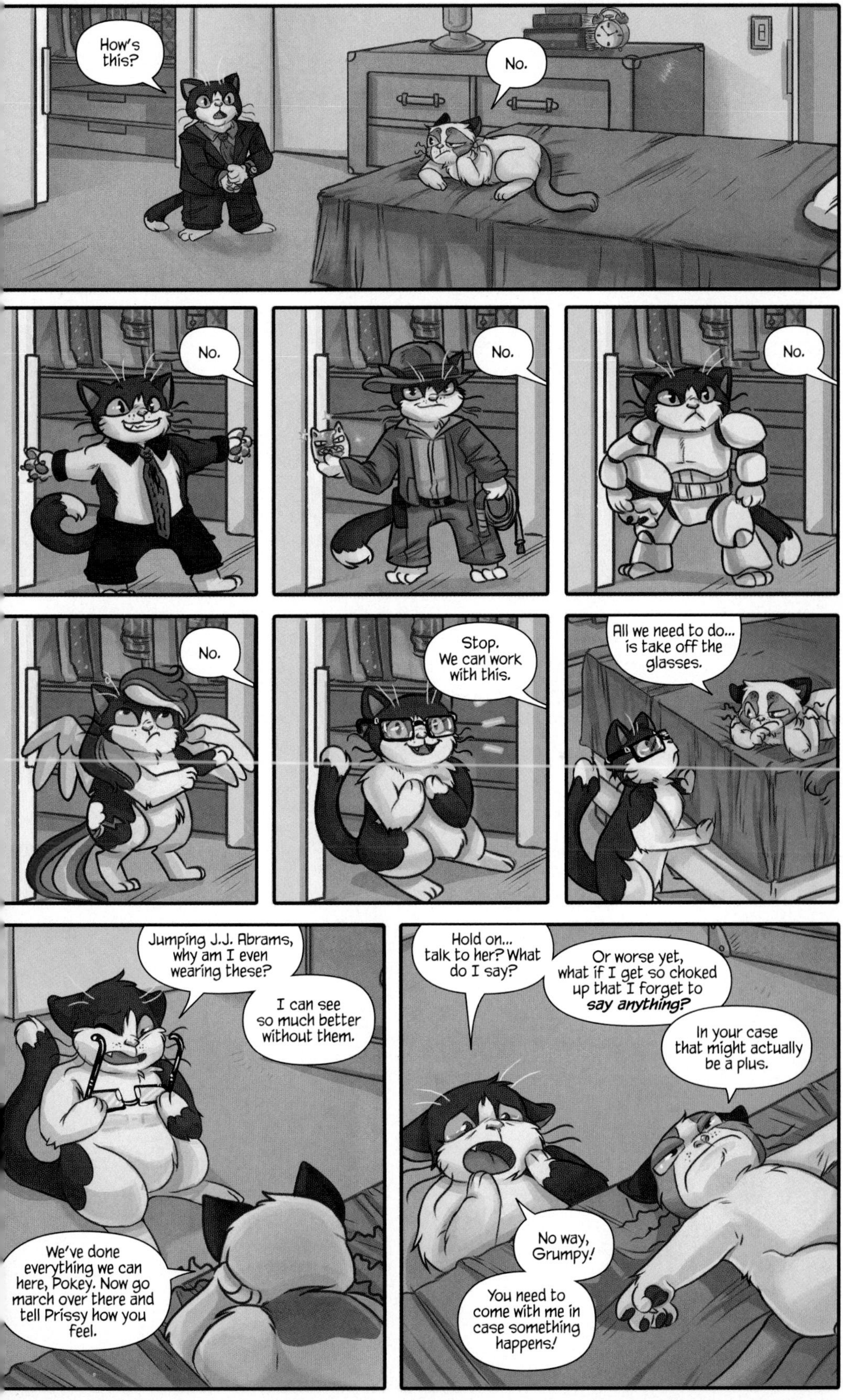

How's this?
No.
No.
No.
No.
No.
Stop. We can work with this.
All we need to do... is take off the glasses.
Jumping J.J. Abrams, why am I even wearing these?
I can see so much better without them.
We've done everything we can here, Pokey. Now go march over there and tell Prissy how you feel.
Hold on... talk to her? What do I say?
Or worse yet, what if I get so choked up that I forget to *say anything?*
In your case that might actually be a plus.
No way, Grumpy!
You need to come with me in case something happens!

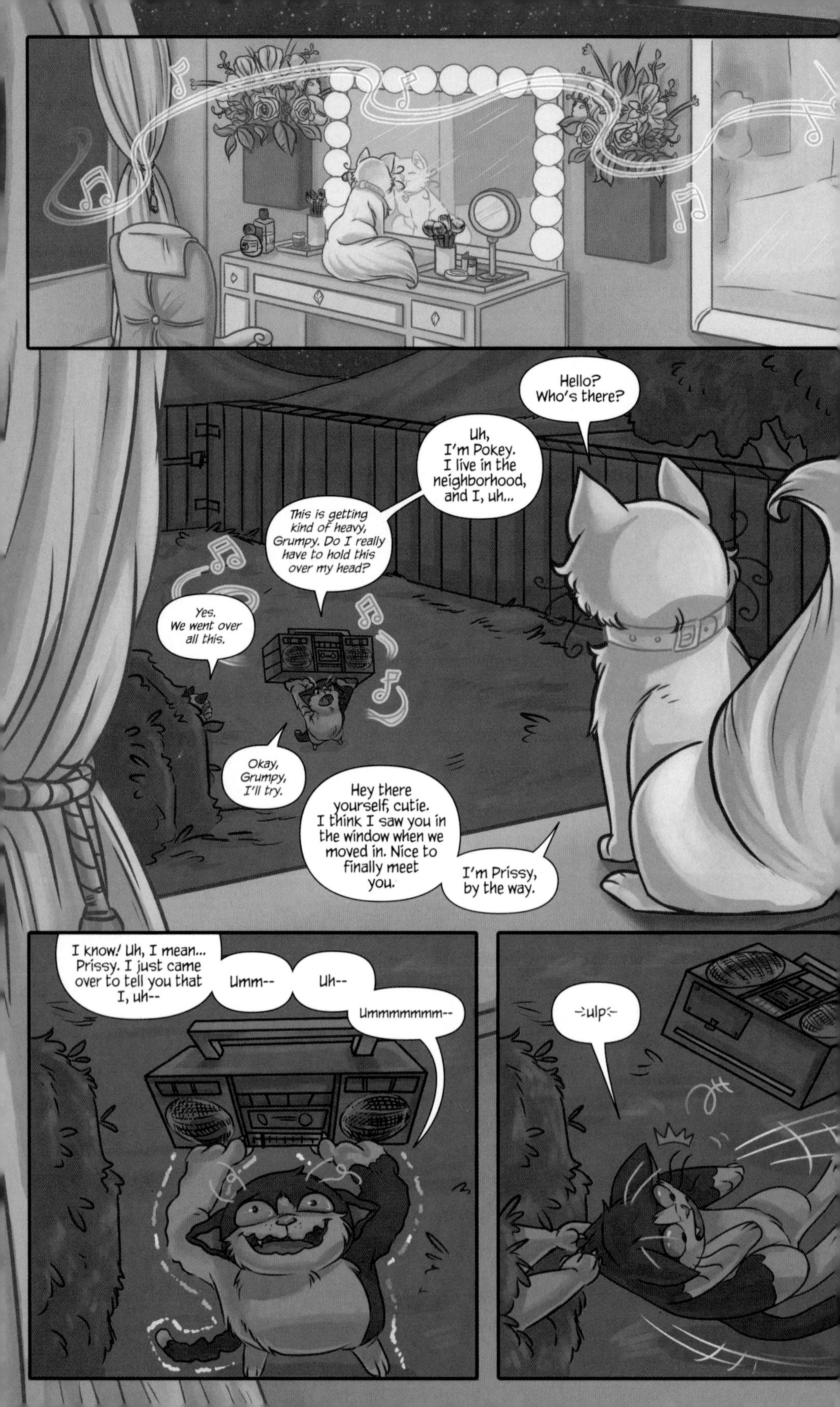
Hello? Who's there?
Uh, I'm Pokey. I live in the neighborhood, and I, uh...
This is getting kind of heavy, Grumpy. Do I really have to hold this over my head?
Yes. We went over all this.
Okay, Grumpy, I'll try.
Hey there yourself, cutie. I think I saw you in the window when we moved in. Nice to finally meet you.
I'm Prissy, by the way.
I know! Uh, I mean... Prissy. I just came over to tell you that I, uh--
Umm--
Uh--
Ummmmmmm--
-ulp-

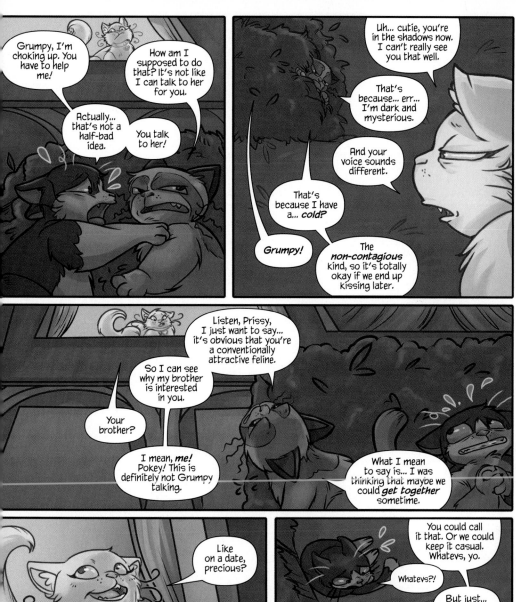

**Panel 1:**

Grumpy, I'm choking up. You have to help me!

How am I supposed to do that? It's not like I can talk to her for you.

Actually... that's not a half-bad idea.

You talk to her!

**Panel 2:**

Uh... cutie, you're in the shadows now. I can't really see you that well.

That's because... err... I'm dark and mysterious.

And your voice sounds different.

That's because I have a... *cold?*

*Grumpy!*

The *non-contagious* kind, so it's totally okay if we end up kissing later.

**Panel 3:**

Listen, Prissy, I just want to say... it's obvious that you're a conventionally attractive feline.

So I can see why my brother is interested in you.

Your brother?

I mean, *me!* Pokey! This is definitely not Grumpy talking.

What I mean to say is... I was thinking that maybe we could *get together* sometime.

**Panel 4:**

Like on a date, precious?

**Panel 5:**

You could call it that. Or we could keep it casual. Whatevs, yo.

Whatevs?!

But just... one last thing, Prissy.

Don't break Pokey's heart, okay?

**Panel 6:**

Prissy! Supper time!

Sorry, I've to go.

Goodnight, Pokey.

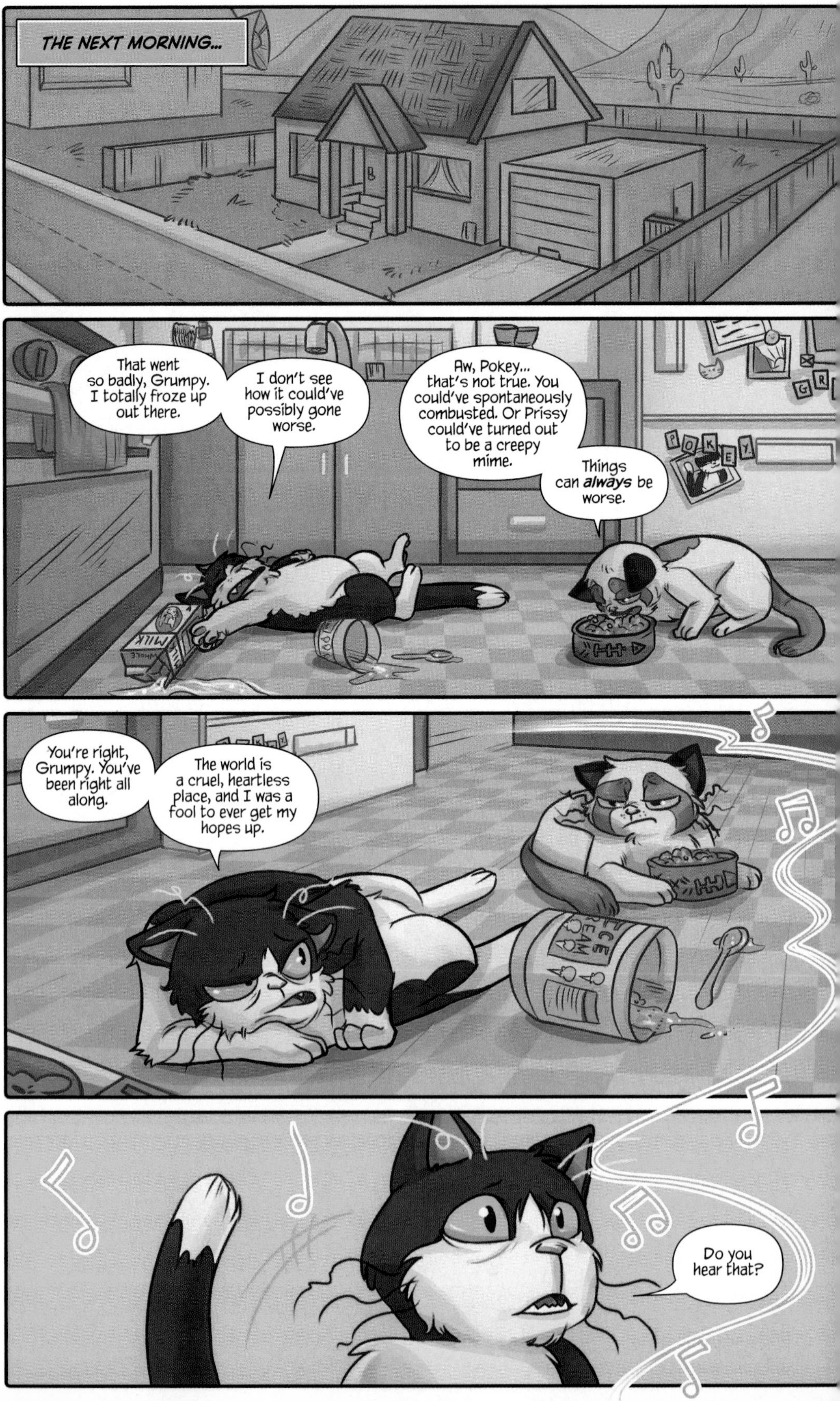
THE NEXT MORNING...
That went so badly, Grumpy. I totally froze up out there.
I don't see how it could've possibly gone worse.
Aw, Pokey... that's not true. You could've spontaneously combusted. Or Prissy could've turned out to be a creepy mime.
Things can *always* be worse.
MILK
WHOLE
POKEY
You're right, Grumpy. You've been right all along.
The world is a cruel, heartless place, and I was a fool to ever get my hopes up.
ICE CREAM
Do you hear that?

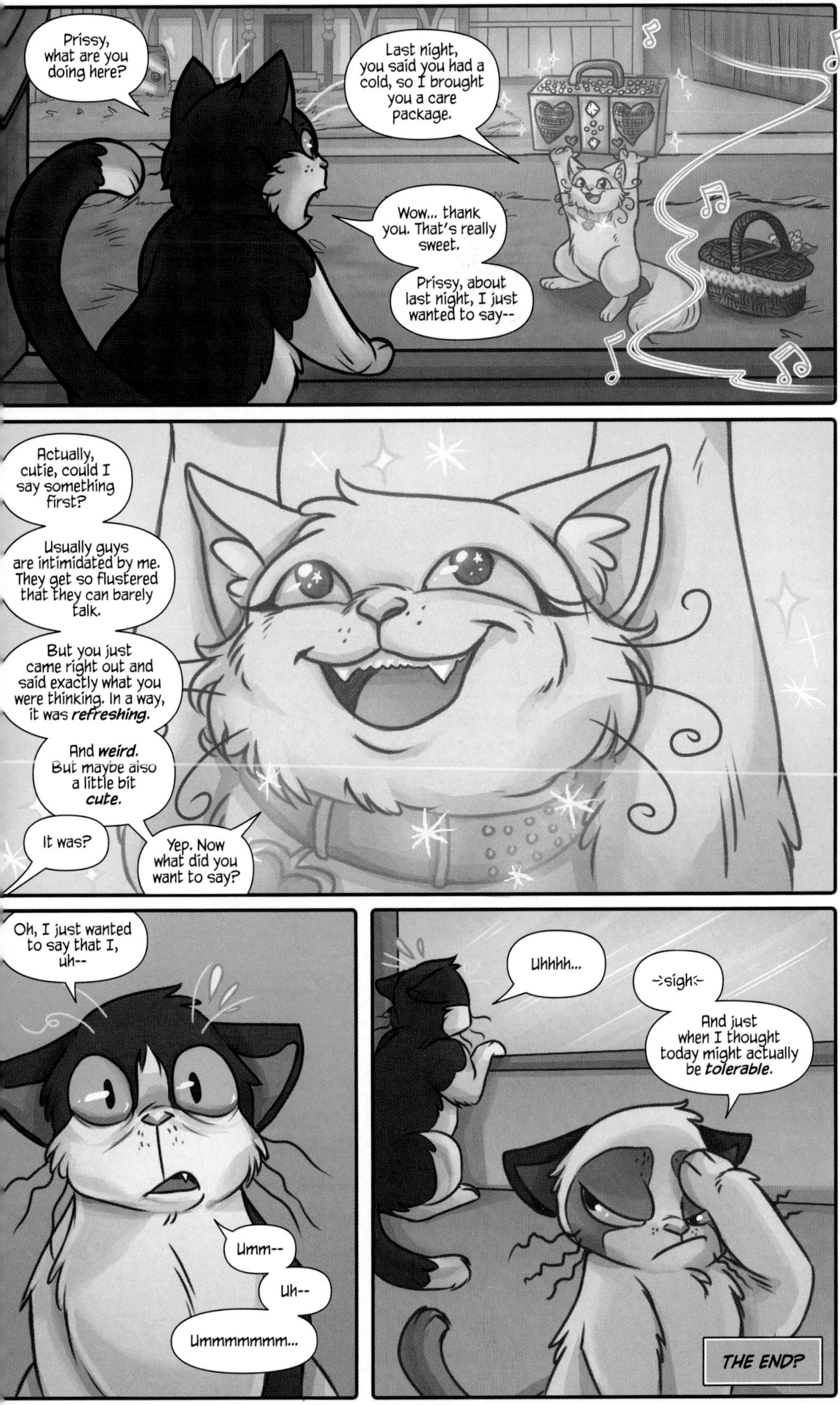
Prissy, what are you doing here?
Last night, you said you had a cold, so I brought you a care package.
Wow... thank you. That's really sweet.
Prissy, about last night, I just wanted to say--
Actually, cutie, could I say something first?
Usually guys are intimidated by me. They get so flustered that they can barely talk.
But you just came right out and said exactly what you were thinking. In a way, it was *refreshing*.
And *weird*. But maybe also a little bit *cute*.
It was?
Yep. Now what did you want to say?
Oh, I just wanted to say that I, uh--
Umm--
Uh--
Ummmmmmm...
Uhhhh...
-sigh-
And just when I thought today might actually be *tolerable*.
THE END?

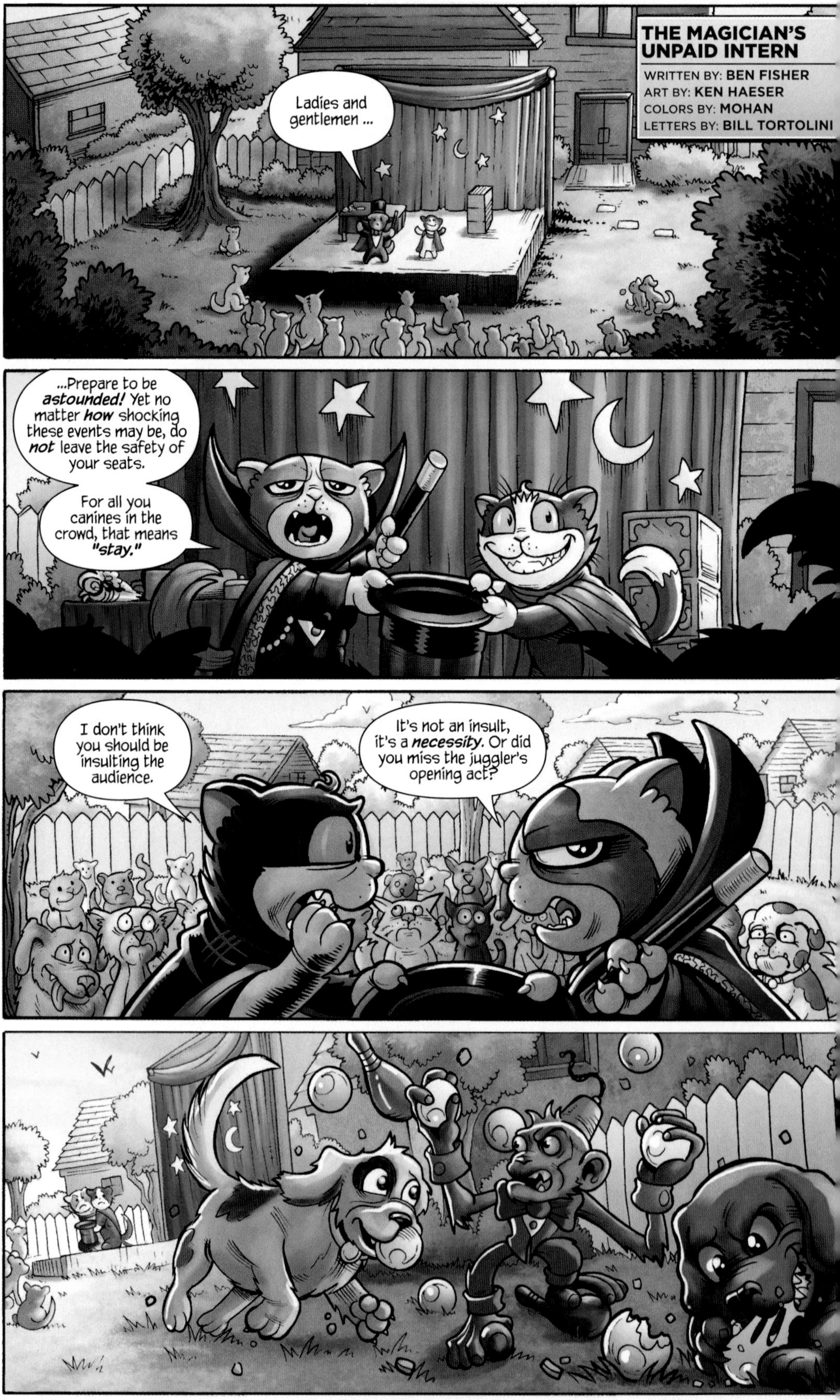
THE MAGICIAN'S UNPAID INTERN
WRITTEN BY: BEN FISHER
ART BY: KEN HAESER
COLORS BY: MOHAN
LETTERS BY: BILL TORTOLINI
Ladies and gentlemen ...
...Prepare to be astounded! Yet no matter how shocking these events may be, do not leave the safety of your seats.
For all you canines in the crowd, that means "stay."
I don't think you should be insulting the audience.
It's not an insult, it's a necessity. Or did you miss the juggler's opening act?

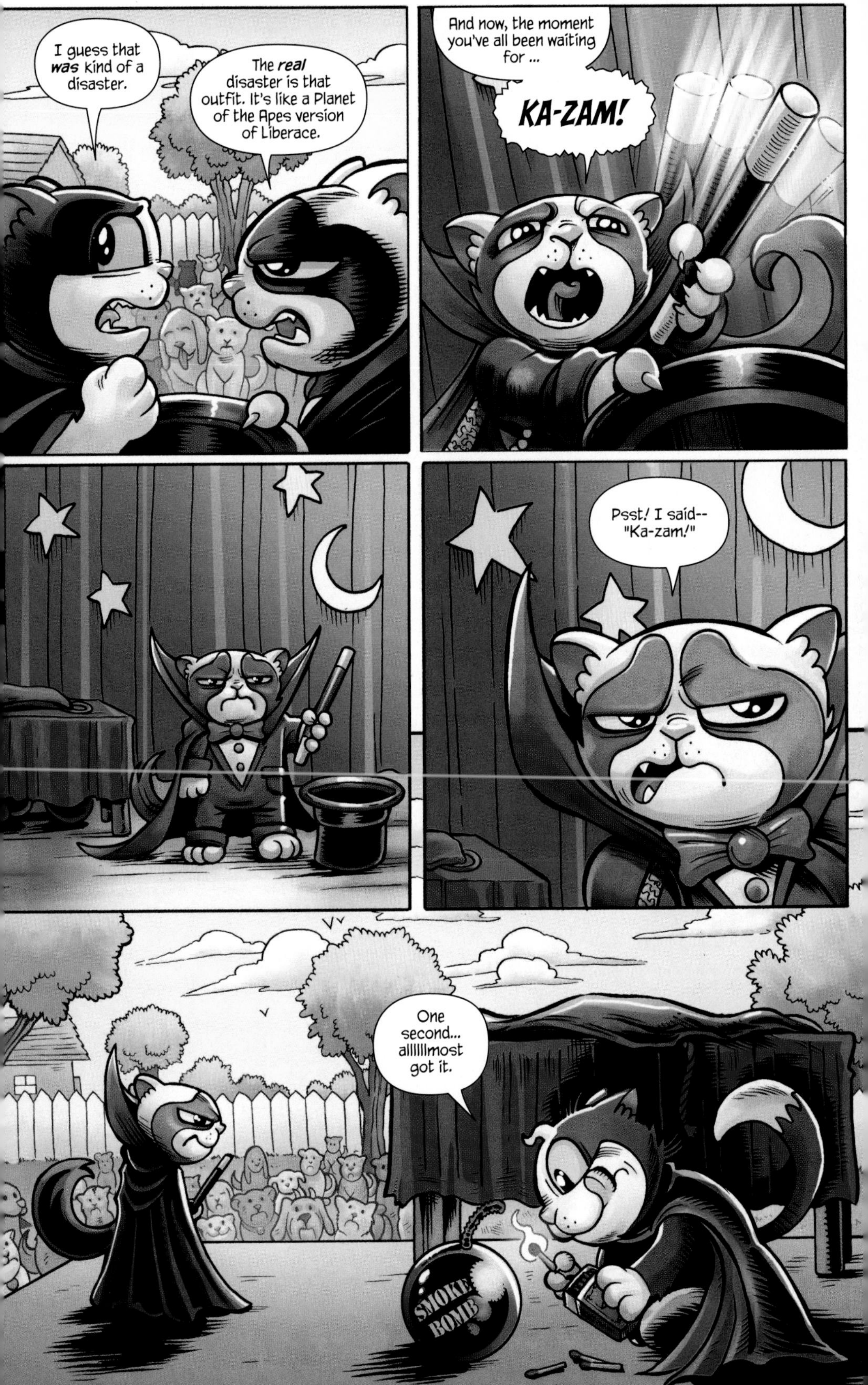
I guess that *was* kind of a disaster.
The *real* disaster is that outfit. It's like a Planet of the Apes version of Liberace.
And now, the moment you've all been waiting for ...
KA-ZAM!
Psst! I said-- "Ka-zam!"
One second... alllllllmost got it.
SMOKE BOMB

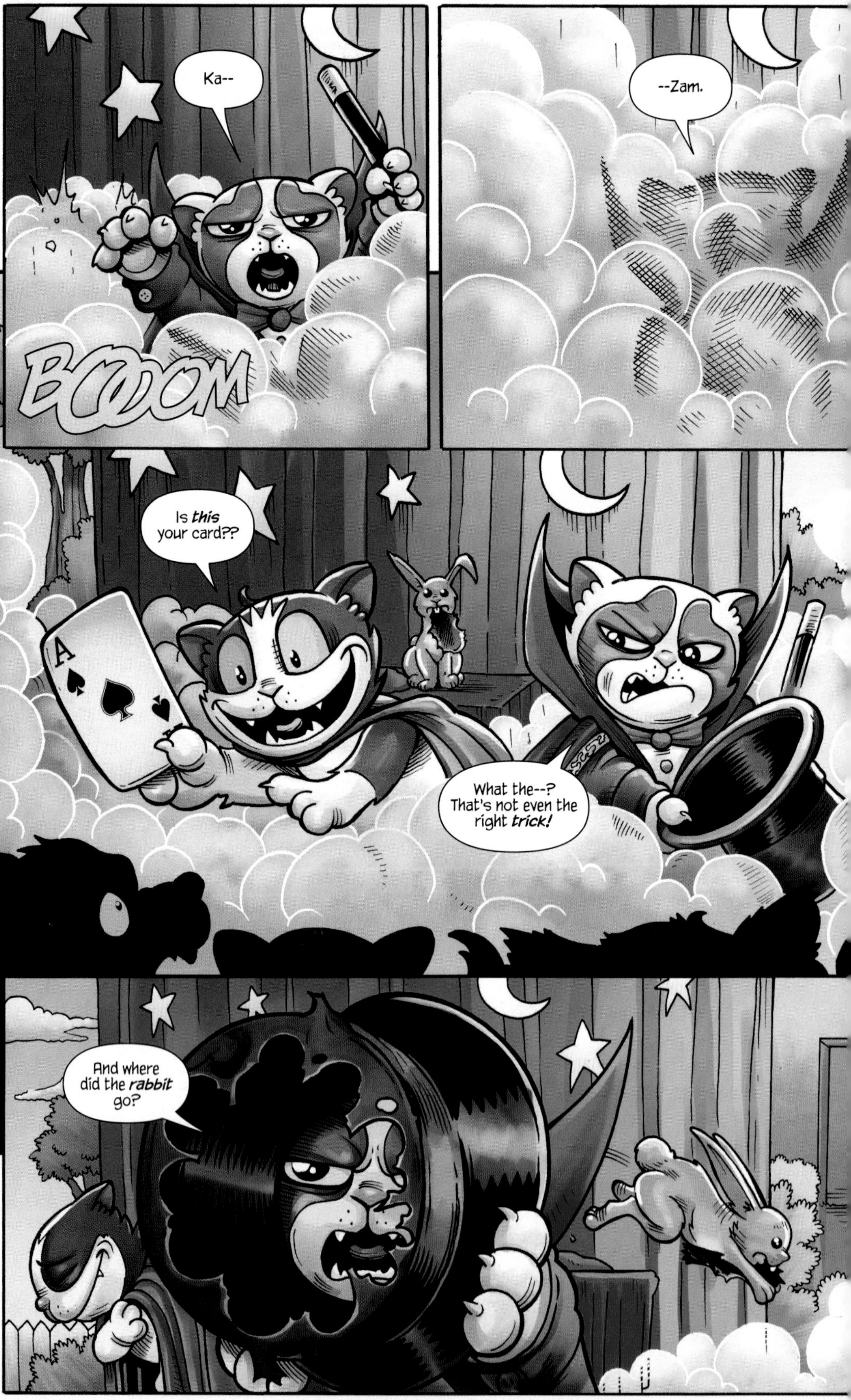
Ka--
BOOOM
--Zam.
Is *this* your card??
What the--? That's not even the right *trick!*
And where did the *rabbit* go?

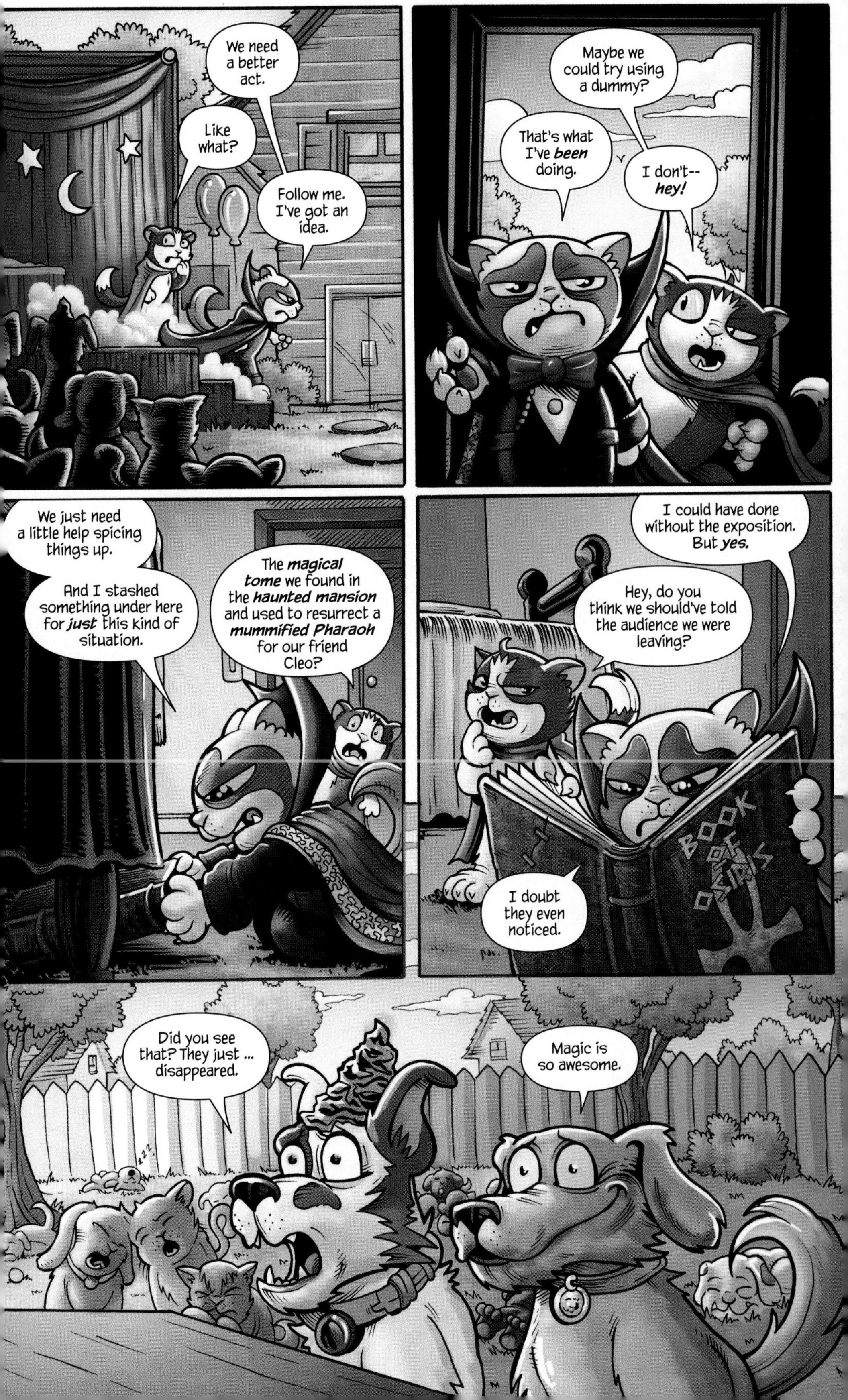

We need a better act.
Like what?
Follow me. I've got an idea.
Maybe we could try using a dummy?
That's what I've *been* doing.
I don't-- *hey!*
We just need a little help spicing things up.
And I stashed something under here for *just* this kind of situation.
The *magical tome* we found in the *haunted mansion* and used to resurrect a *mummified Pharaoh* for our friend Cleo?
I could have done without the exposition. But *yes.*
Hey, do you think we should've told the audience we were leaving?
I doubt they even noticed.
BOOK OF OSIRIS
Did you see that? They just ... disappeared.
Magic is so awesome.

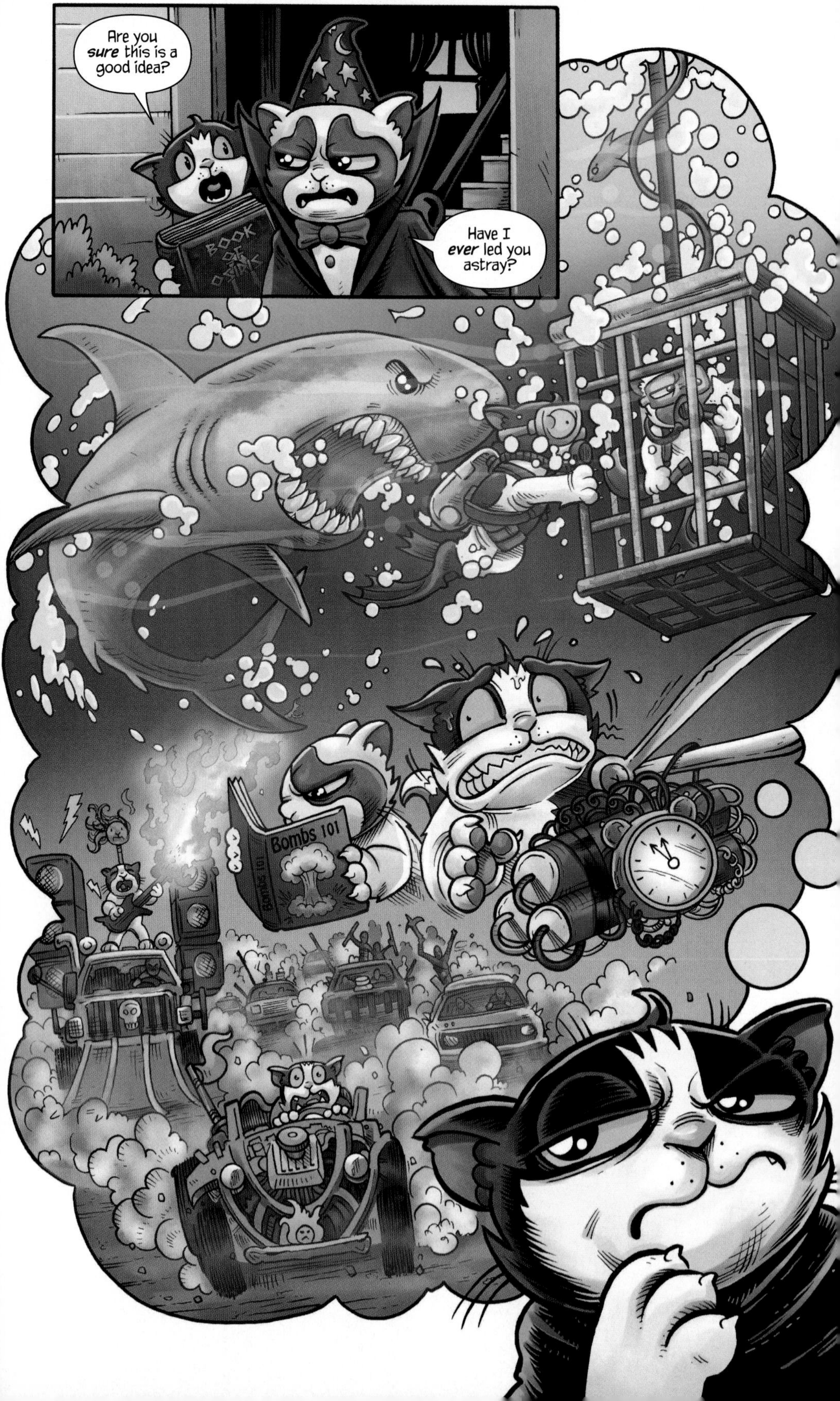
Are you *sure* this is a good idea?
Have I *ever* led you astray?
BOOK OF OSIRIS
Bombs 101

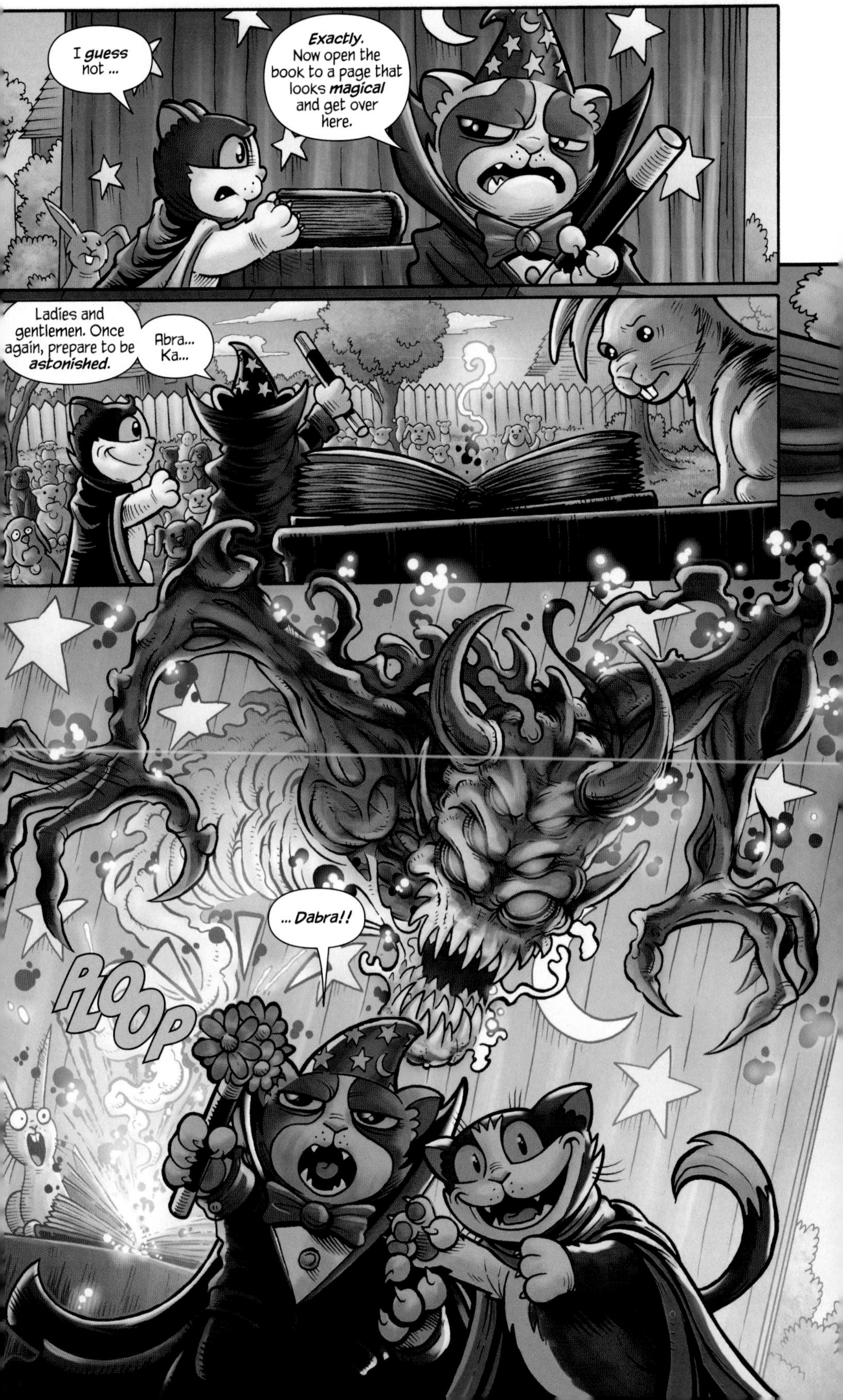

I *guess* not ...
***Exactly.*** Now open the book to a page that looks ***magical*** and get over here.
Ladies and gentlemen. Once again, prepare to be ***astonished.***
Abra... Ka...
*... Dabra!!*
PLOOP

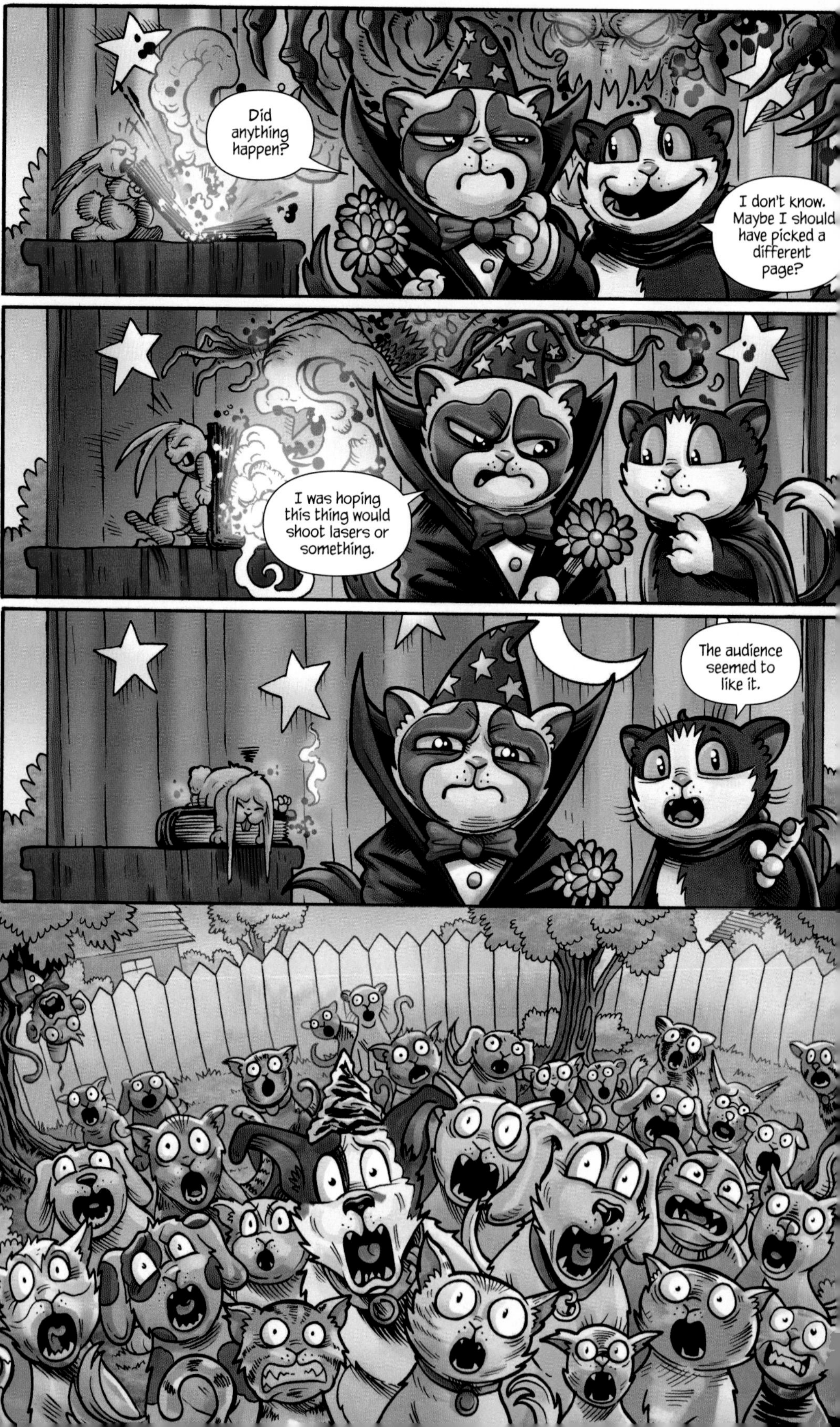
Did anything happen?
I don't know. Maybe I should have picked a different page?
I was hoping this thing would shoot lasers or something.
The audience seemed to like it.

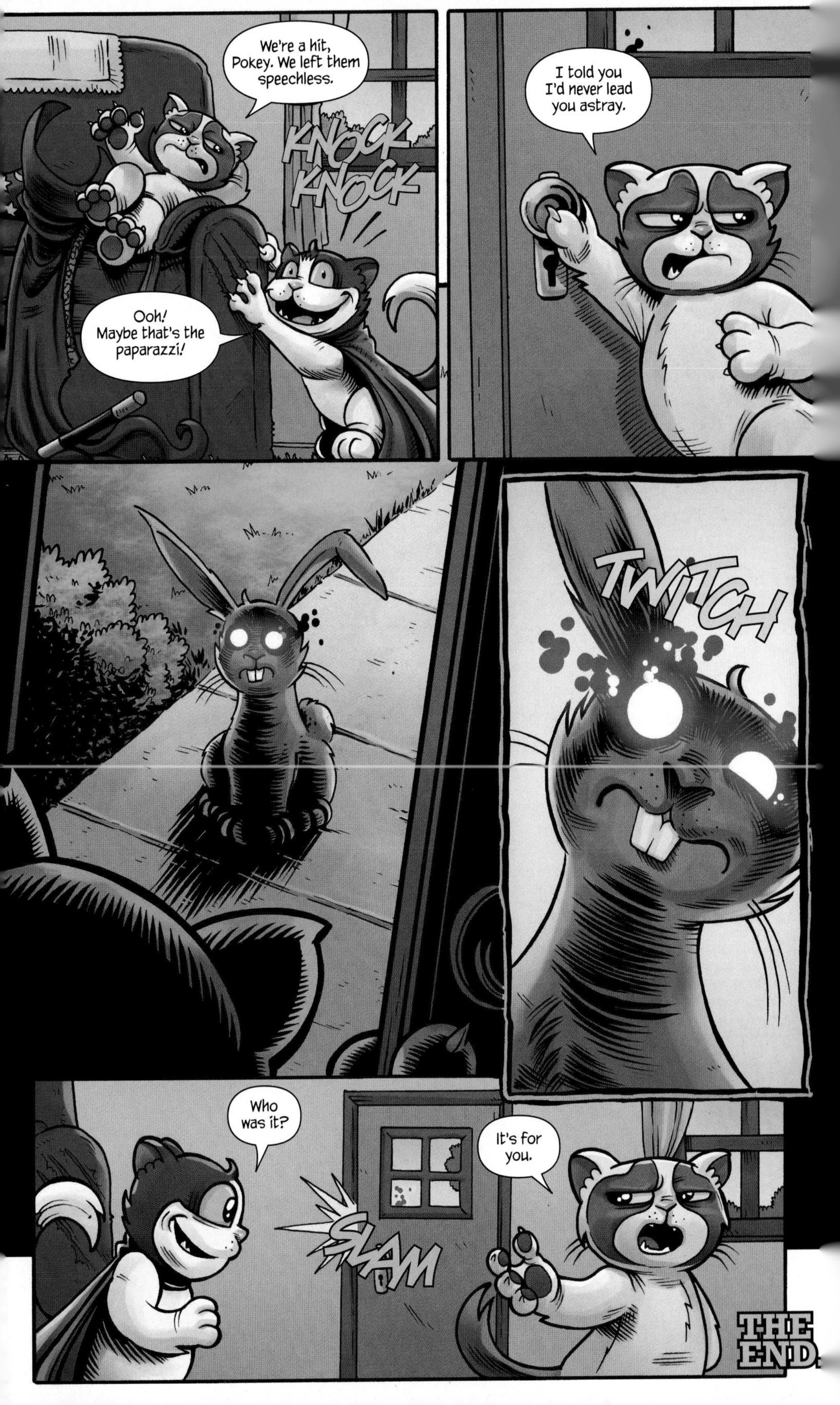
We're a hit, Pokey. We left them speechless.
KNOCK KNOCK
Ooh! Maybe that's the paparazzi!
I told you I'd never lead you astray.
TWITCH
Who was it?
SLAM
It's for you.
THE END.

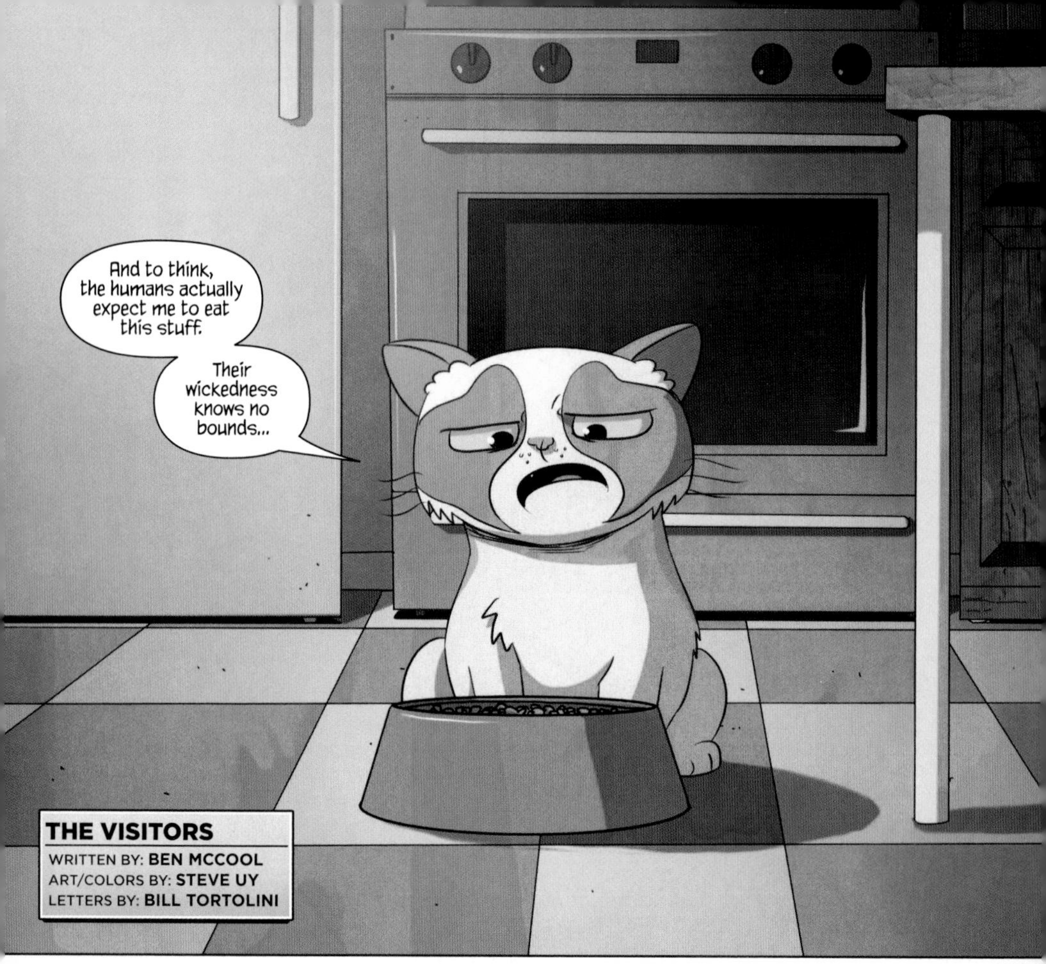
And to think, the humans actually expect me to eat this stuff.
Their wickedness knows no bounds...
THE VISITORS
WRITTEN BY: BEN MCCOOL
ART/COLORS BY: STEVE UY
LETTERS BY: BILL TORTOLINI

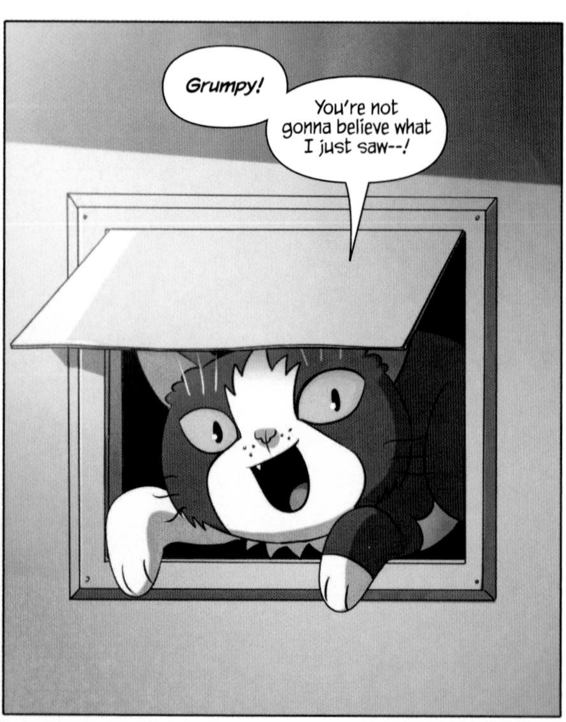
*Grumpy!*
You're not gonna believe what I just saw--!

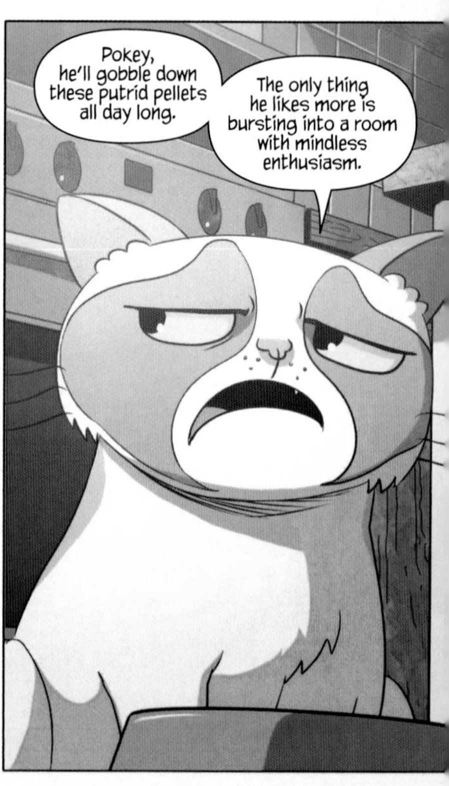
Pokey, he'll gobble down these putrid pellets all day long.
The only thing he likes more is bursting into a room with mindless enthusiasm.

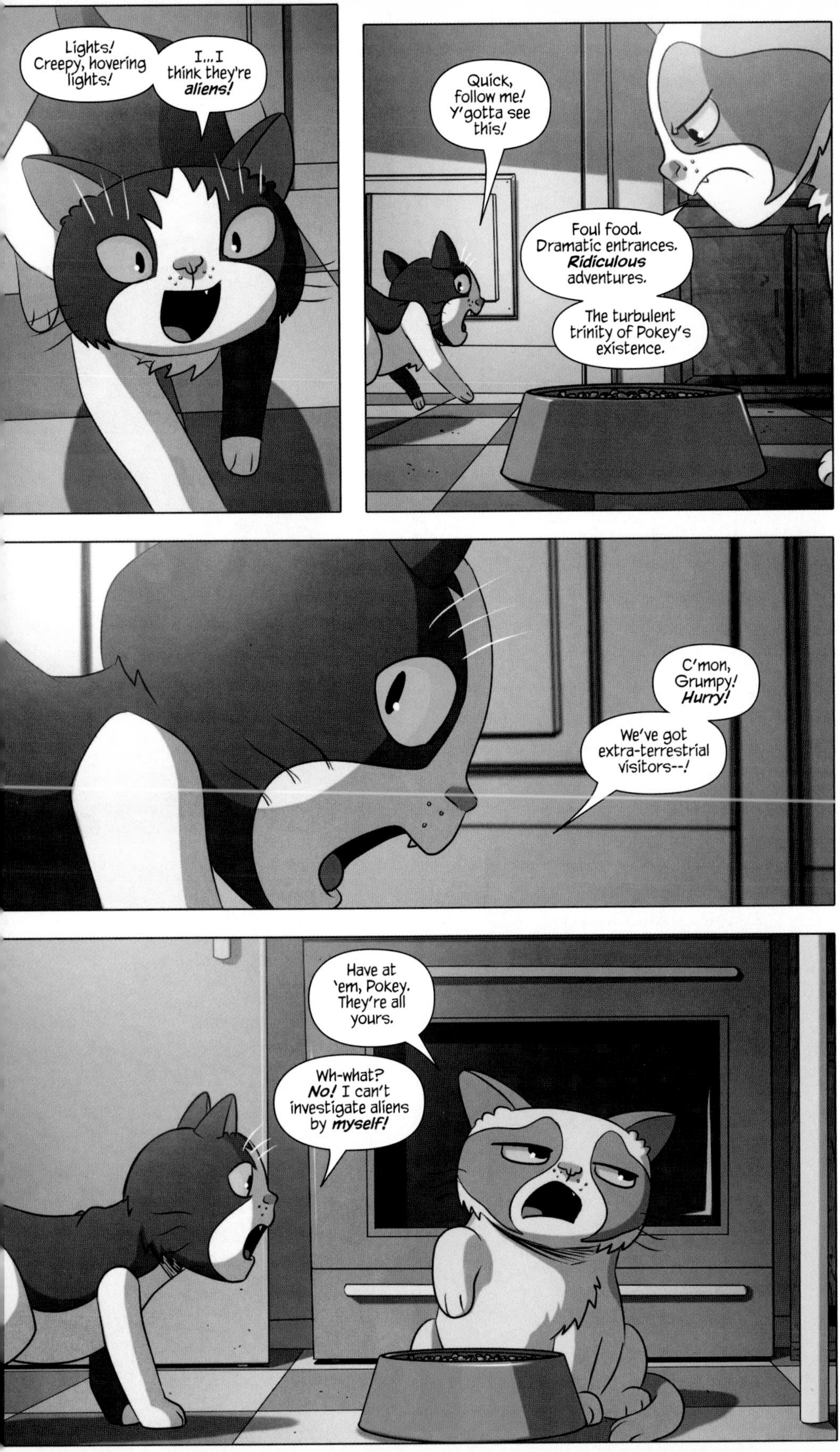
Lights! Creepy, hovering lights!
I...I think they're ***aliens!***
Quick, follow me! Y'gotta see this!
Foul food. Dramatic entrances. ***Ridiculous*** adventures.
The turbulent trinity of Pokey's existence.
C'mon, Grumpy! ***Hurry!***
We've got extra-terrestrial visitors--!
Have at 'em, Pokey. They're all yours.
Wh-what? ***No!*** I can't investigate aliens by ***myself!***

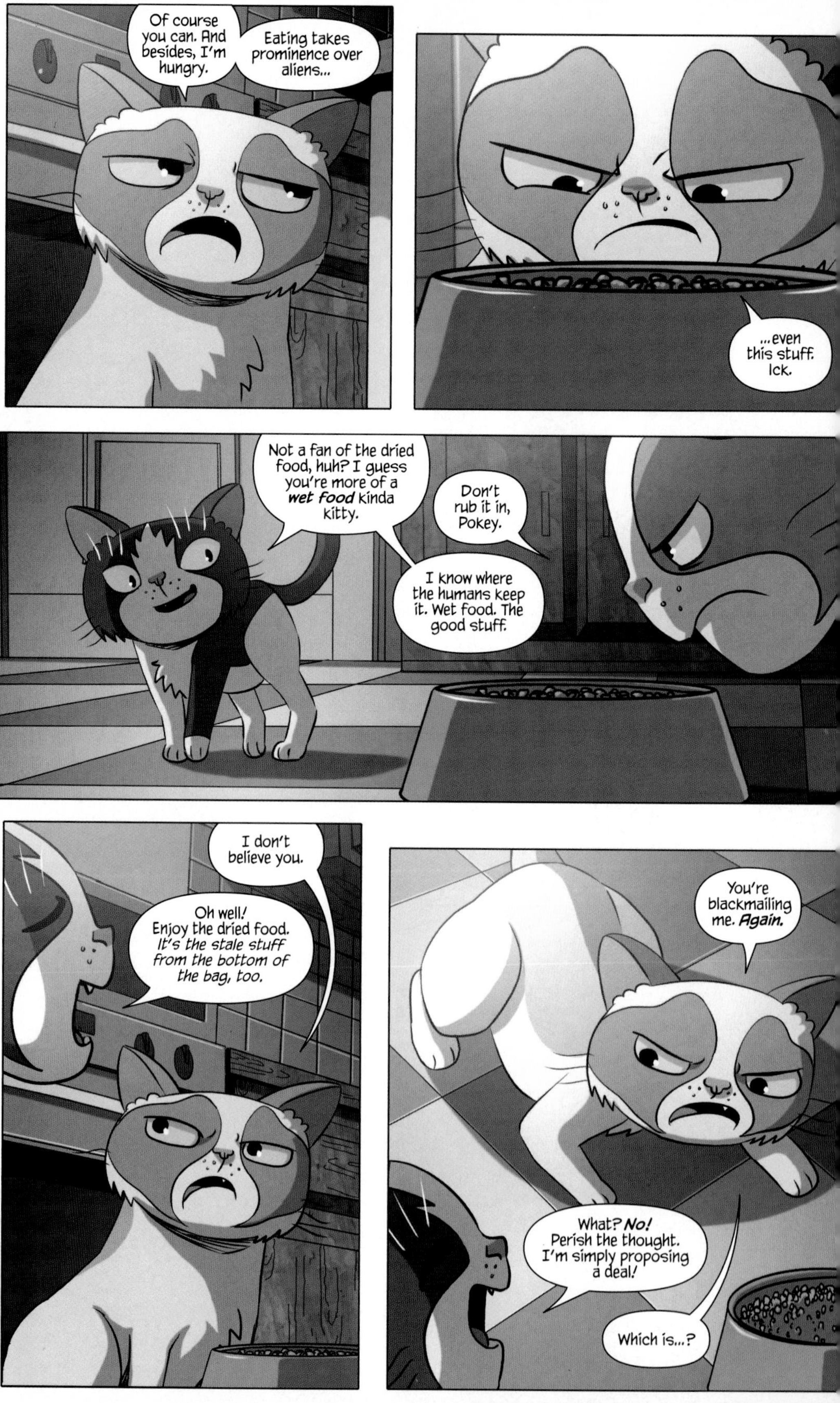

Of course you can. And besides, I'm hungry.
Eating takes prominence over aliens...
...even this stuff. Ick.
Not a fan of the dried food, huh? I guess you're more of a *wet food* kinda kitty.
Don't rub it in, Pokey.
I know where the humans keep it. Wet food. The good stuff.
I don't believe you.
Oh well! Enjoy the dried food. *It's the stale stuff from the bottom of the bag, too.*
You're blackmailing me. *Again.*
What? *No!* Perish the thought. I'm simply proposing a deal!
Which is...?

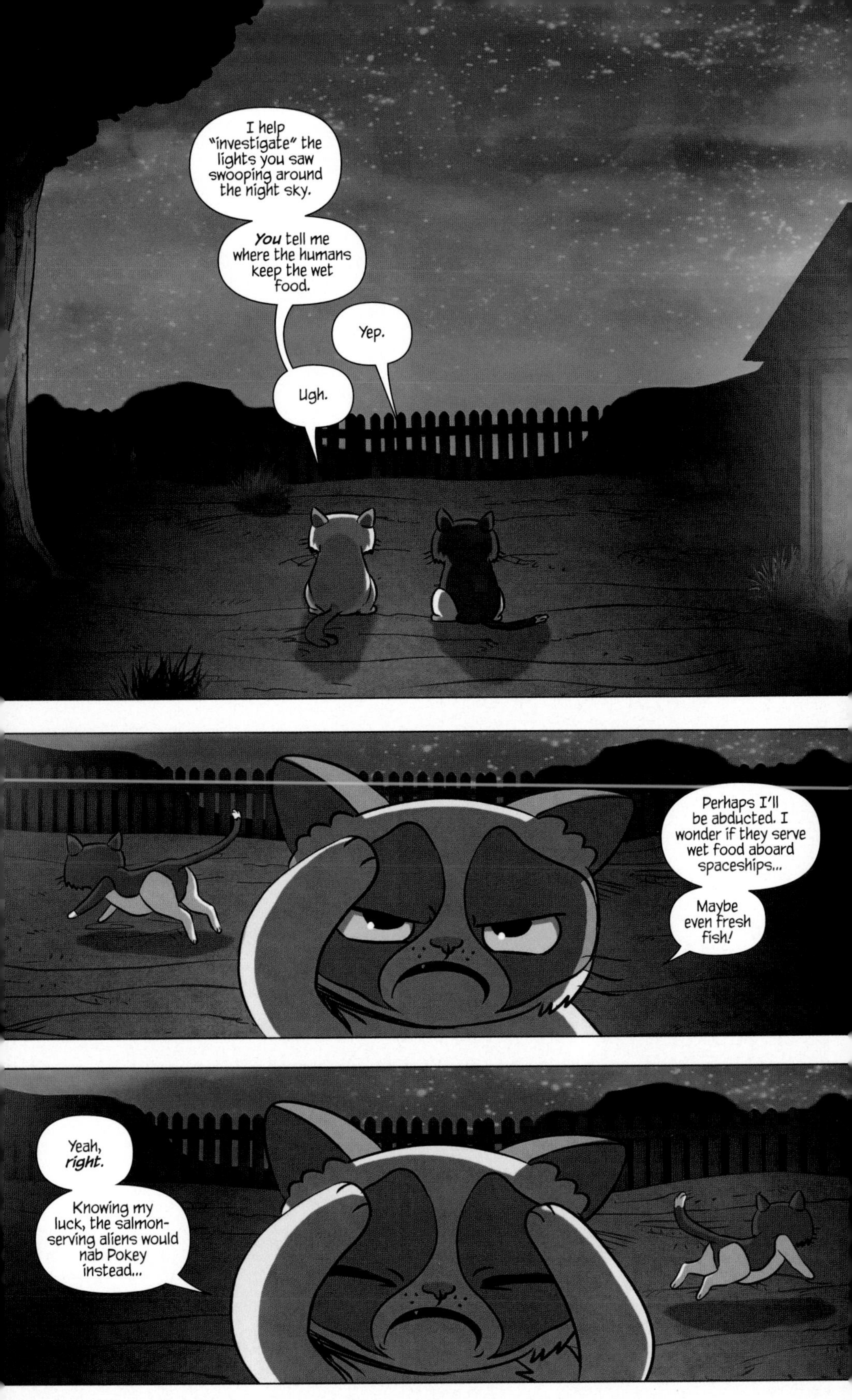

I help "investigate" the lights you saw swooping around the night sky.
*You* tell me where the humans keep the wet food.
Yep.
Ugh.
Perhaps I'll be abducted. I wonder if they serve wet food aboard spaceships...
Maybe even fresh fish!
Yeah, *right*.
Knowing my luck, the salmon-serving aliens would nab Pokey instead...

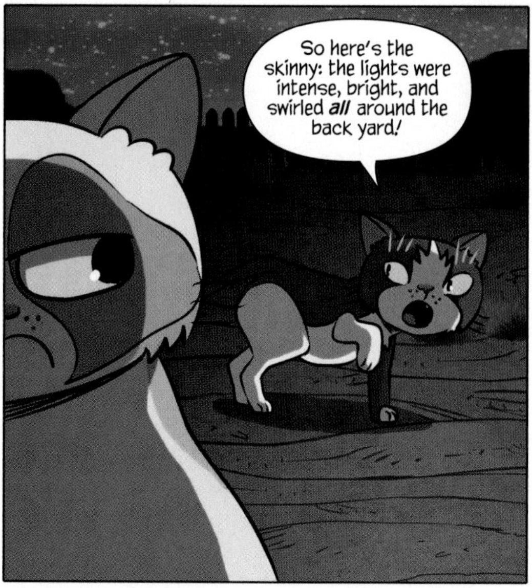
So here's the skinny: the lights were intense, bright, and swirled *all* around the back yard!

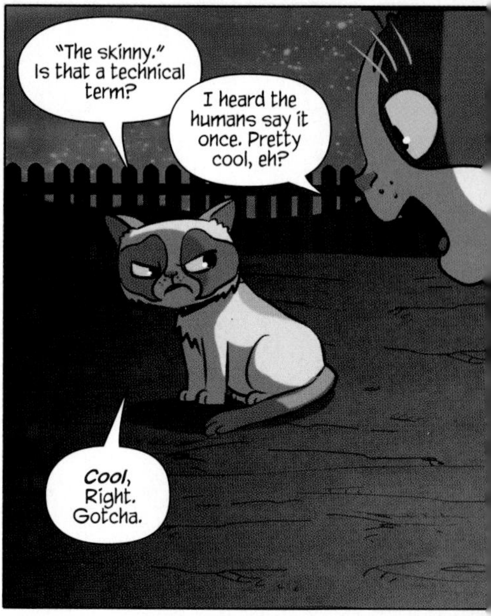
"The skinny." Is that a technical term?
I heard the humans say it once. Pretty cool, eh?
*Cool*, Right. Gotcha.

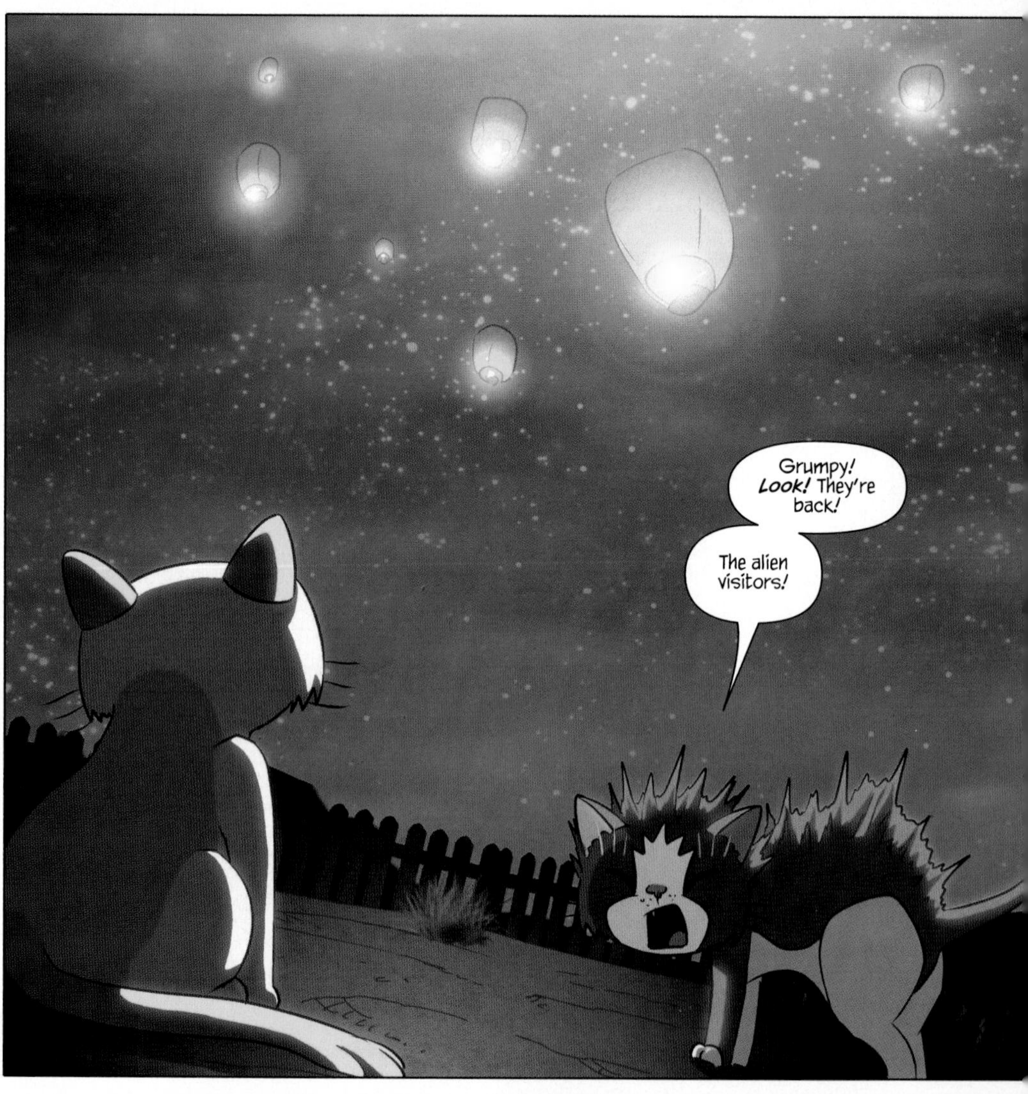
Grumpy! *Look!* They're back!
The alien visitors!

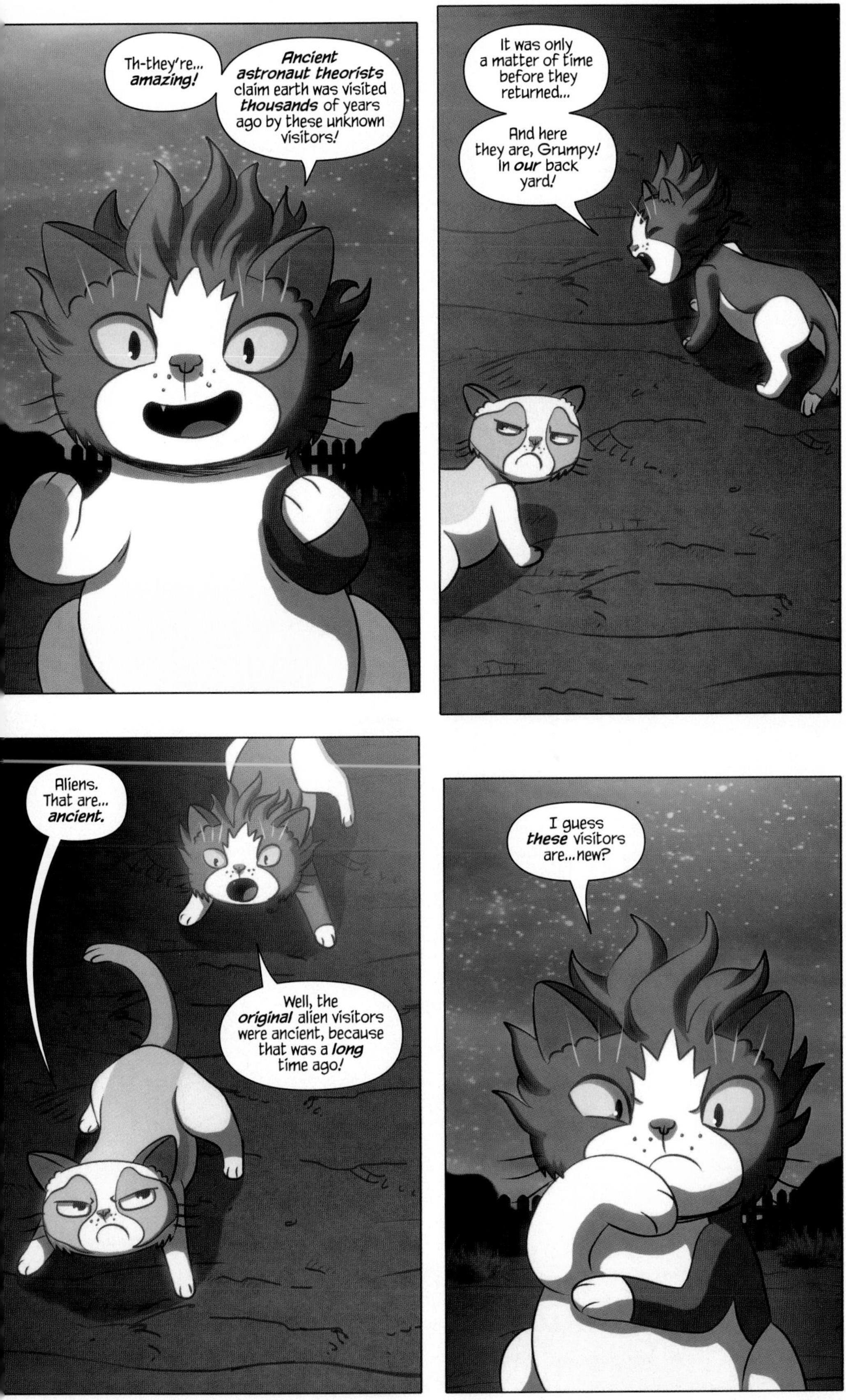
Th-they're... *amazing!*
***Ancient astronaut theorists*** claim earth was visited ***thousands*** of years ago by these unknown visitors!
It was only a matter of time before they returned...
And here they are, Grumpy! In ***our*** back yard!
Aliens. That are... ***ancient.***
Well, the ***original*** alien visitors were ancient, because that was a ***long*** time ago!
I guess ***these*** visitors are...new?

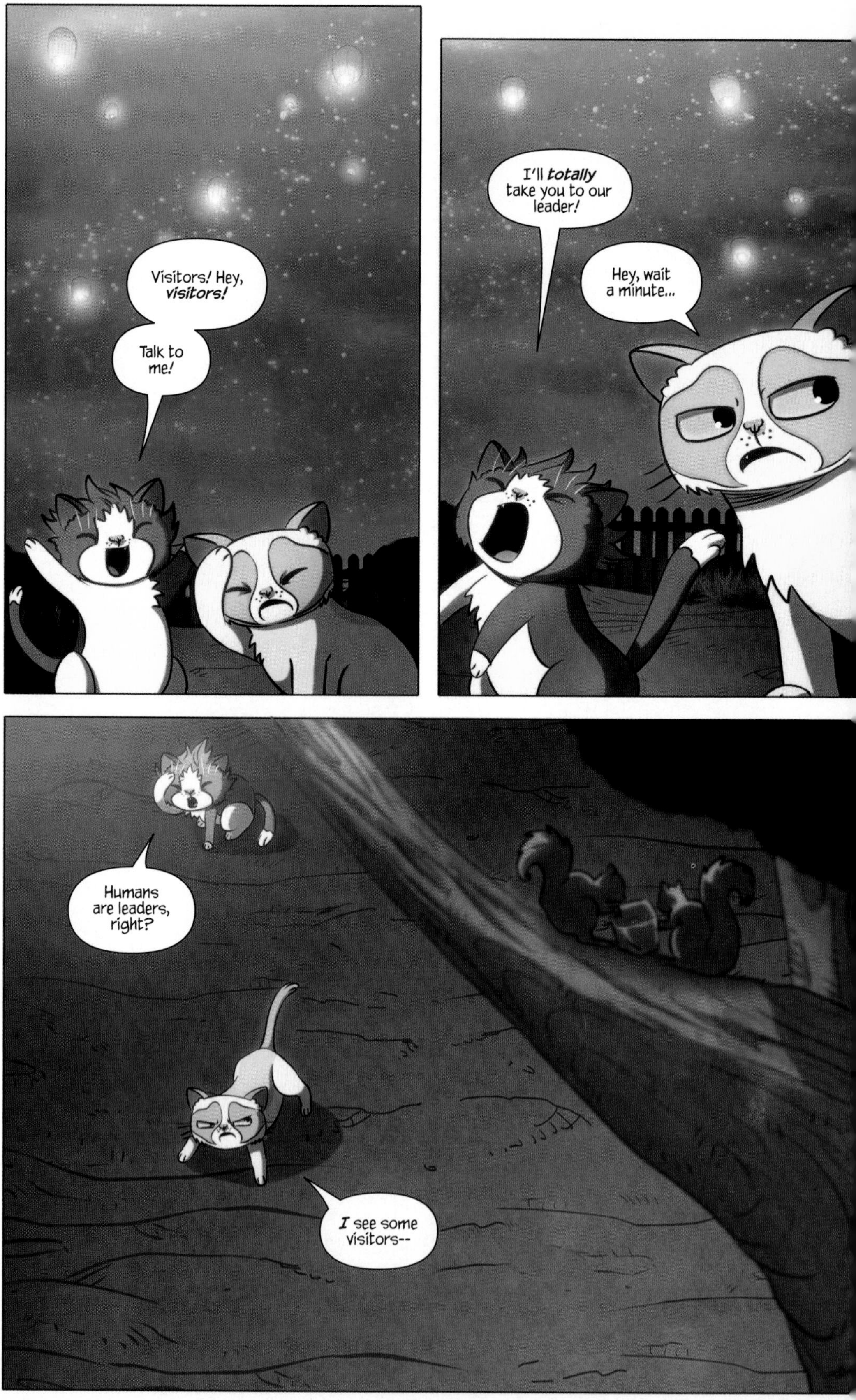
Visitors! Hey, *visitors!*
Talk to me!
I'll ***totally*** take you to our leader!
Hey, wait a minute...
Humans are leaders, right?
*I* see some visitors--

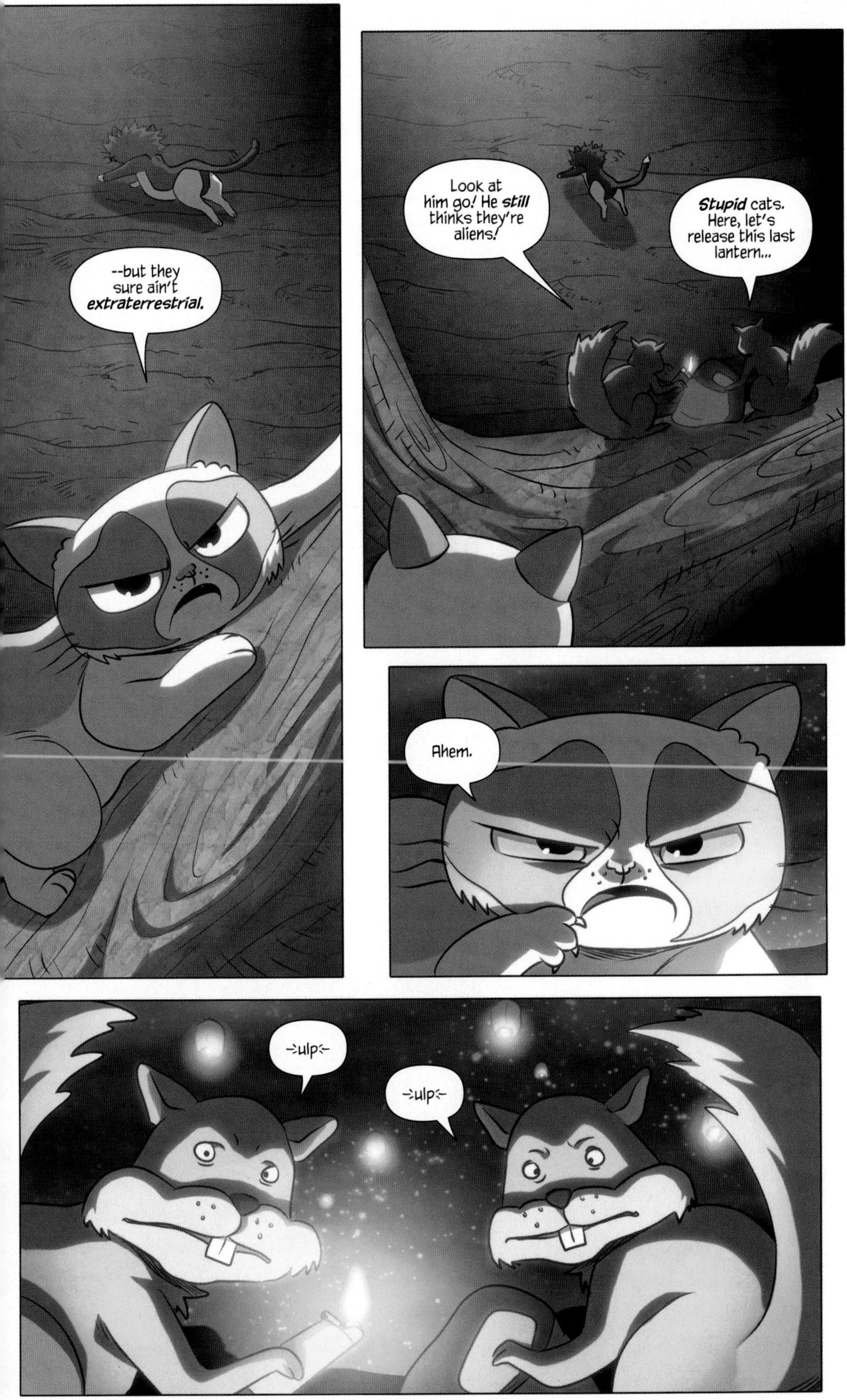
--but they sure ain't *extraterrestrial.*
Look at him go! He *still* thinks they're aliens!
*Stupid* cats. Here, let's release this last lantern...
Ahem.
-ulp-
-ulp-

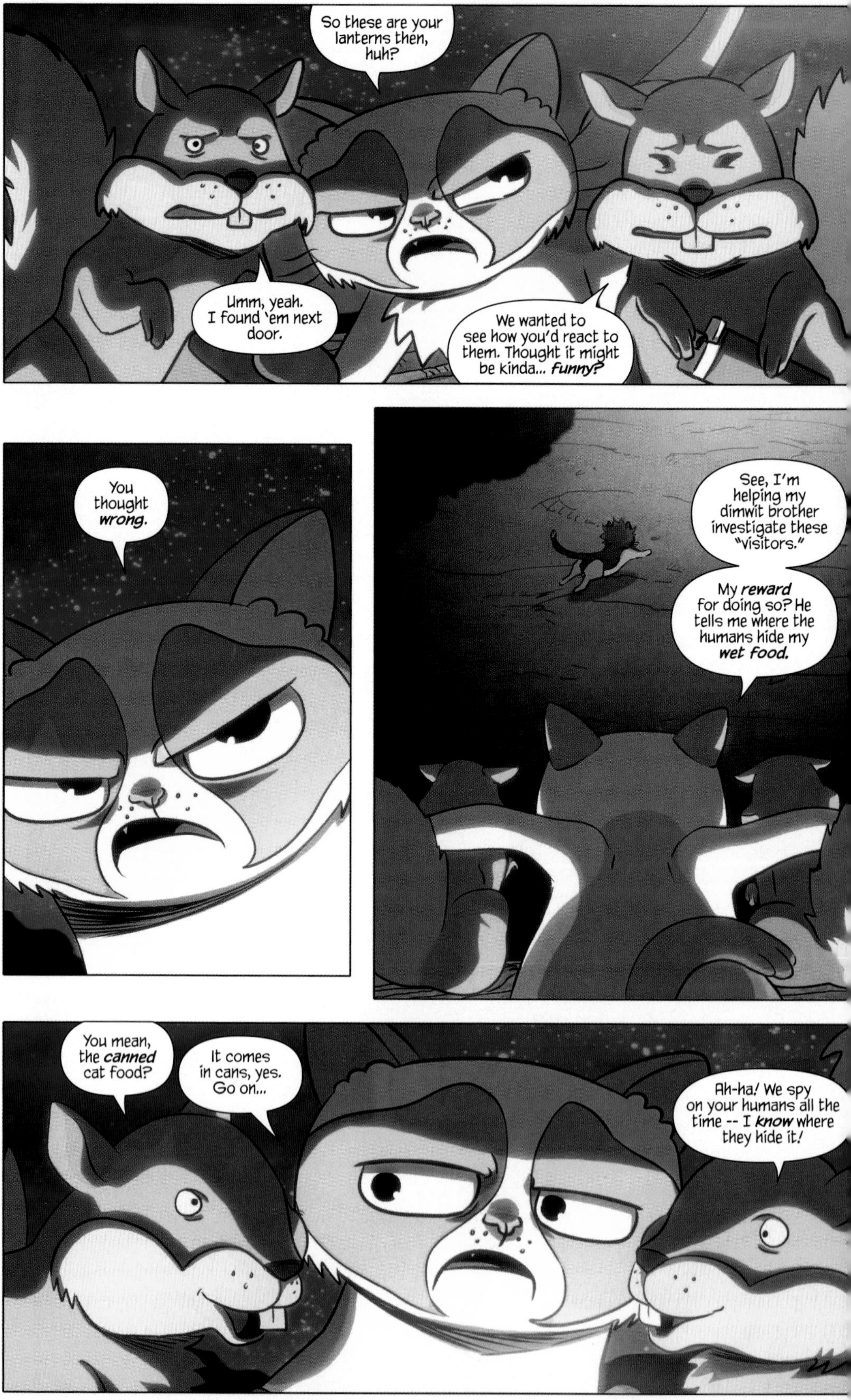

So these are your lanterns then, huh?
Umm, yeah. I found 'em next door.
We wanted to see how you'd react to them. Thought it might be kinda... *funny?*
You thought *wrong.*
See, I'm helping my dimwit brother investigate these "visitors."
My *reward* for doing so? He tells me where the humans hide my *wet food.*
You mean, the *canned* cat food?
It comes in cans, yes. Go on...
Ah-ha! We spy on your humans all the time -- I *know* where they hide it!

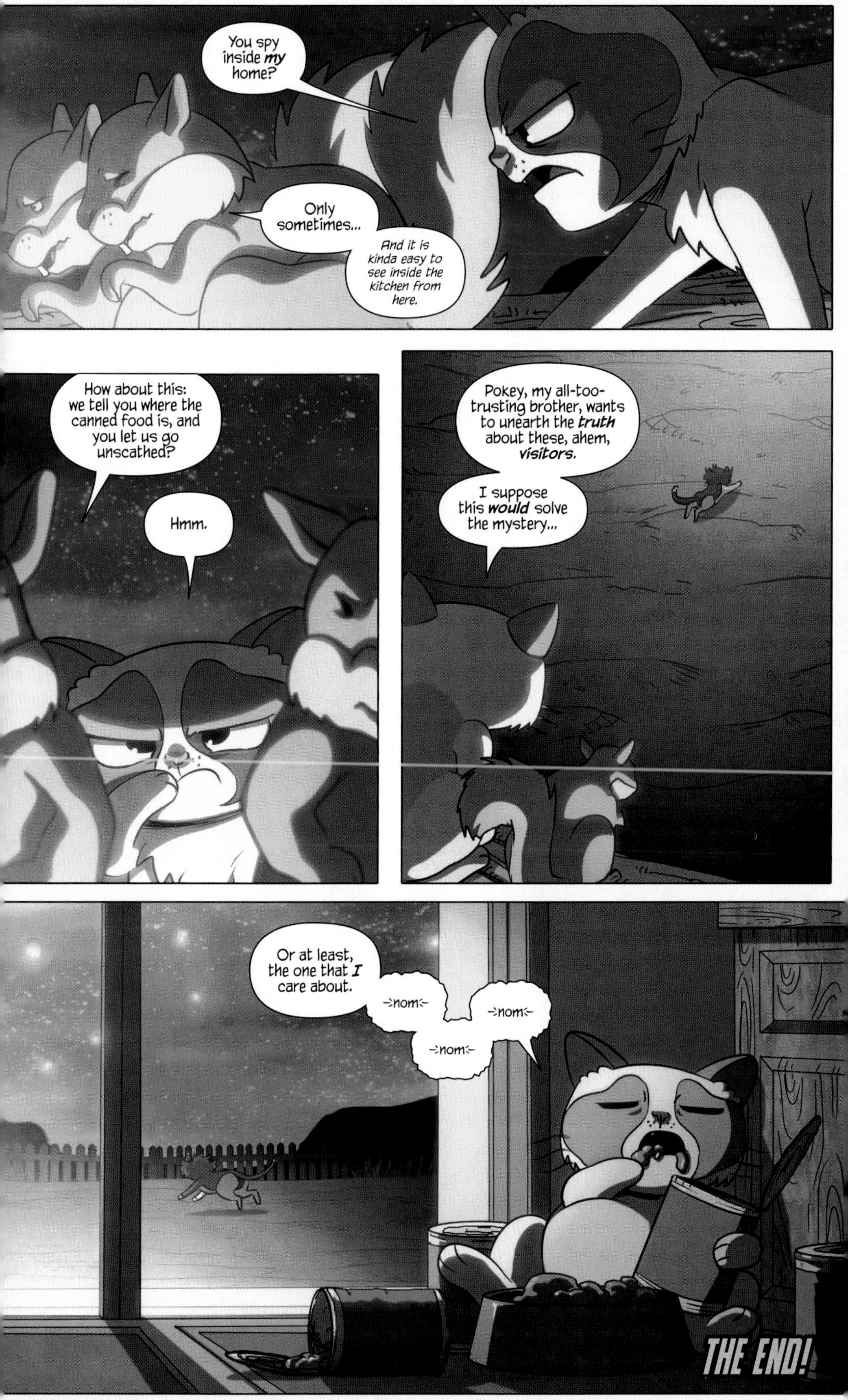

You spy inside *my* home?
Only sometimes...
*And it is kinda easy to see inside the kitchen from here.*
How about this: we tell you where the canned food is, and you let us go unscathed?
Hmm.
Pokey, my all-too-trusting brother, wants to unearth the *truth* about these, ahem, *visitors*.
I suppose this *would* solve the mystery...
Or at least, the one that *I* care about.
nom
nom
nom
THE END!

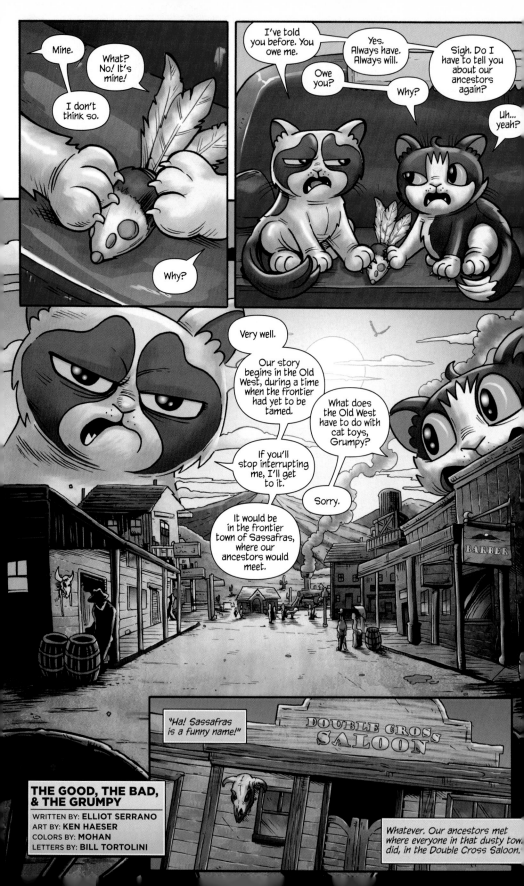

Mine.

What? No! It's mine!

I don't think so.

Why?

I've told you before. You owe me.

Owe you?

Why?

Yes. Always have. Always will.

Sigh. Do I have to tell you about our ancestors again?

Uh... yeah?

Very well.

Our story begins in the Old West, during a time when the frontier had yet to be tamed.

What does the Old West have to do with cat toys, Grumpy?

If you'll stop interrupting me, I'll get to it.

Sorry.

It would be in the frontier town of Sassafras, where our ancestors would meet.

"Ha! Sassafras is a funny name!"

DOUBLE CROSS SALOON

BARBER

**THE GOOD, THE BAD, & THE GRUMPY**
WRITTEN BY: ELLIOT SERRANO
ART BY: KEN HAESER
COLORS BY: MOHAN
LETTERS BY: BILL TORTOLINI

Whatever. Our ancestors met where everyone in that dusty tow did, in the Double Cross Saloon.

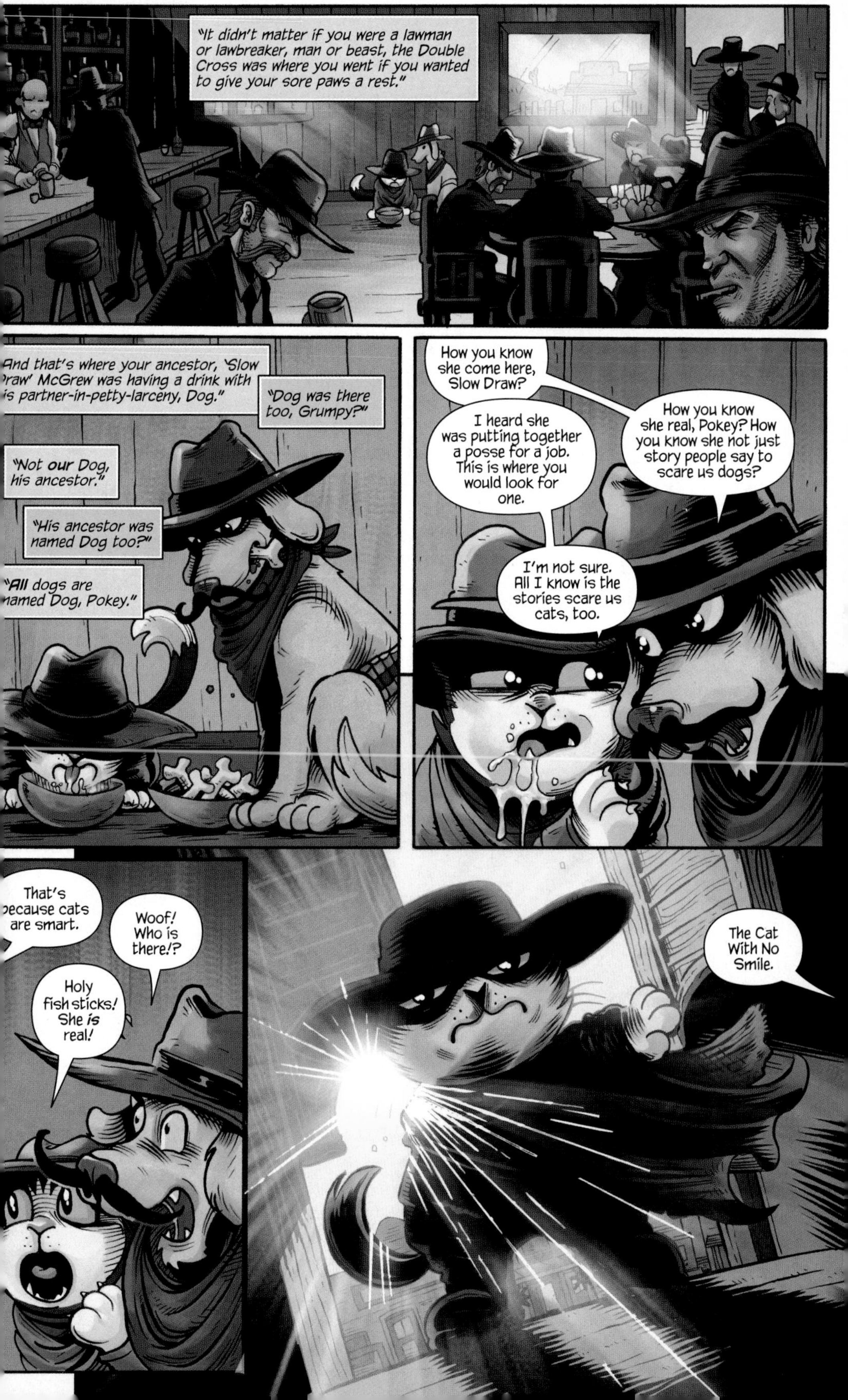
"It didn't matter if you were a lawman or lawbreaker, man or beast, the Double Cross was where you went if you wanted to give your sore paws a rest."
And that's where your ancestor, 'Slow Draw' McGrew was having a drink with is partner-in-petty-larceny, Dog."
"Dog was there too, Grumpy?"
"Not our Dog, his ancestor."
"His ancestor was named Dog too?"
"All dogs are named Dog, Pokey."
How you know she come here, Slow Draw?
I heard she was putting together a posse for a job. This is where you would look for one.
How you know she real, Pokey? How you know she not just story people say to scare us dogs?
I'm not sure. All I know is the stories scare us cats, too.
That's because cats are smart.
Woof! Who is there!?
Holy fish sticks! She is real!
The Cat With No Smile.

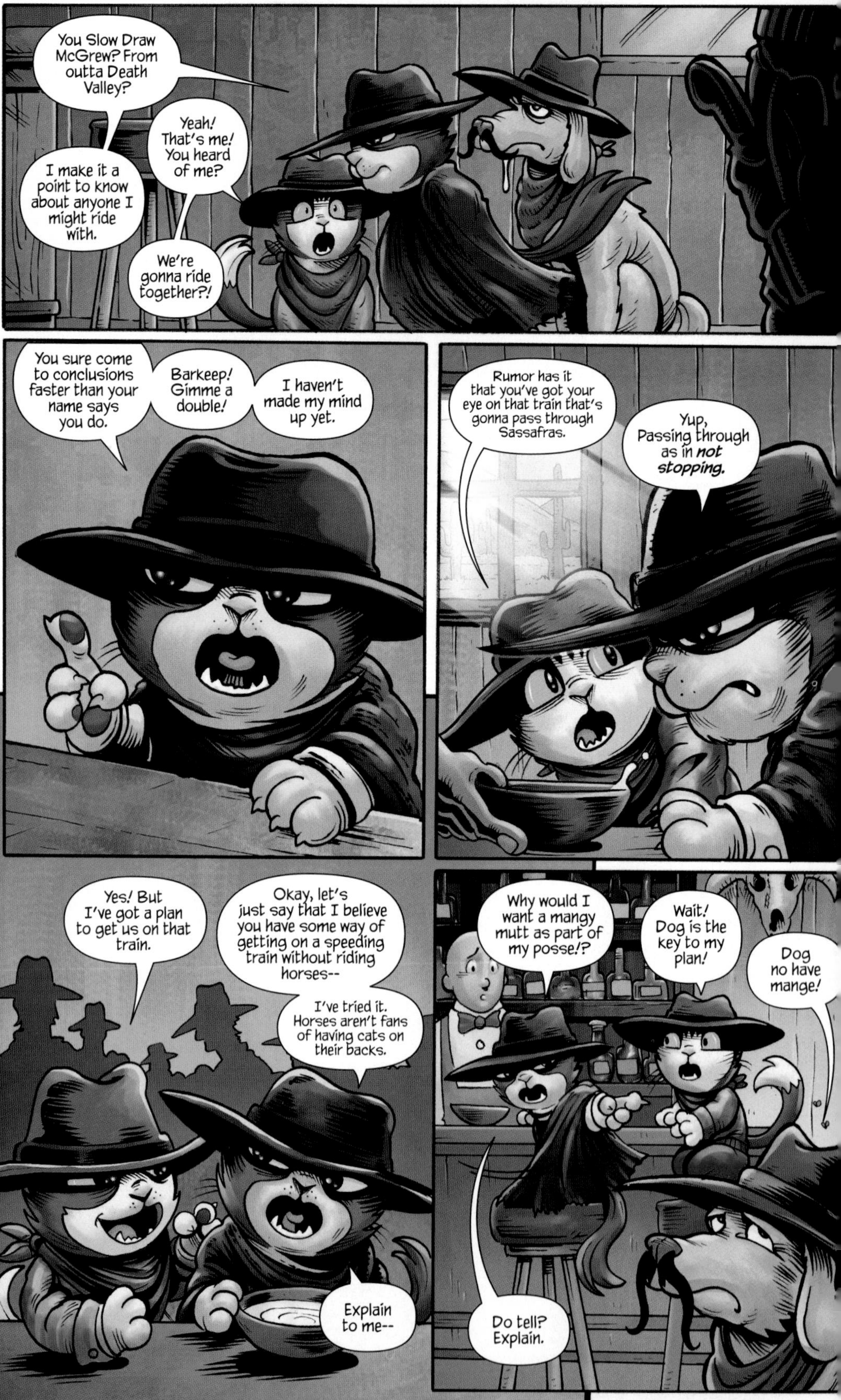

You Slow Draw McGrew? From outta Death Valley?
Yeah! That's me! You heard of me?
I make it a point to know about anyone I might ride with.
We're gonna ride together?!
You sure come to conclusions faster than your name says you do.
Barkeep! Gimme a double!
I haven't made my mind up yet.
Rumor has it that you've got your eye on that train that's gonna pass through Sassafras.
Yup, Passing through as in ***not stopping.***
Yes! But I've got a plan to get us on that train.
Okay, let's just say that I believe you have some way of getting on a speeding train without riding horses--
I've tried it. Horses aren't fans of having cats on their backs.
Explain to me--
Why would I want a mangy mutt as part of my posse!?
Wait! Dog is the key to my plan!
Dog no have mange!
Do tell? Explain.

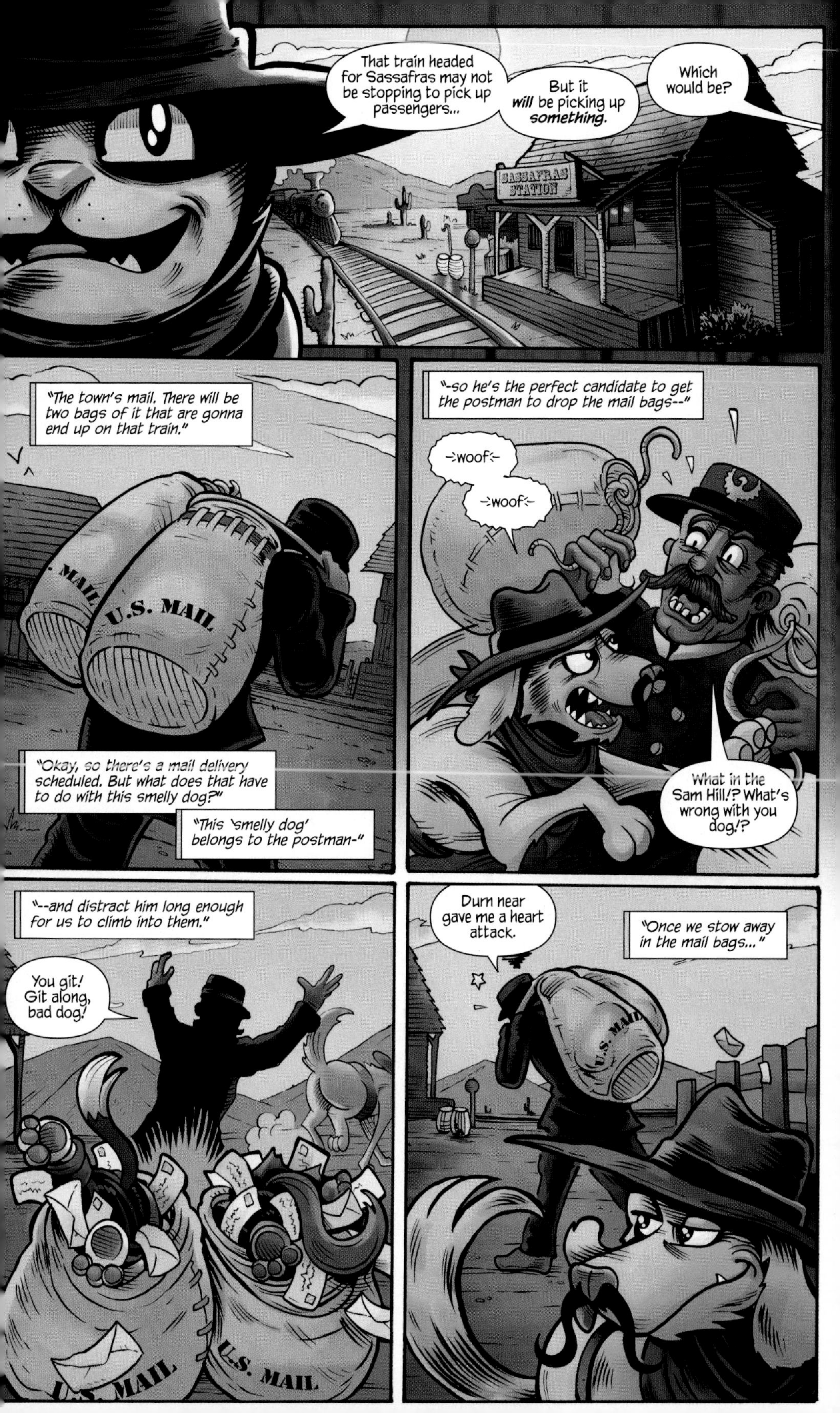
That train headed for Sassafras may not be stopping to pick up passengers...
But it *will* be picking up *something.*
Which would be?
SASSAFRAS STATION
"The town's mail. There will be two bags of it that are gonna end up on that train."
U.S. MAIL
U.S. MAIL
"Okay, so there's a mail delivery scheduled. But what does that have to do with this smelly dog?"
"This 'smelly dog' belongs to the postman-"
"-so he's the perfect candidate to get the postman to drop the mail bags--"
woof
woof
What in the Sam Hill!? What's wrong with you dog!?
"--and distract him long enough for us to climb into them."
You git! Git along, bad dog!
U.S. MAIL
U.S. MAIL
Durn near gave me a heart attack.
"Once we stow away in the mail bags..."
U.S. MAIL

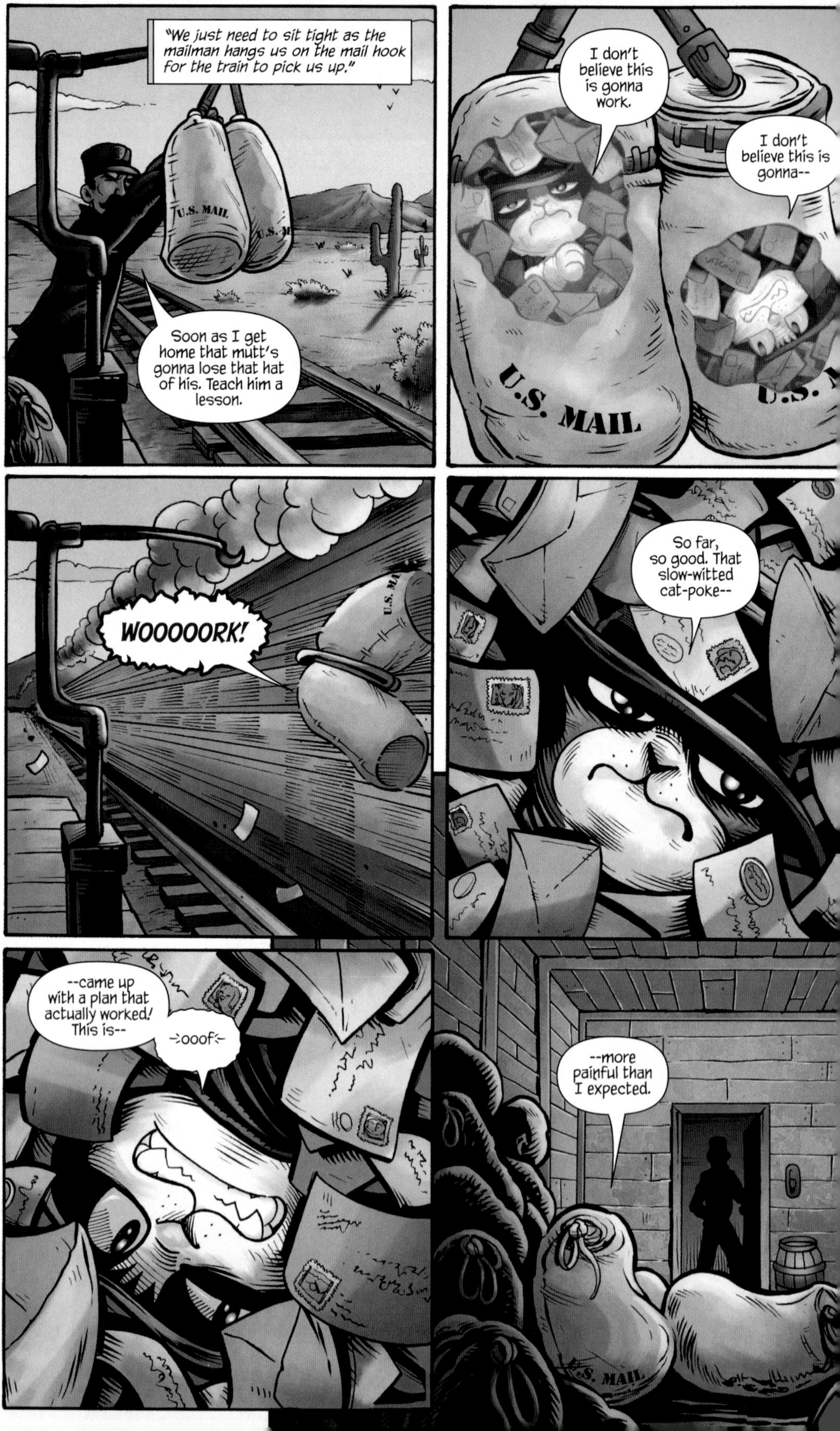
"We just need to sit tight as the mailman hangs us on the mail hook for the train to pick us up."
U.S. MAIL
Soon as I get home that mutt's gonna lose that hat of his. Teach him a lesson.
I don't believe this is gonna work.
I don't believe this is gonna--
U.S. MAIL
WOOOOORK!
So far, so good. That slow-witted cat-poke--
--came up with a plan that actually worked! This is--
ooof
--more painful than I expected.
U.S. MAIL

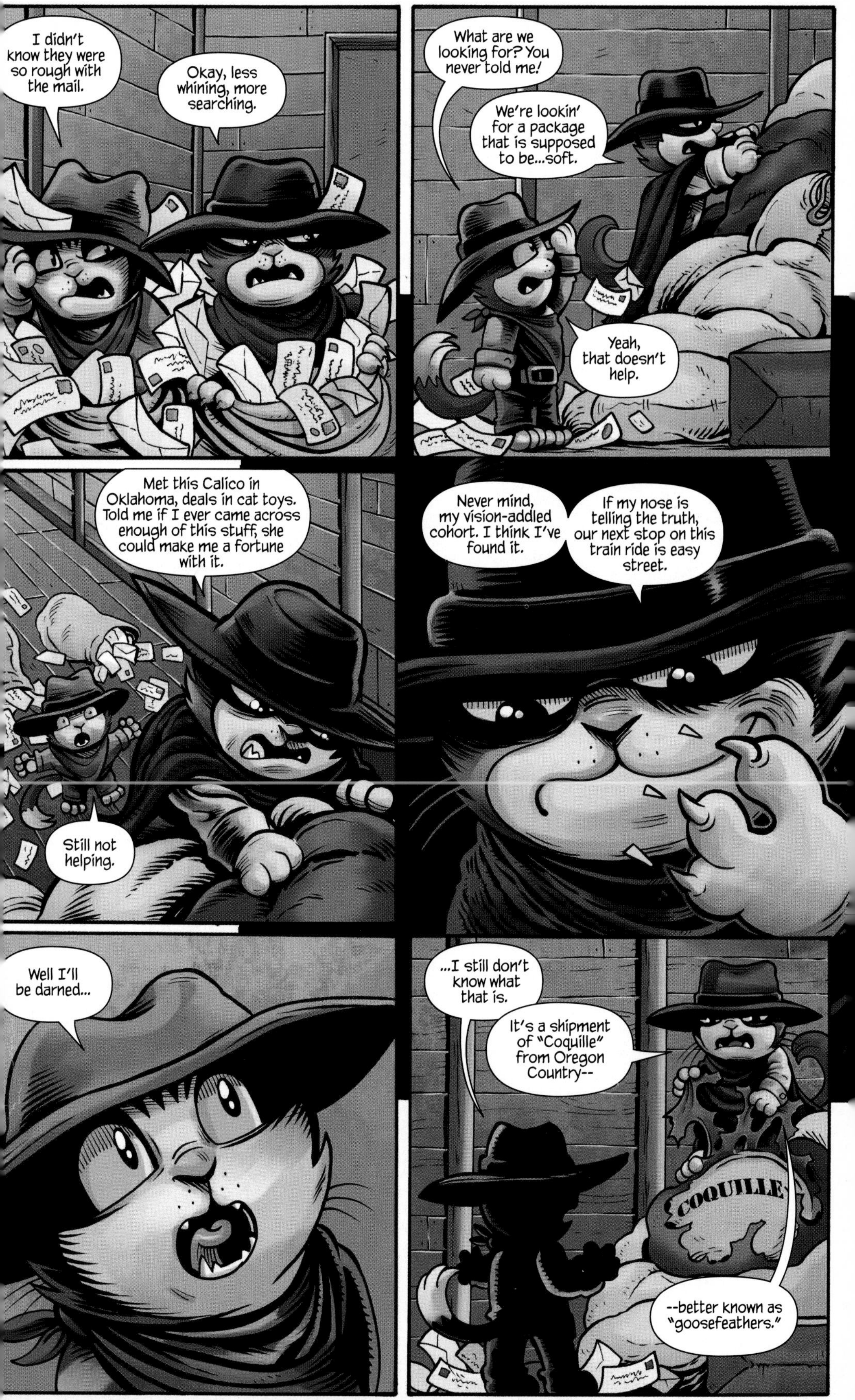
I didn't know they were so rough with the mail.
Okay, less whining, more searching.
What are we looking for? You never told me!
We're lookin' for a package that is supposed to be...soft.
Yeah, that doesn't help.
Met this Calico in Oklahoma, deals in cat toys. Told me if I ever came across enough of this stuff, she could make me a fortune with it.
Still not helping.
Never mind, my vision-addled cohort. I think I've found it.
If my nose is telling the truth, our next stop on this train ride is easy street.
Well I'll be darned...
...I still don't know what that is.
It's a shipment of "Coquille" from Oregon Country--
COQUILLE
--better known as "goosefeathers."

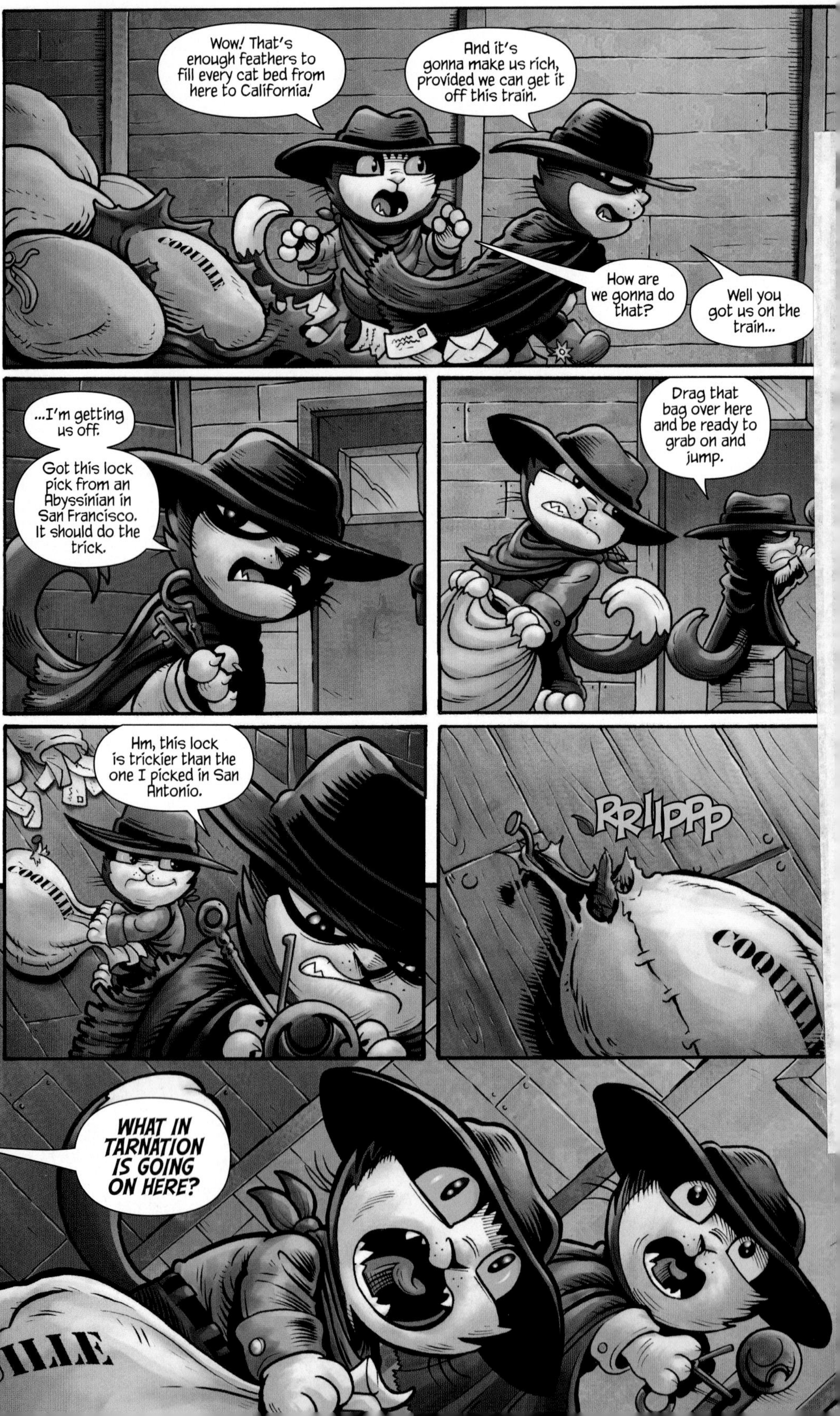

Wow! That's enough feathers to fill every cat bed from here to California!
And it's gonna make us rich, provided we can get it off this train.
COQUILLE
How are we gonna do that?
Well you got us on the train...
...I'm getting us off.
Got this lock pick from an Abyssinian in San Francisco. It should do the trick.
Drag that bag over here and be ready to grab on and jump.
Hm, this lock is trickier than the one I picked in San Antonio.
COQUILLE
RRIIPPP
COQUILLE
WHAT IN TARNATION IS GOING ON HERE?

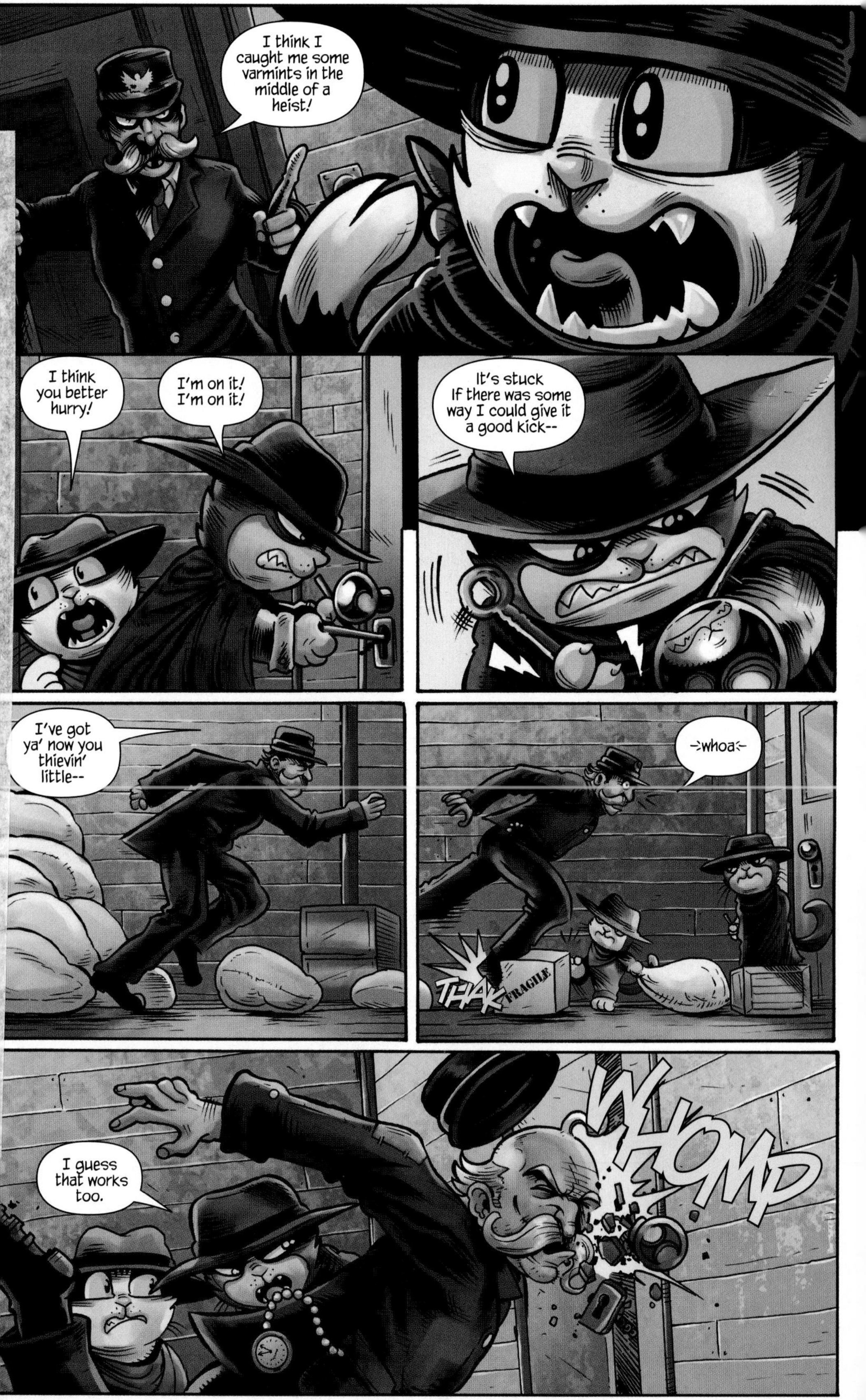

I think I caught me some varmints in the middle of a heist!
I think you better hurry!
I'm on it! I'm on it!
It's stuck If there was some way I could give it a good kick--
I've got ya' now you thievin' little--
whoa
THAK
FRAGILE
WHOMP!
I guess that works too.

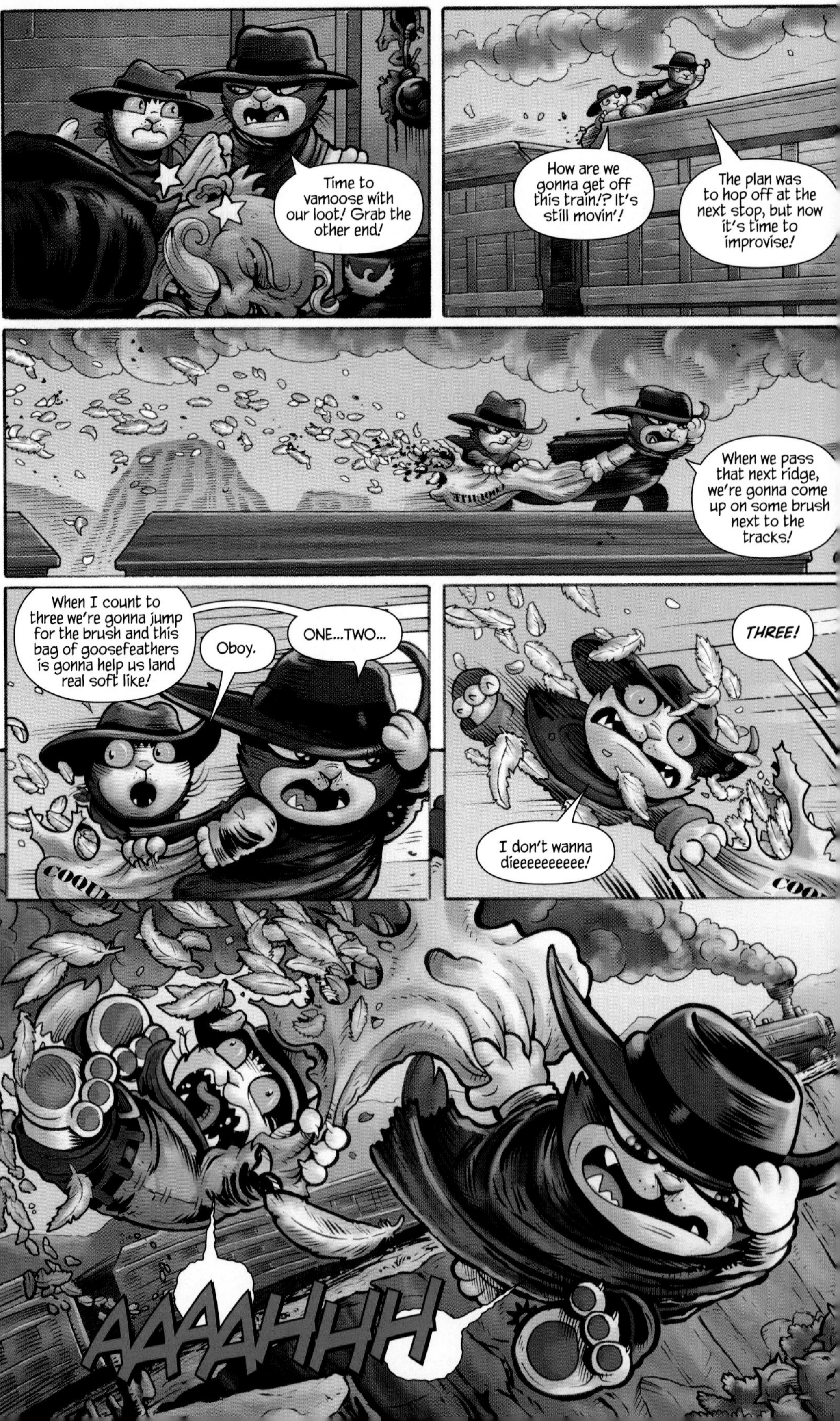

Time to vamoose with our loot! Grab the other end!
How are we gonna get off this train!? It's still movin'!
The plan was to hop off at the next stop, but now it's time to improvise!
When we pass that next ridge, we're gonna come up on some brush next to the tracks!
When I count to three we're gonna jump for the brush and this bag of goosefeathers is gonna help us land real soft like!
Oboy.
ONE...TWO...
THREE!
I don't wanna dieeeeeeeeee!
AAAAHHH

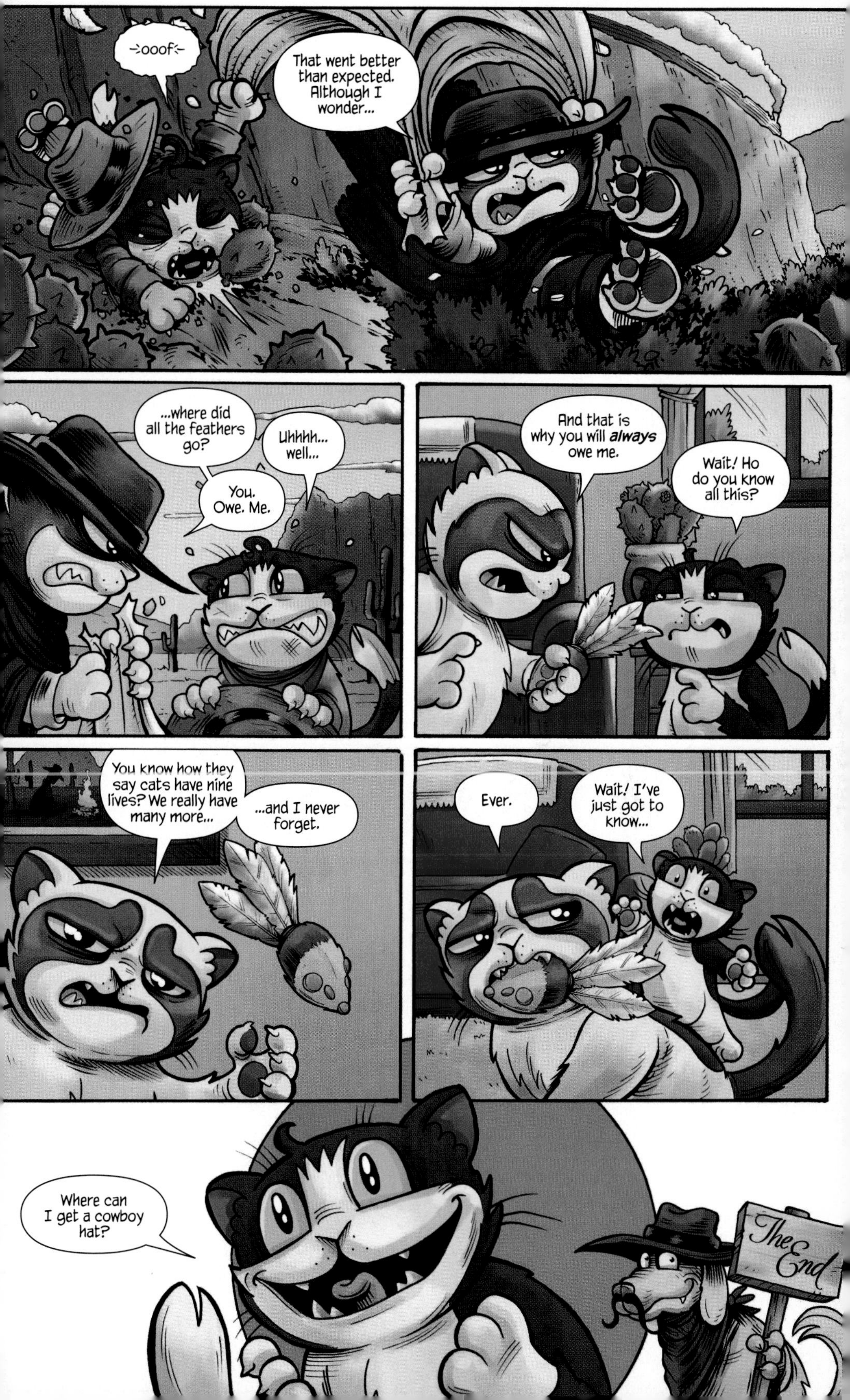

-ooof-
That went better than expected. Although I wonder...
...where did all the feathers go?
Uhhhh... well...
You. Owe. Me.
And that is why you will *always* owe me.
Wait! Ho do you know all this?
You know how they say cats have nine lives? We really have many more...
...and I never forget.
Ever.
Wait! I've just got to know...
Where can I get a cowboy hat?
The End

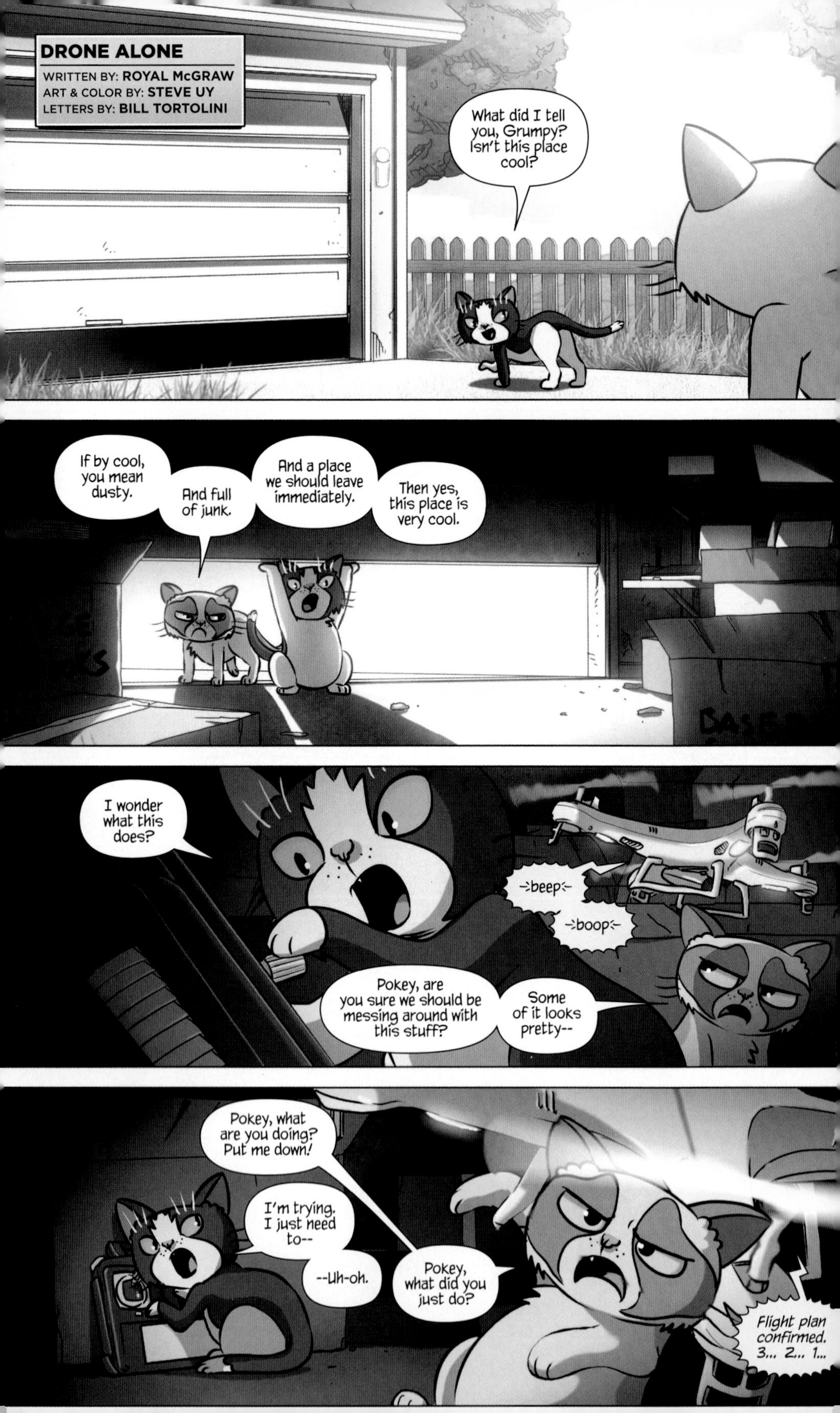
DRONE ALONE
WRITTEN BY: ROYAL McGRAW
ART & COLOR BY: STEVE UY
LETTERS BY: BILL TORTOLINI
What did I tell you, Grumpy? Isn't this place cool?
If by cool, you mean dusty.
And full of junk.
And a place we should leave immediately.
Then yes, this place is very cool.
I wonder what this does?
-beep-
-boop-
Pokey, are you sure we should be messing around with this stuff?
Some of it looks pretty--
Pokey, what are you doing? Put me down!
I'm trying. I just need to--
--Uh-oh.
Pokey, what did you just do?
Flight plan confirmed. 3... 2... 1...

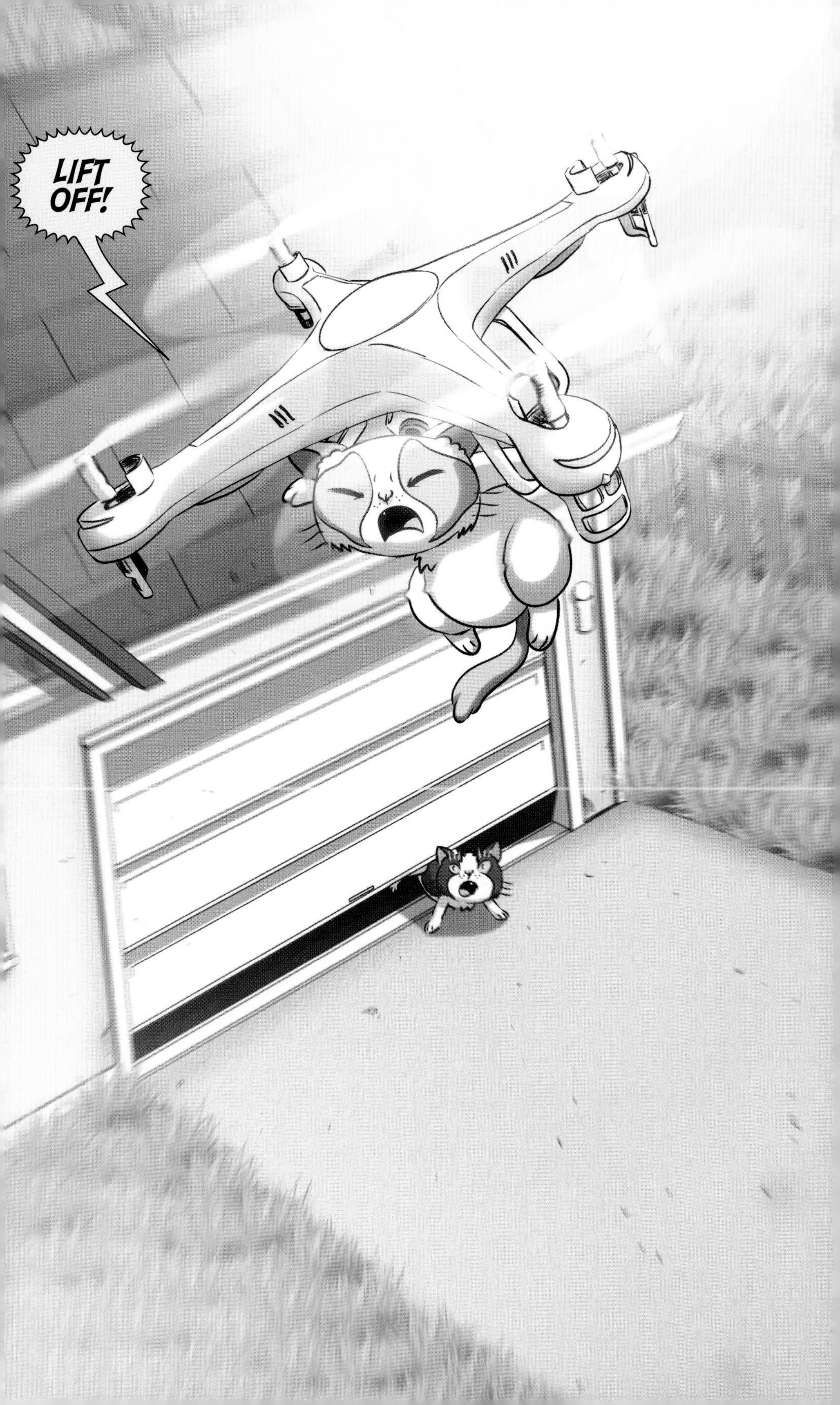
LIFT OFF!

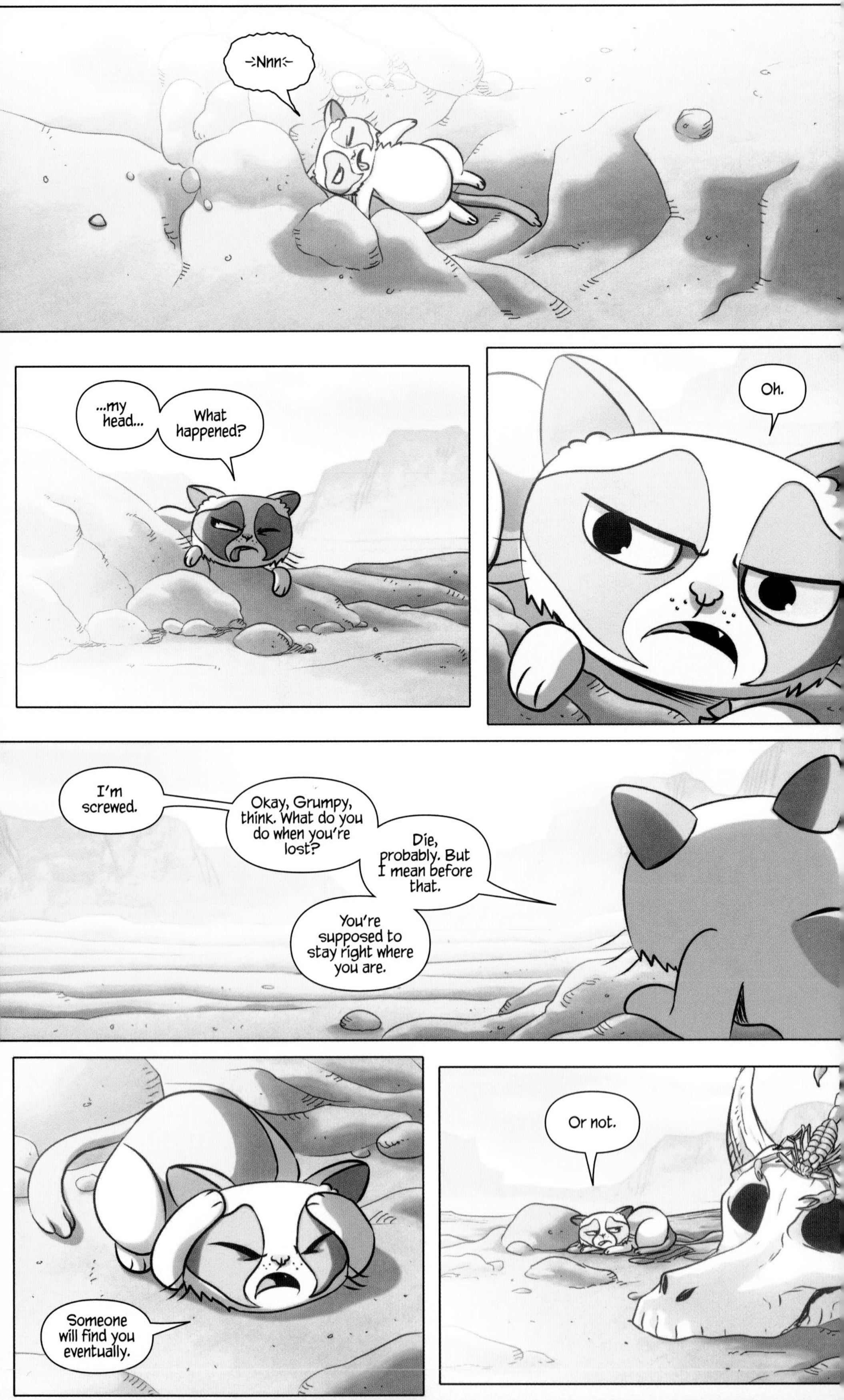
-Nnn-
...my head...
What happened?
Oh.
I'm screwed.
Okay, Grumpy, think. What do you do when you're lost?
Die, probably. But I mean before that.
You're supposed to stay right where you are.
Someone will find you eventually.
Or not.

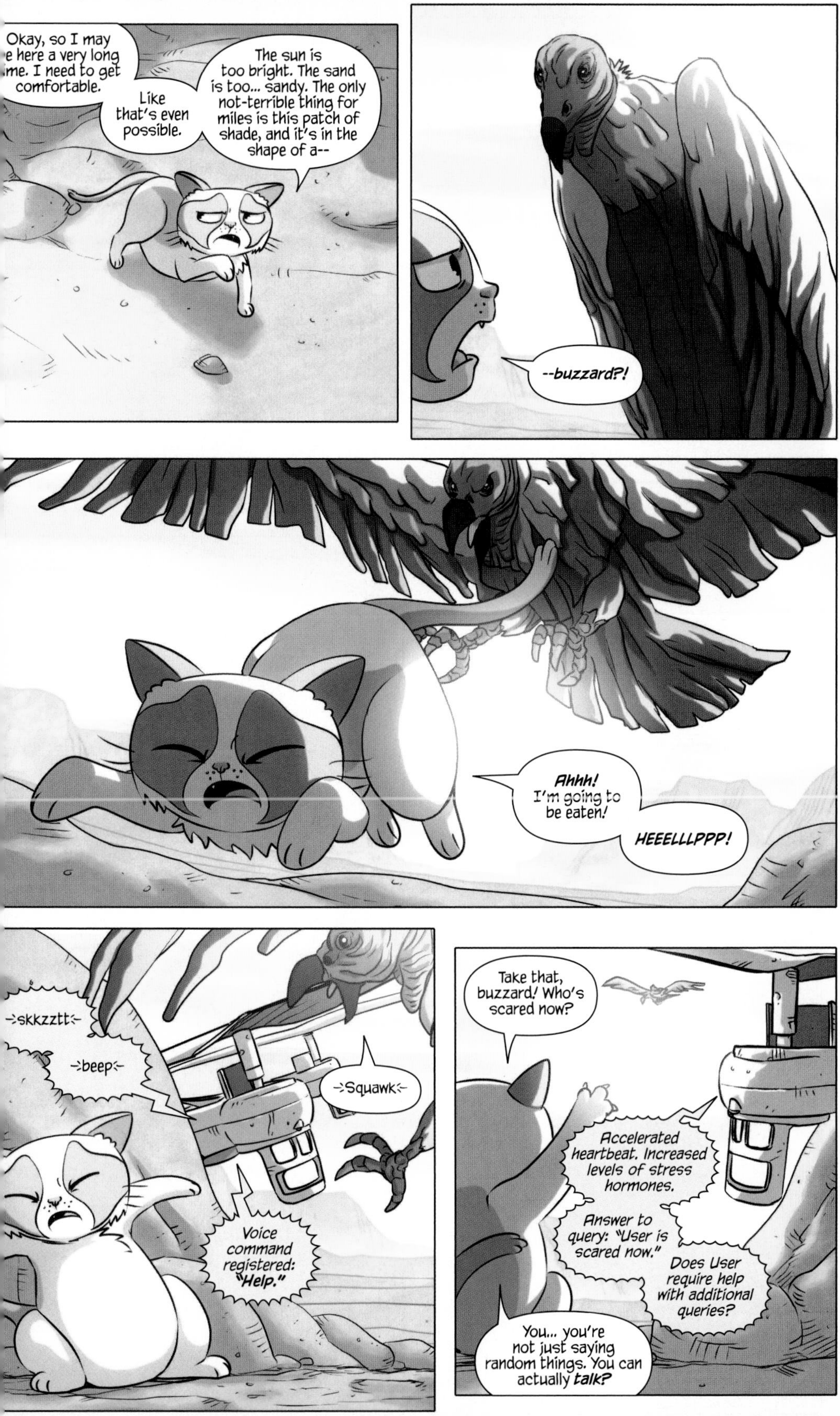
Okay, so I may
e here a very long
me. I need to get
comfortable.
Like that's even possible.
The sun is too bright. The sand is too... sandy. The only not-terrible thing for miles is this patch of shade, and it's in the shape of a--
--buzzard?!
Ahhh! I'm going to be eaten!
HEEELLLPPP!
-skkzztt-
-beep-
-Squawk-
Voice command registered: "Help."
Take that, buzzard! Who's scared now?
Accelerated heartbeat. Increased levels of stress hormones.
Answer to query: "User is scared now."
Does User require help with additional queries?
You... you're not just saying random things. You can actually talk?

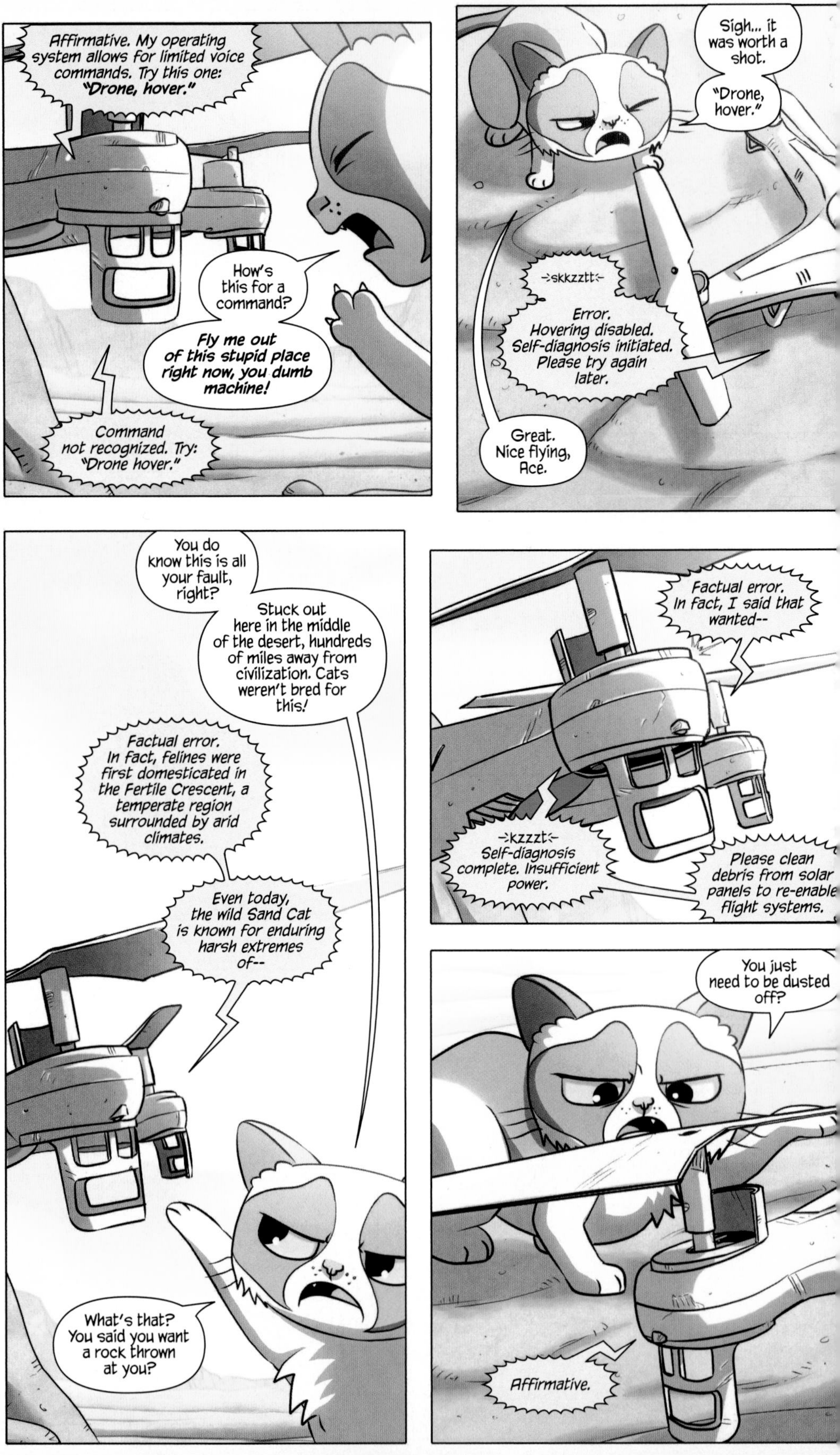
Affirmative. My operating system allows for limited voice commands. Try this one: "Drone, hover."
How's this for a command?
Fly me out of this stupid place right now, you dumb machine!
Command not recognized. Try: "Drone hover."
Sigh... it was worth a shot.
"Drone, hover."
-skkzztt-
Error. Hovering disabled. Self-diagnosis initiated. Please try again later.
Great. Nice flying, Ace.
You do know this is all your fault, right?
Stuck out here in the middle of the desert, hundreds of miles away from civilization. Cats weren't bred for this!
Factual error. In fact, felines were first domesticated in the Fertile Crescent, a temperate region surrounded by arid climates.
Even today, the wild Sand Cat is known for enduring harsh extremes of--
What's that? You said you want a rock thrown at you?
Factual error. In fact, I said that wanted--
-kzzzt-
Self-diagnosis complete. Insufficient power.
Please clean debris from solar panels to re-enable flight systems.
You just need to be dusted off?
Affirmative.

I usually have strict rules against performing manual labor.

But in this case, I'm making an exception.

Battery rapid-charging. Power levels at 23%...

34%...

48%...

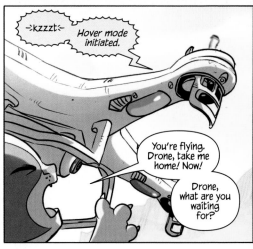

-›kzzzt‹-

Hover mode initiated.

You're flying. Drone, take me home! Now!

Drone, what are you waiting for?

Voice command not recognized.

Please input flight plan into external controller unit.

But... but that's the way back at home. Is there some other way?

Flight commands require use of external controller unit.

Then there's no way out.

I'm going to die out here, all alone.

Negative, User. I'm here with--

All alone.

This isn't so terrible. Honestly, I always assumed my death would be much worse.

And involve sharks.

And clowns.

And an eerie, unsettling silence.

Drone, there's no such thing as clown sharks in the desert, right?

Did you hear my question?

I'm not loving this eerie, unsettling silence.

-›ba-beep‹-

Flight plan accepted. Flight route plotted--

--HANG ON TO YOUR MITTENS!

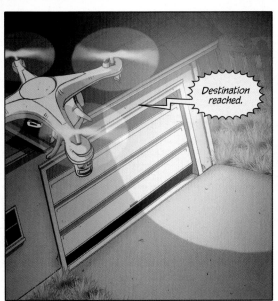

Destination reached.

Landing systems go.

Grumpy, you're back! I was so worried about you!

I kept trying to enter commands, but the batteries were too low to bring you home.

Are you okay?

Yeah, I mean... obviously.

Cats are basically desert creatures. I was in my natural element out there.

Apex predator. Top of the food chain.

Oh, that's a relief, because you sure looked scared.

What do you mean looked?

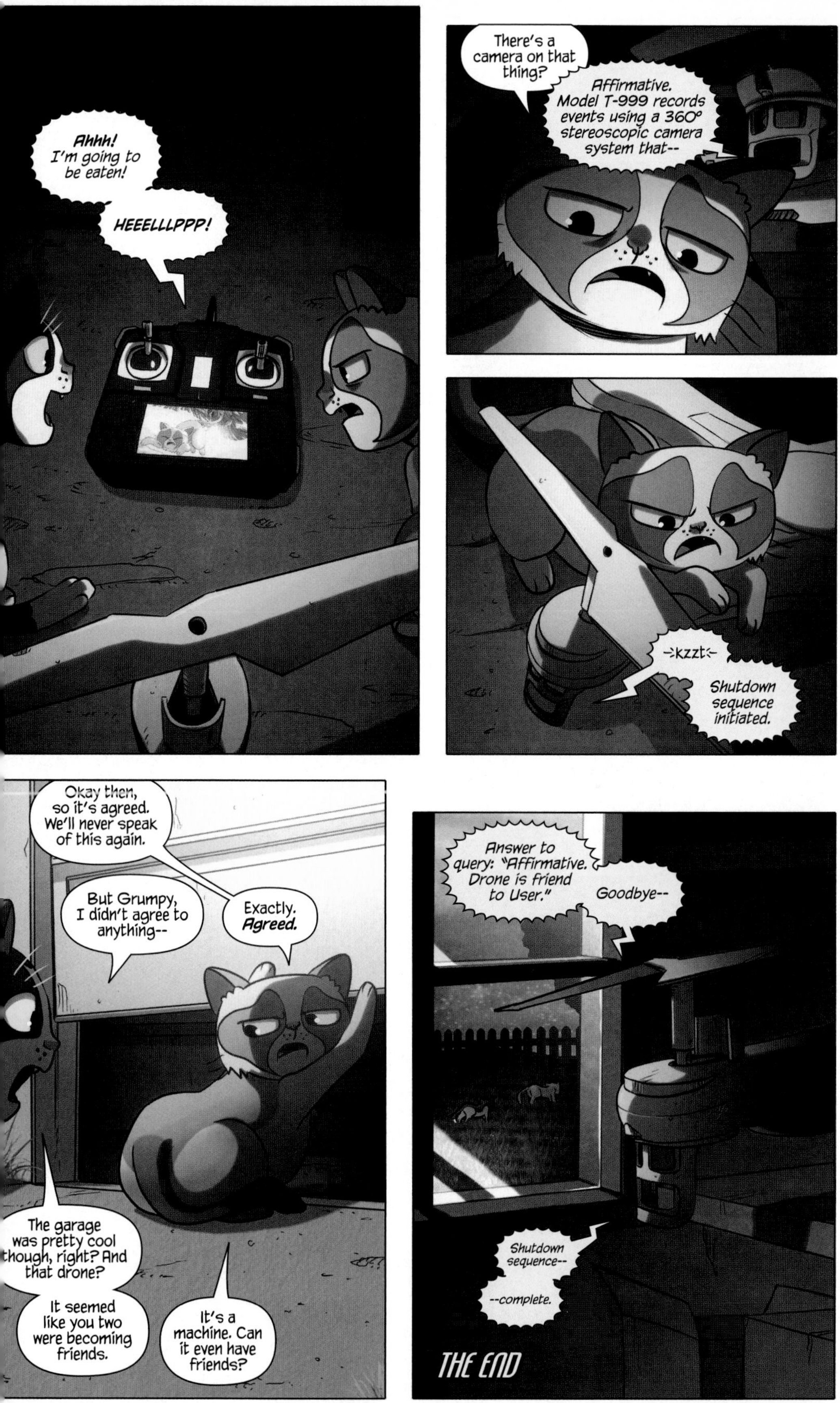

Ahhh! I'm going to be eaten!
HEEELLLPPP!
There's a camera on that thing?
Affirmative. Model T-999 records events using a 360° stereoscopic camera system that--
-kzzt-
Shutdown sequence initiated.
Okay then, so it's agreed. We'll never speak of this again.
But Grumpy, I didn't agree to anything--
Exactly. Agreed.
The garage was pretty cool though, right? And that drone?
It seemed like you two were becoming friends.
It's a machine. Can it even have friends?
Answer to query: "Affirmative. Drone is friend to User."
Goodbye--
Shutdown sequence--
--complete.
THE END

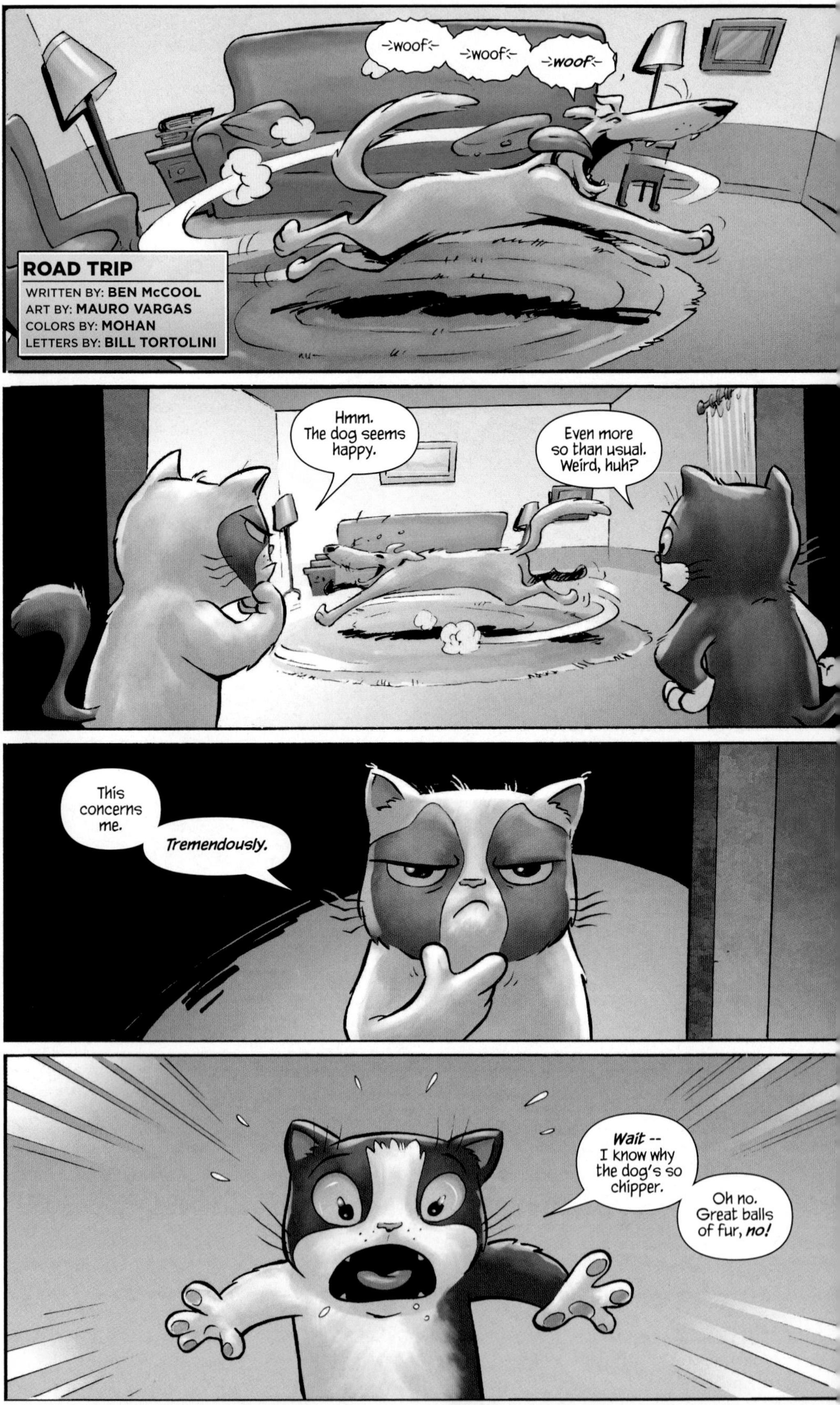

woof
woof
woof
ROAD TRIP
WRITTEN BY: BEN McCOOL
ART BY: MAURO VARGAS
COLORS BY: MOHAN
LETTERS BY: BILL TORTOLINI
Hmm. The dog seems happy.
Even more so than usual. Weird, huh?
This concerns me.
Tremendously.
Wait -- I know why the dog's so chipper.
Oh no. Great balls of fur, no!

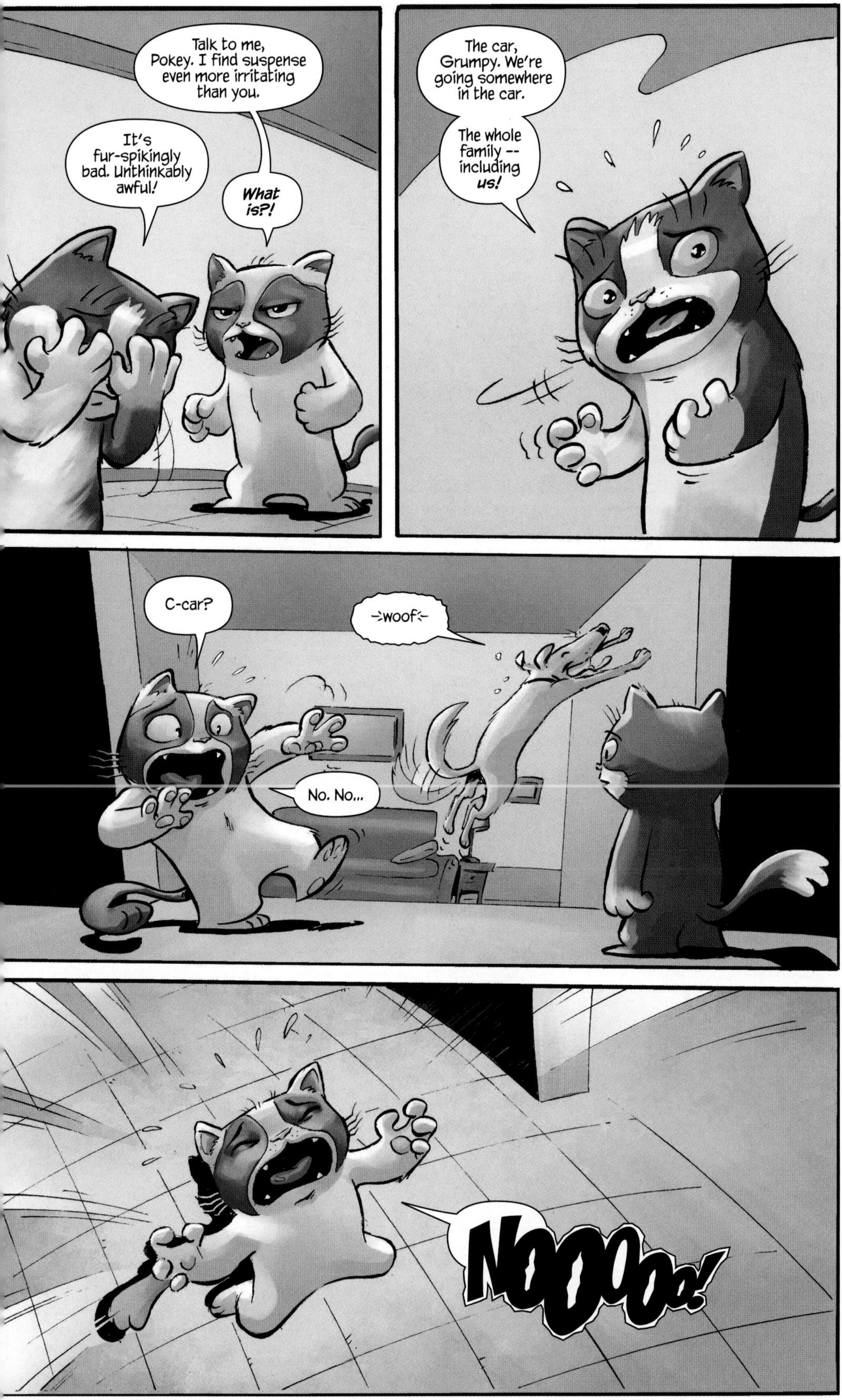
Talk to me, Pokey. I find suspense even more irritating than you.
It's fur-spikingly bad. Unthinkably awful!
What is?!
The car, Grumpy. We're going somewhere in the car.
The whole family -- including us!
C-car?
woof
No. No...
NOOOoo!

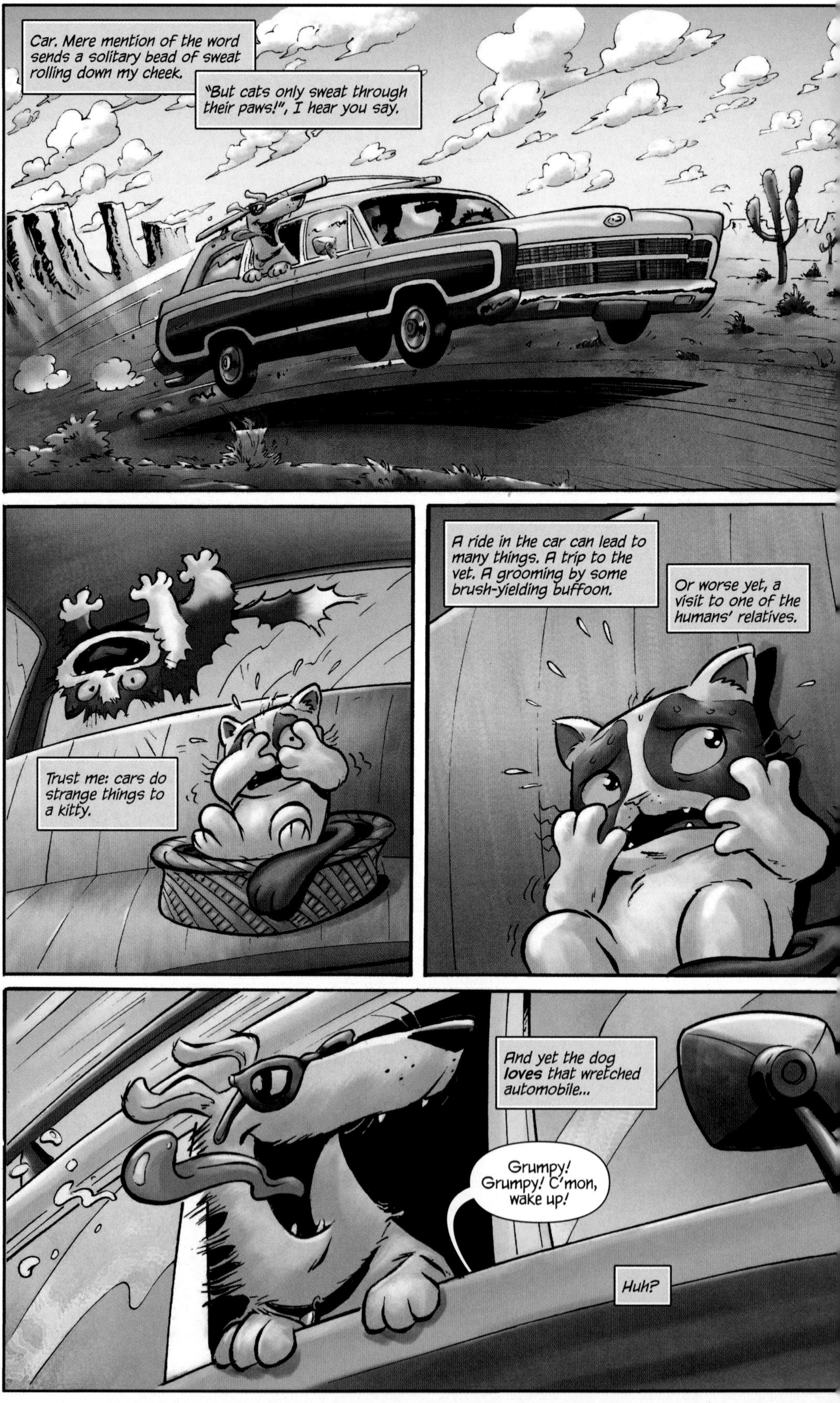
Car. Mere mention of the word sends a solitary bead of sweat rolling down my cheek.
"But cats only sweat through their paws!", I hear you say.
Trust me: cars do strange things to a kitty.
A ride in the car can lead to many things. A trip to the vet. A grooming by some brush-yielding buffoon.
Or worse yet, a visit to one of the humans' relatives.
And yet the dog **loves** that wretched automobile...
Grumpy! Grumpy! C'mon, wake up!
Huh?

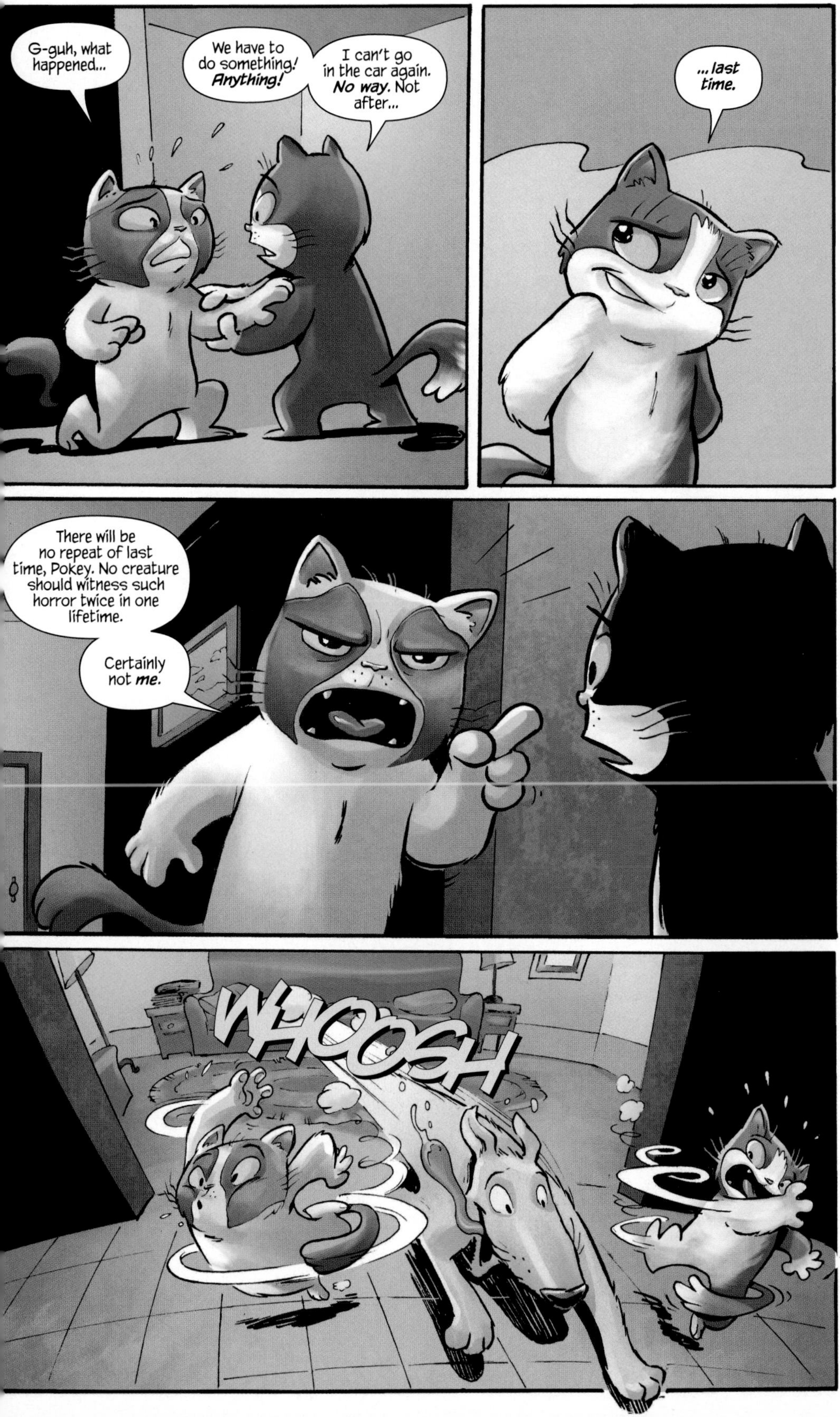
G-guh, what happened...
We have to do something! *Anything!*
I can't go in the car again. *No way.* Not after...
...*last time.*
There will be no repeat of last time, Pokey. No creature should witness such horror twice in one lifetime.
Certainly not *me.*
WHOOSH

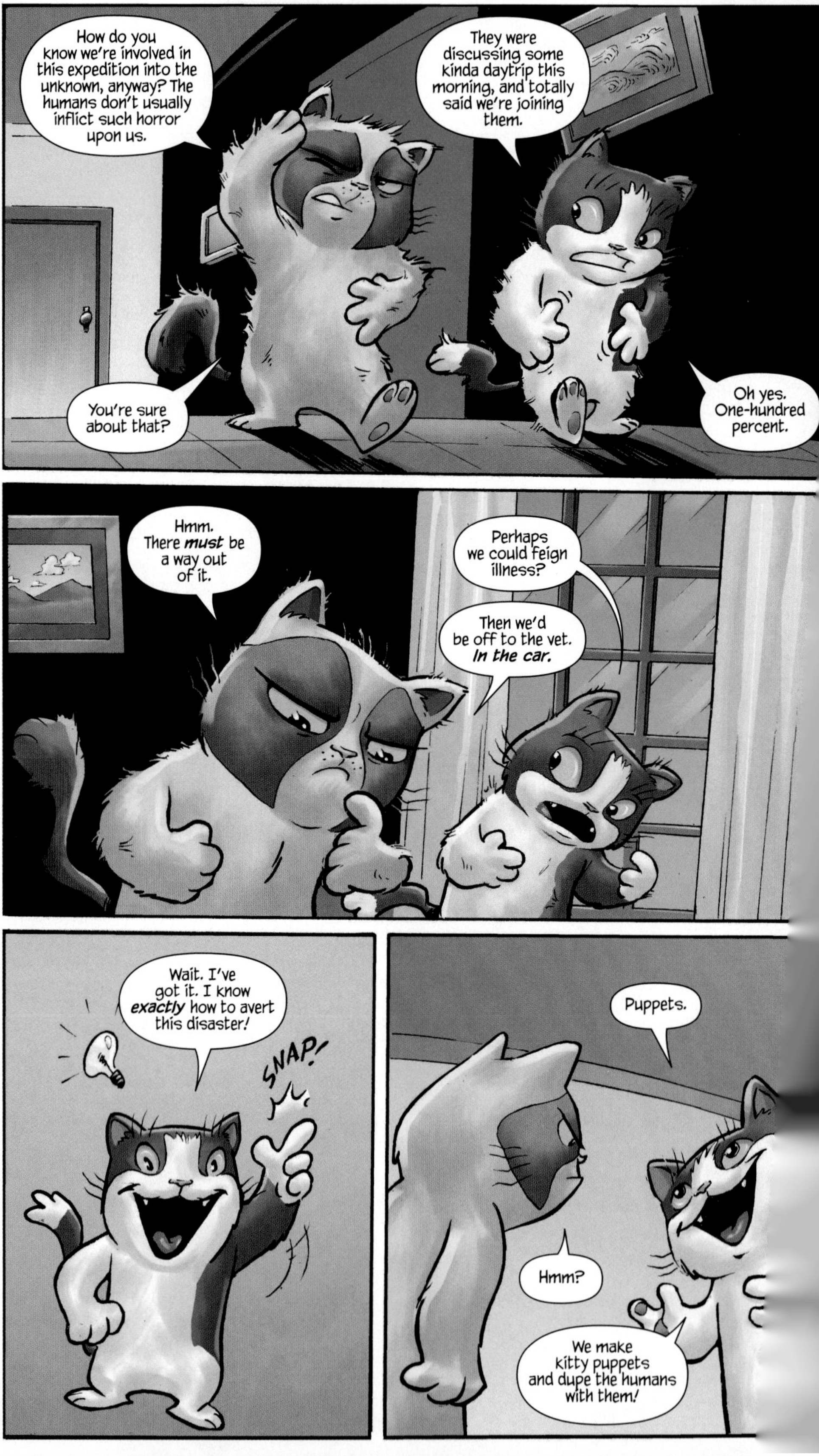
How do you know we're involved in this expedition into the unknown, anyway? The humans don't usually inflict such horror upon us.
They were discussing some kinda daytrip this morning, and totally said we're joining them.
You're sure about that?
Oh yes. One-hundred percent.
Hmm. There *must* be a way out of it.
Perhaps we could feign illness?
Then we'd be off to the vet. ***In the car.***
Wait. I've got it. I know *exactly* how to avert this disaster!
SNAP!
Puppets.
Hmm?
We make kitty puppets and dupe the humans with them!

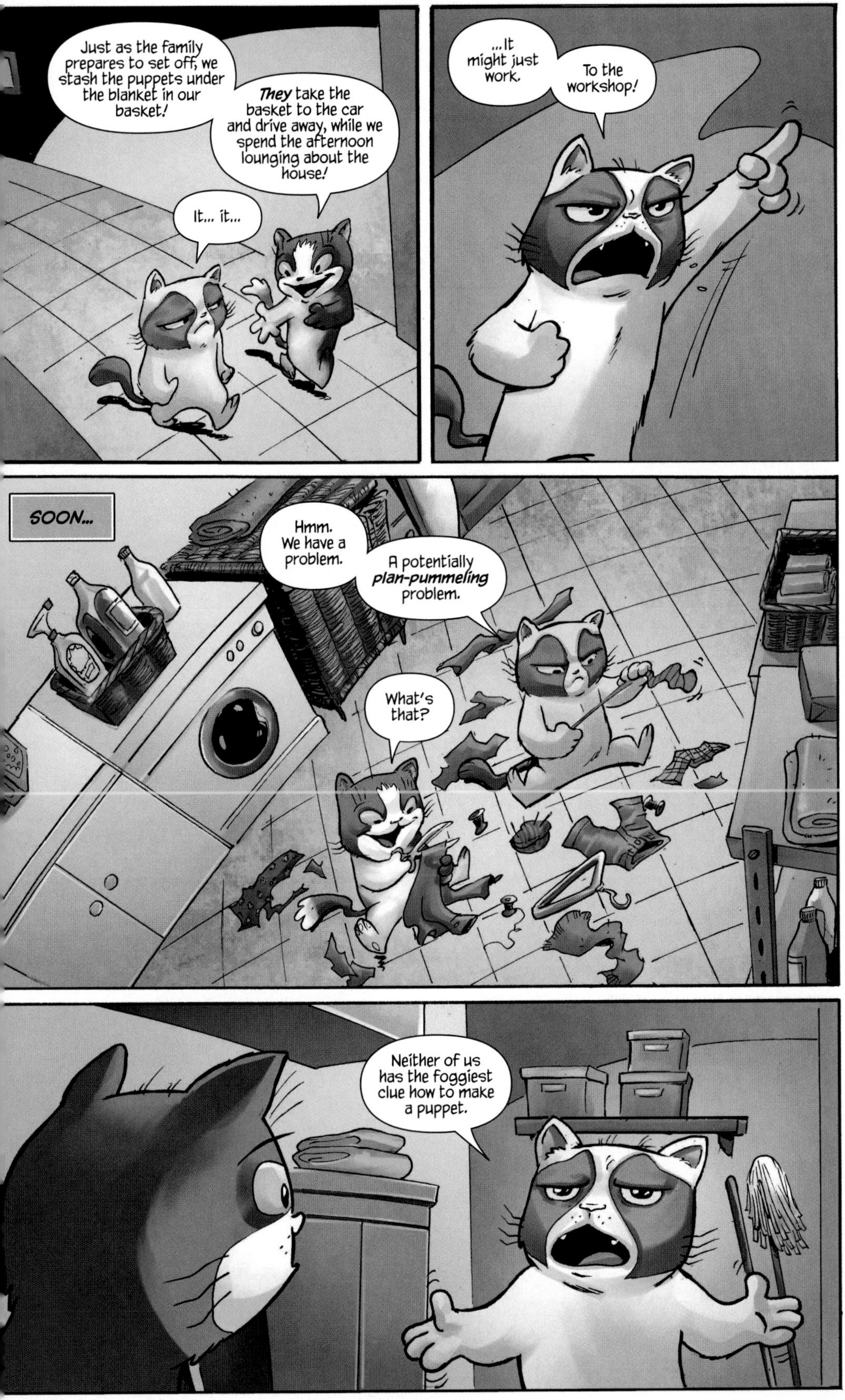
Just as the family prepares to set off, we stash the puppets under the blanket in our basket!
They take the basket to the car and drive away, while we spend the afternoon lounging about the house!
It... it...
...It might just work.
To the workshop!
SOON...
Hmm. We have a problem.
A potentially plan-pummeling problem.
What's that?
Neither of us has the foggiest clue how to make a puppet.

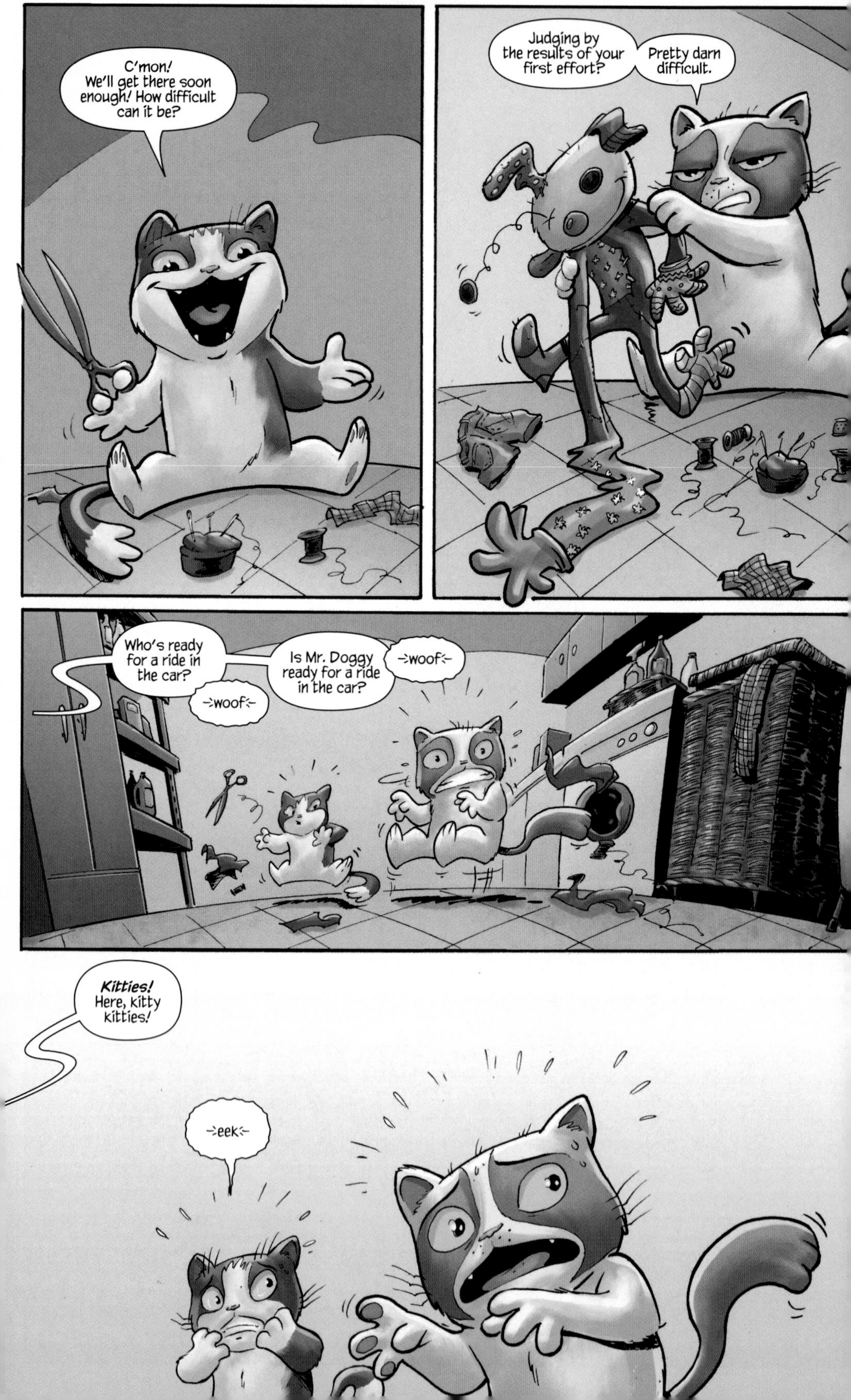
C'mon! We'll get there soon enough! How difficult can it be?
Judging by the results of your first effort?
Pretty darn difficult.
Who's ready for a ride in the car?
-woof-
Is Mr. Doggy ready for a ride in the car?
-woof-
Kitties! Here, kitty kitties!
-eek-

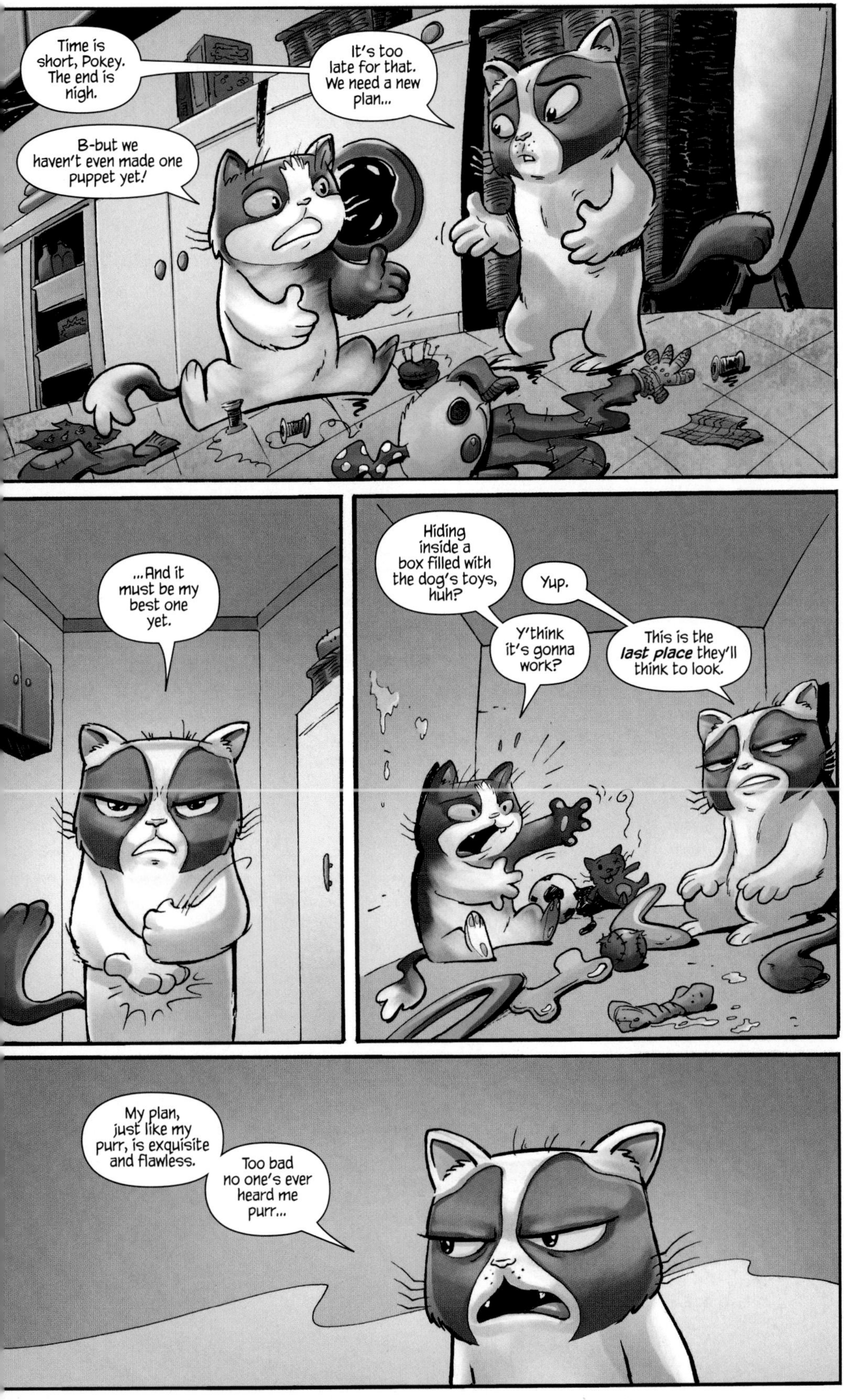
Time is short, Pokey. The end is nigh.
It's too late for that. We need a new plan...
B-but we haven't even made one puppet yet!
...And it must be my best one yet.
Hiding inside a box filled with the dog's toys, huh?
Yup.
Y'think it's gonna work?
This is the *last place* they'll think to look.
My plan, just like my purr, is exquisite and flawless.
Too bad no one's ever heard me purr...

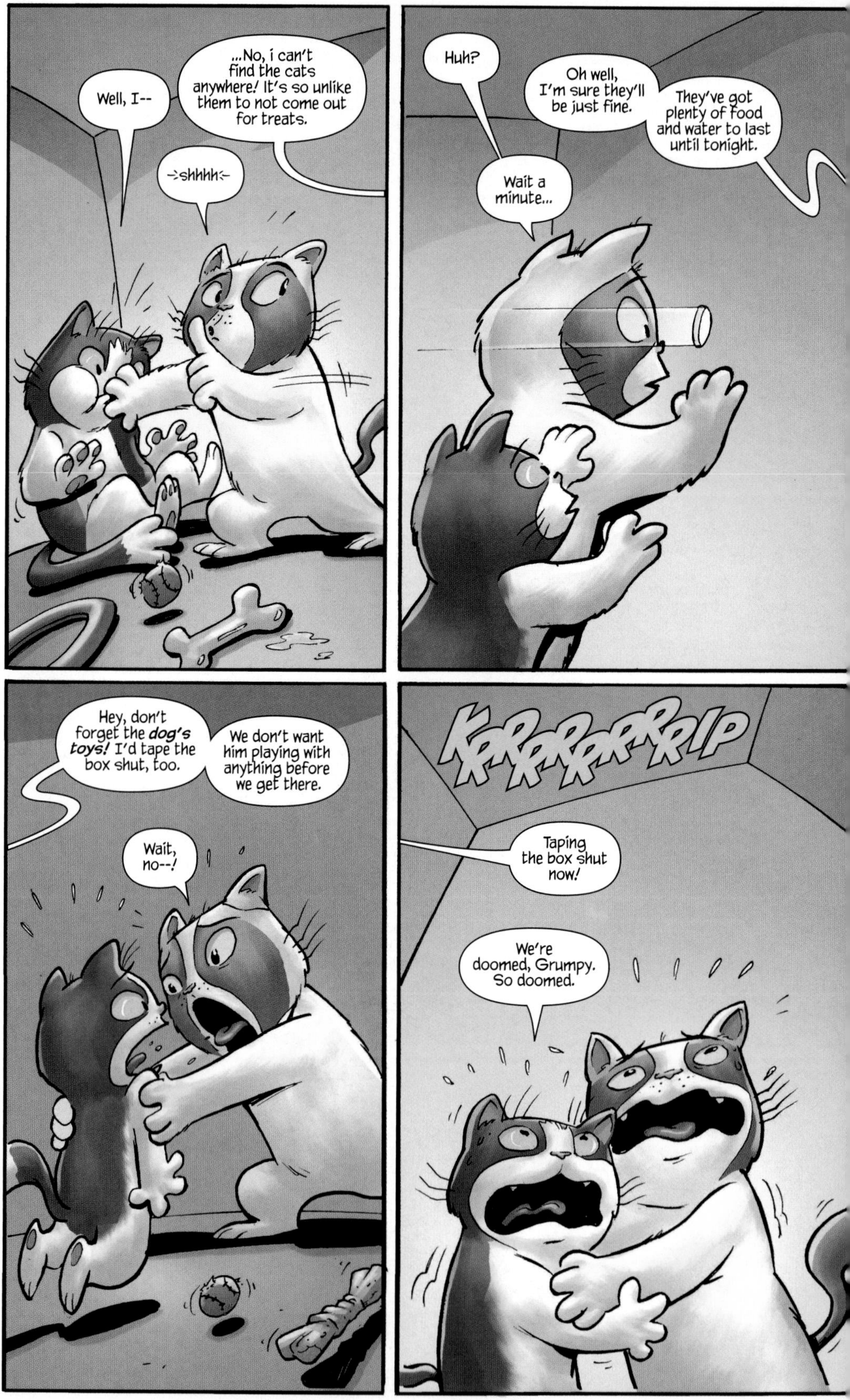
Well, I--
...No, i can't find the cats anywhere! It's so unlike them to not come out for treats.
-shhhh-
Huh?
Oh well, I'm sure they'll be just fine.
They've got plenty of food and water to last until tonight.
Wait a minute...
Hey, don't forget the *dog's toys!* I'd tape the box shut, too.
We don't want him playing with anything before we get there.
Wait, no--!
KRRRRRRRIP
Taping the box shut now!
We're doomed, Grumpy. So doomed.

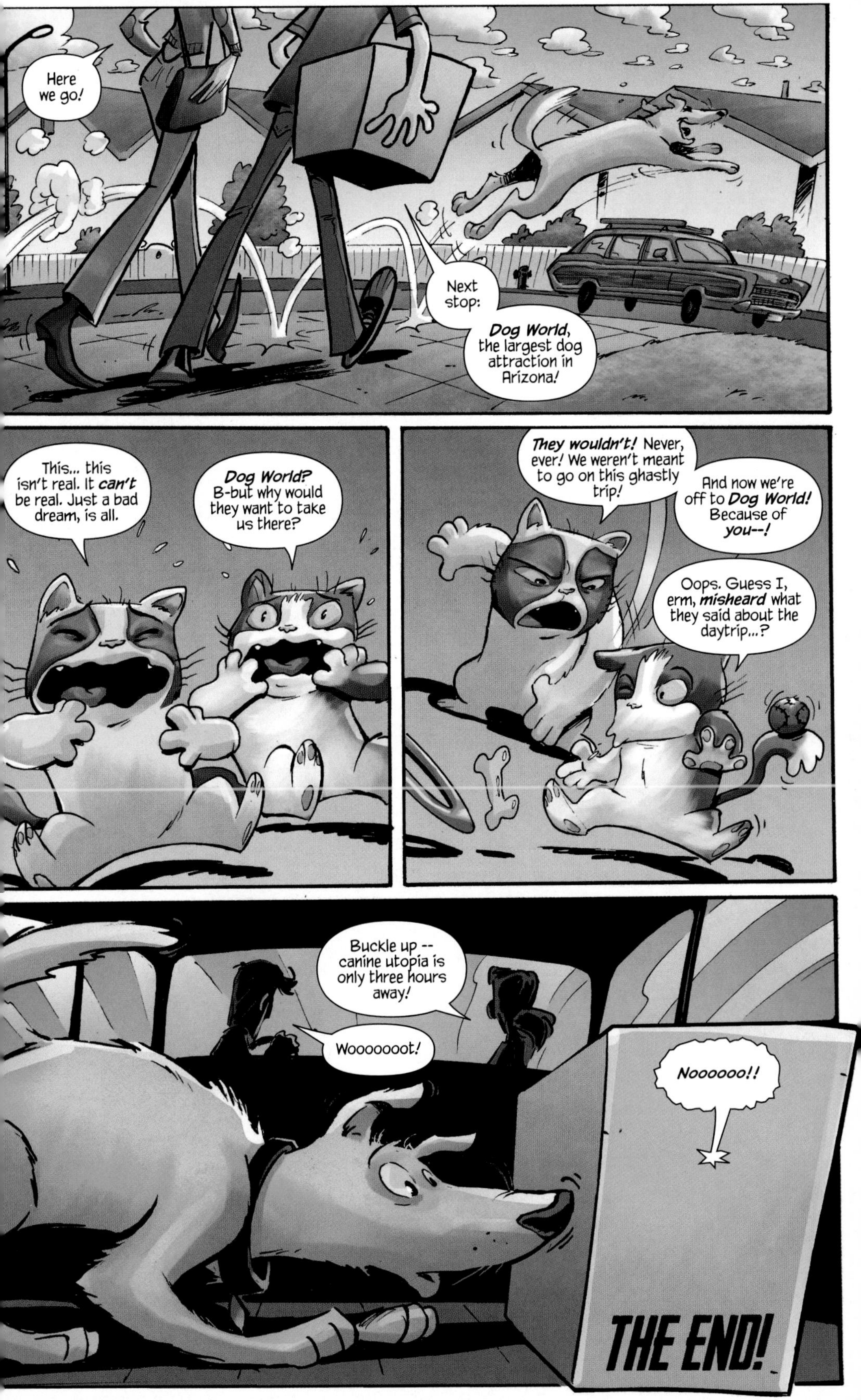
Here we go!
Next stop:
Dog World, the largest dog attraction in Arizona!
This... this isn't real. It can't be real. Just a bad dream, is all.
Dog World? B-but why would they want to take us there?
They wouldn't! Never, ever! We weren't meant to go on this ghastly trip!
And now we're off to Dog World! Because of you--!
Oops. Guess I, erm, misheard what they said about the daytrip...?
Buckle up -- canine utopia is only three hours away!
Woooooooot!
Noooooo!!
THE END!

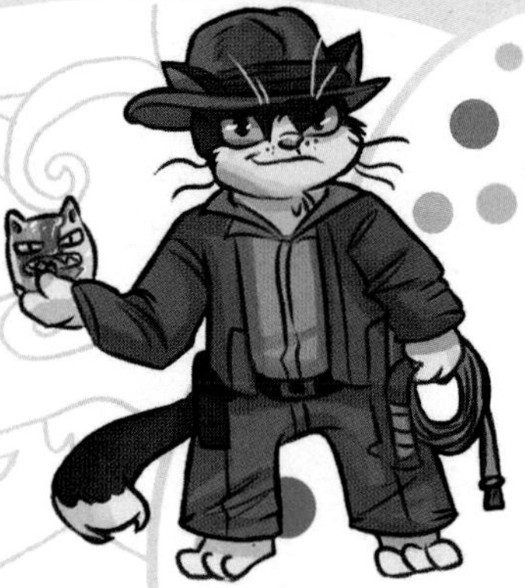

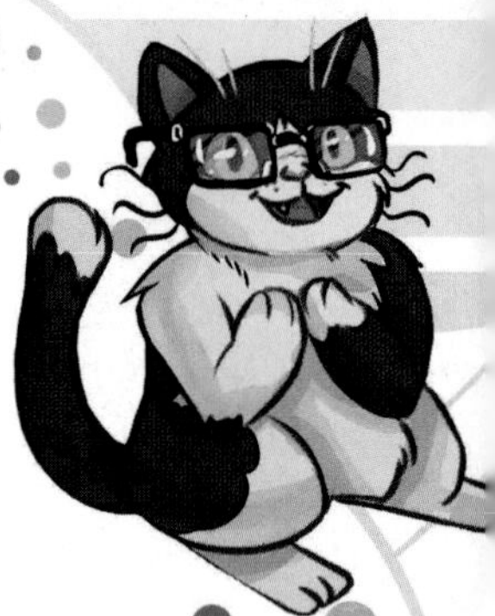

# Bonus Materials

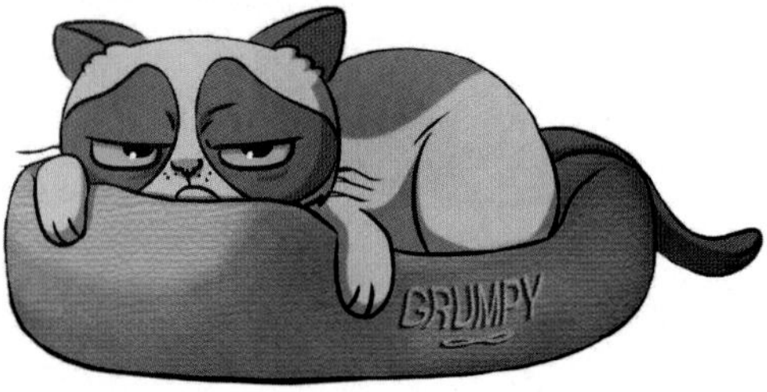
GRUMPY

Wait. The fun isn't over yet.

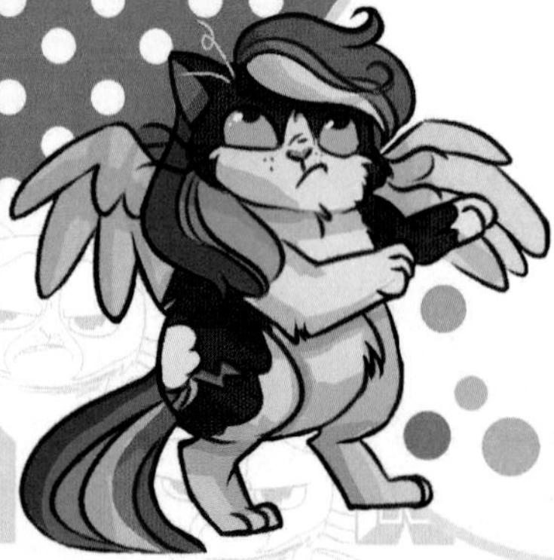

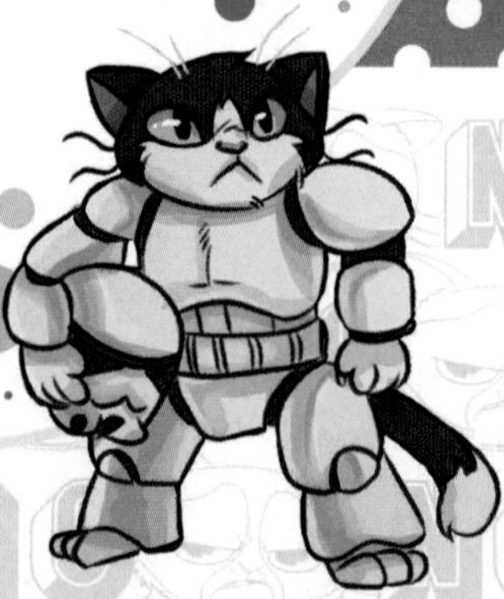

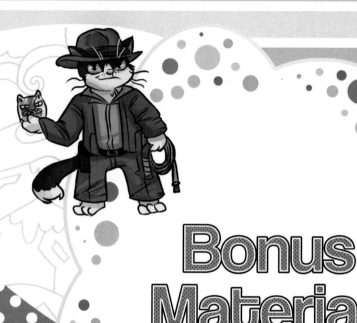

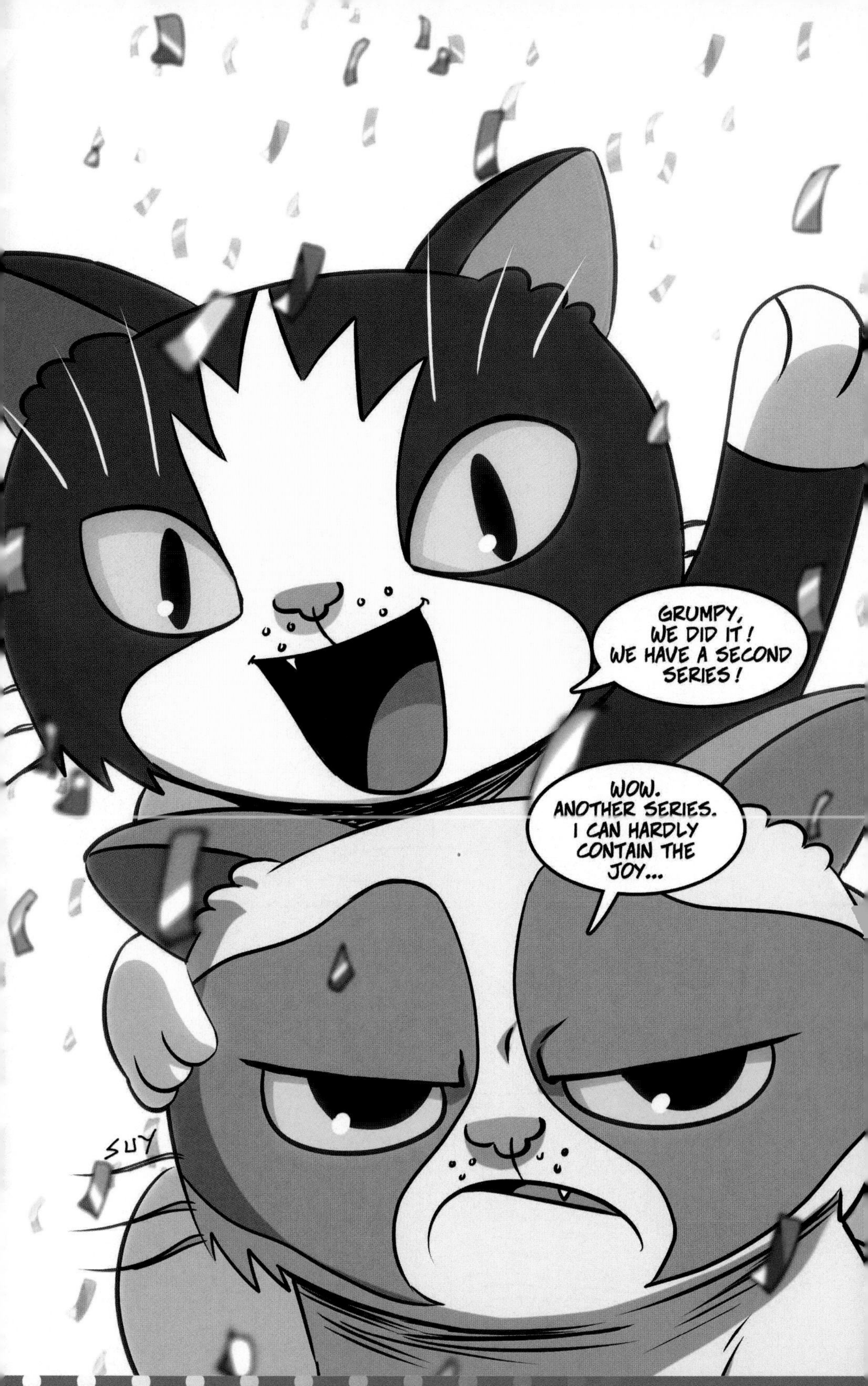
GRUMPY, WE DID IT! WE HAVE A SECOND SERIES!
WOW. ANOTHER SERIES. I CAN HARDLY CONTAIN THE JOY...
SUY

Issue 1, Cover A By **STEVE UY**

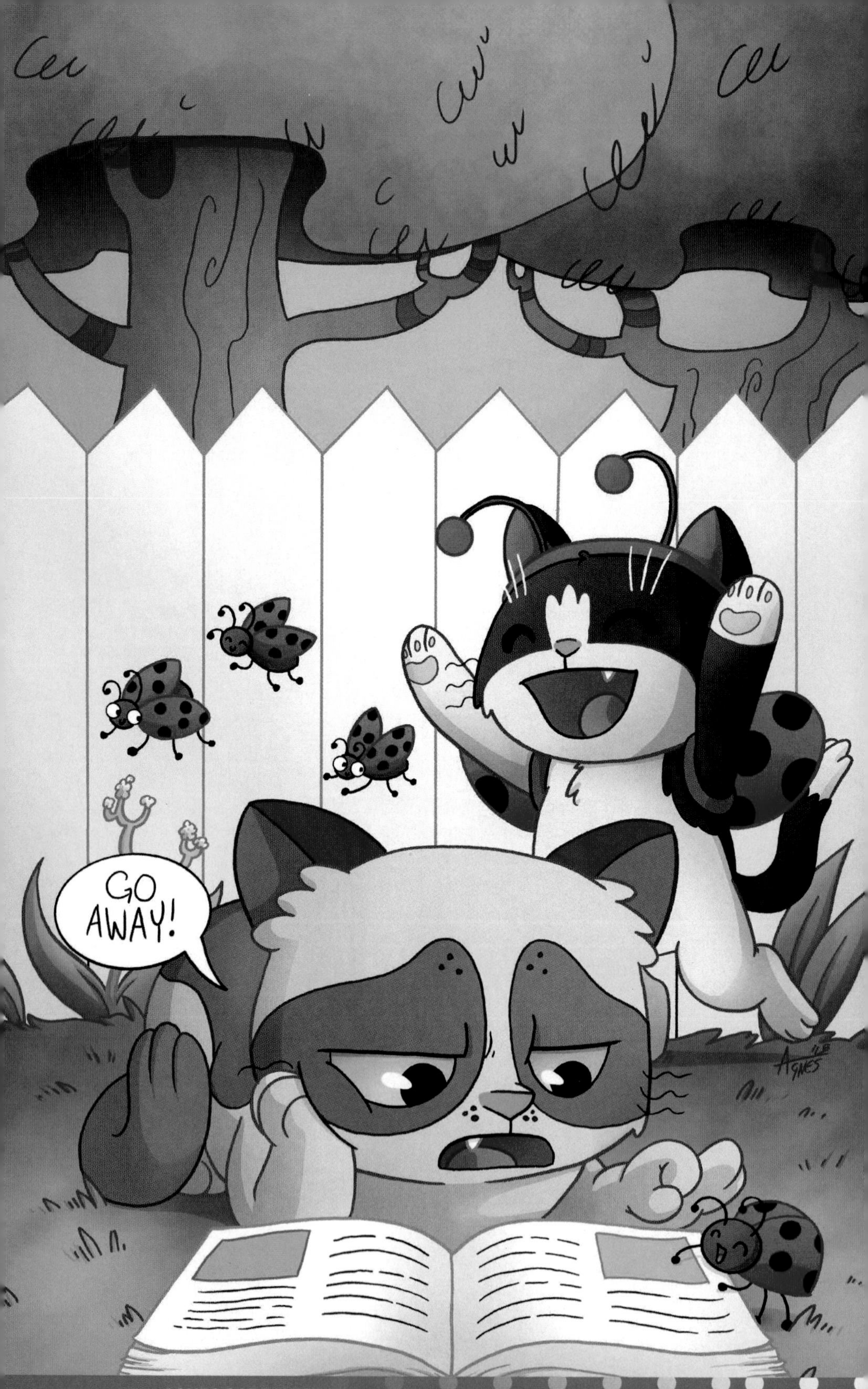
GO AWAY!

Issue 1, Cover B By **AGNES GARBOWSKA**

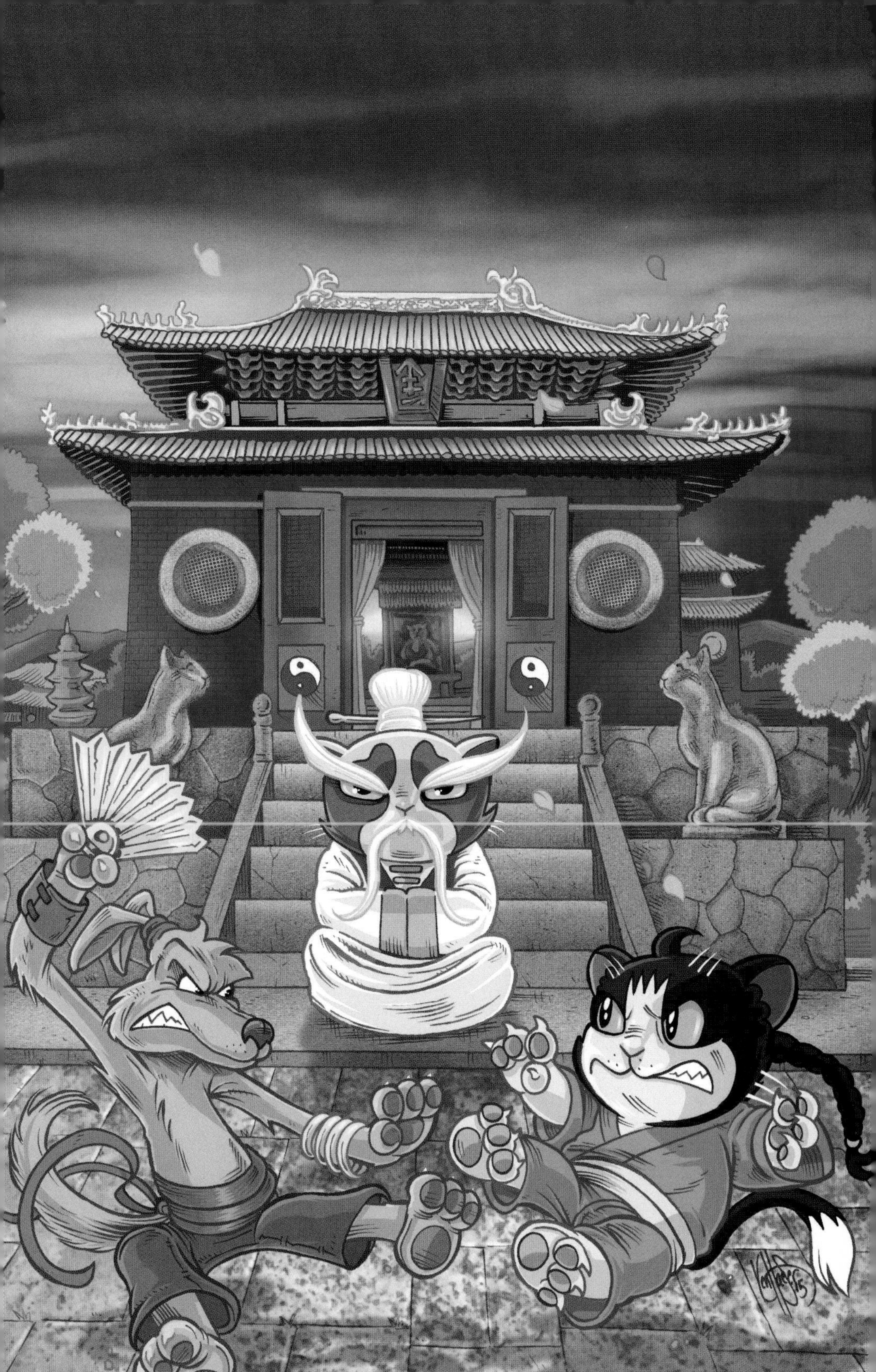

Issue 1, Cover C By **KEN HAESER**

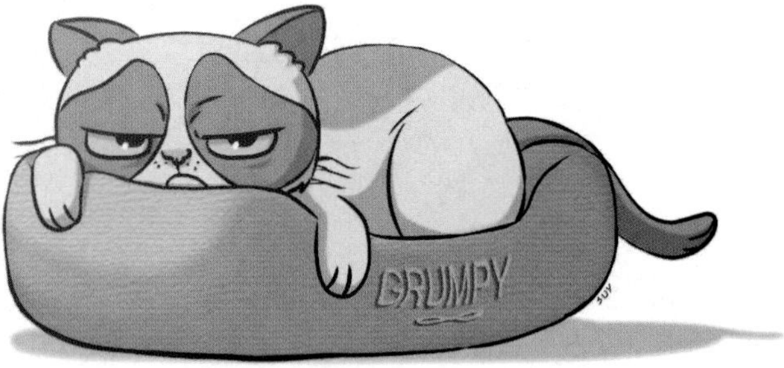
GRUMPY

Issue 1, Meme Authentix Cover By **STEVE UY**

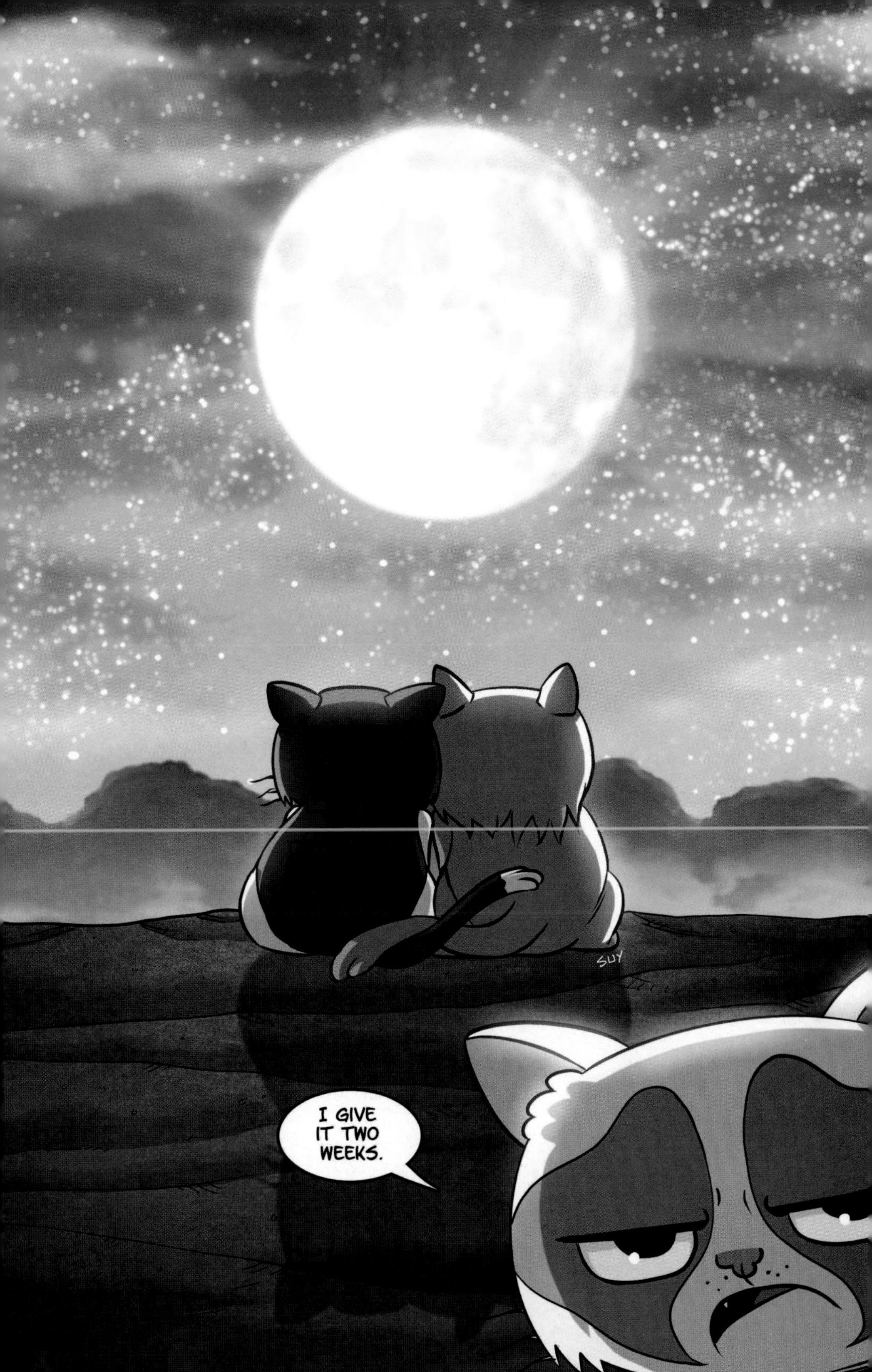
I GIVE IT TWO WEEKS.
SUY

Issue 2, Cover A By **STEVE UY**

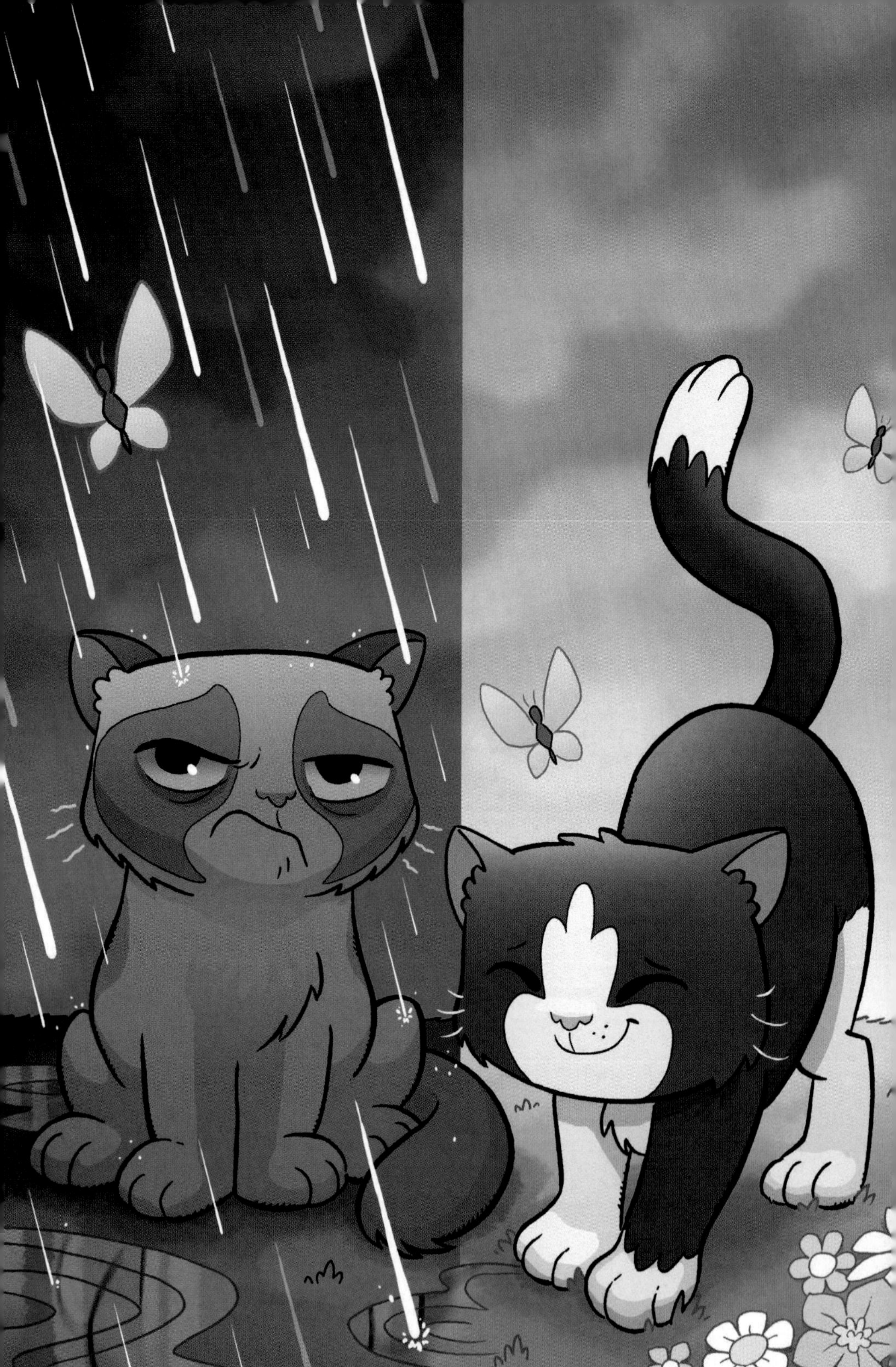

Issue 2, Cover B By **TONY FLEECS**

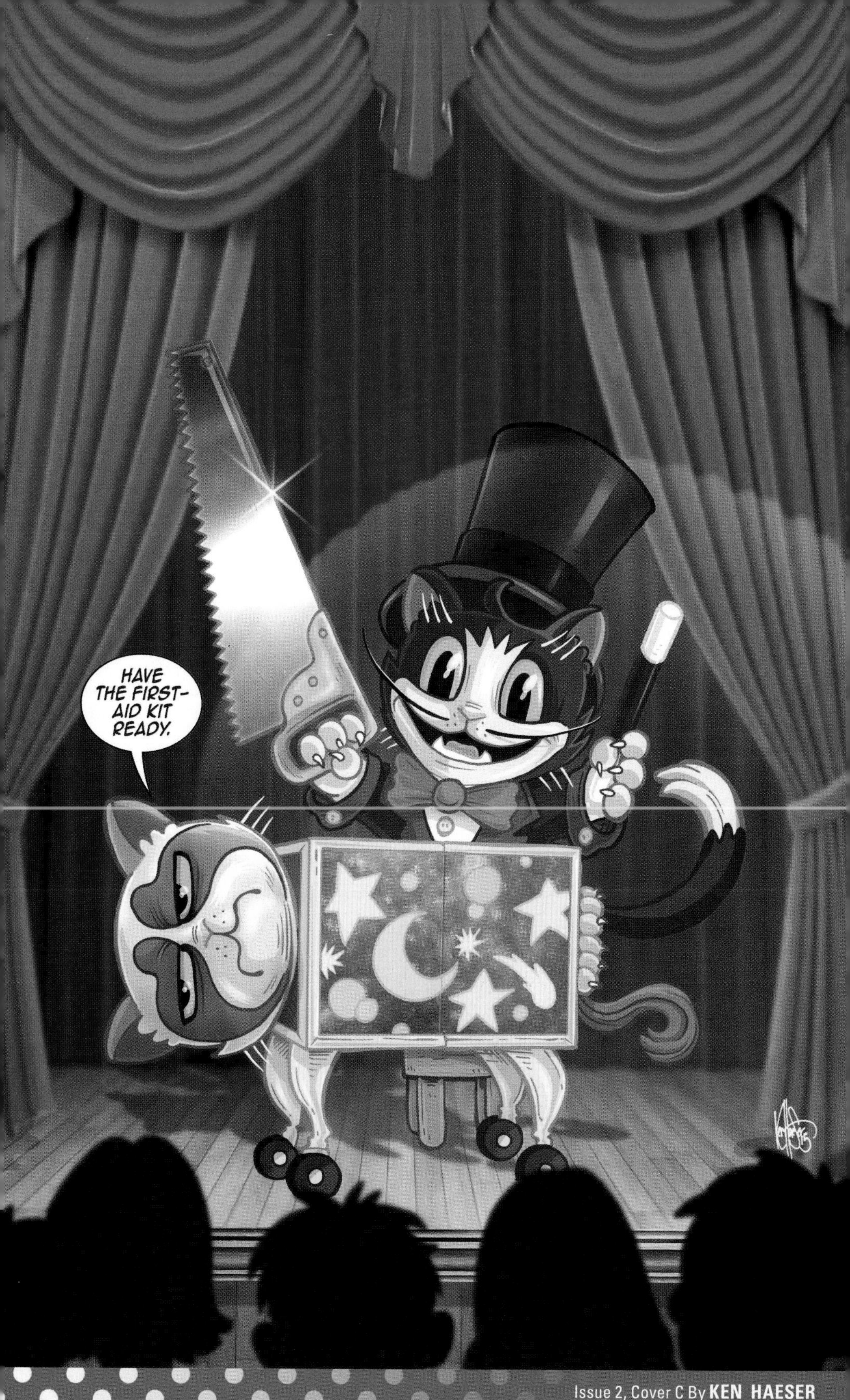
HAVE THE FIRST-AID KIT READY.

Issue 2, Cover C By **KEN HAESER**

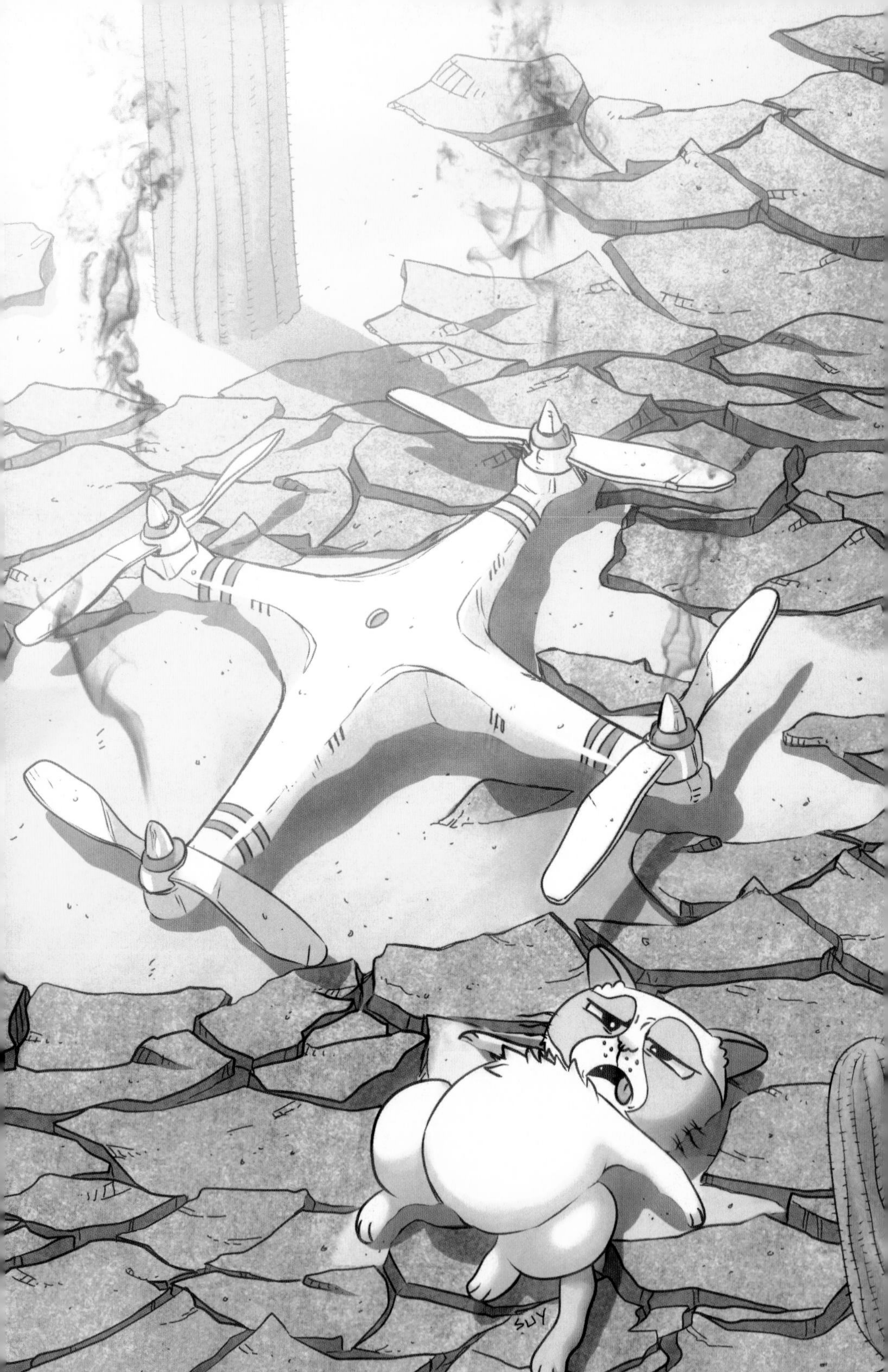
SUY

Issue 3, Cover A By **STEVE UY**

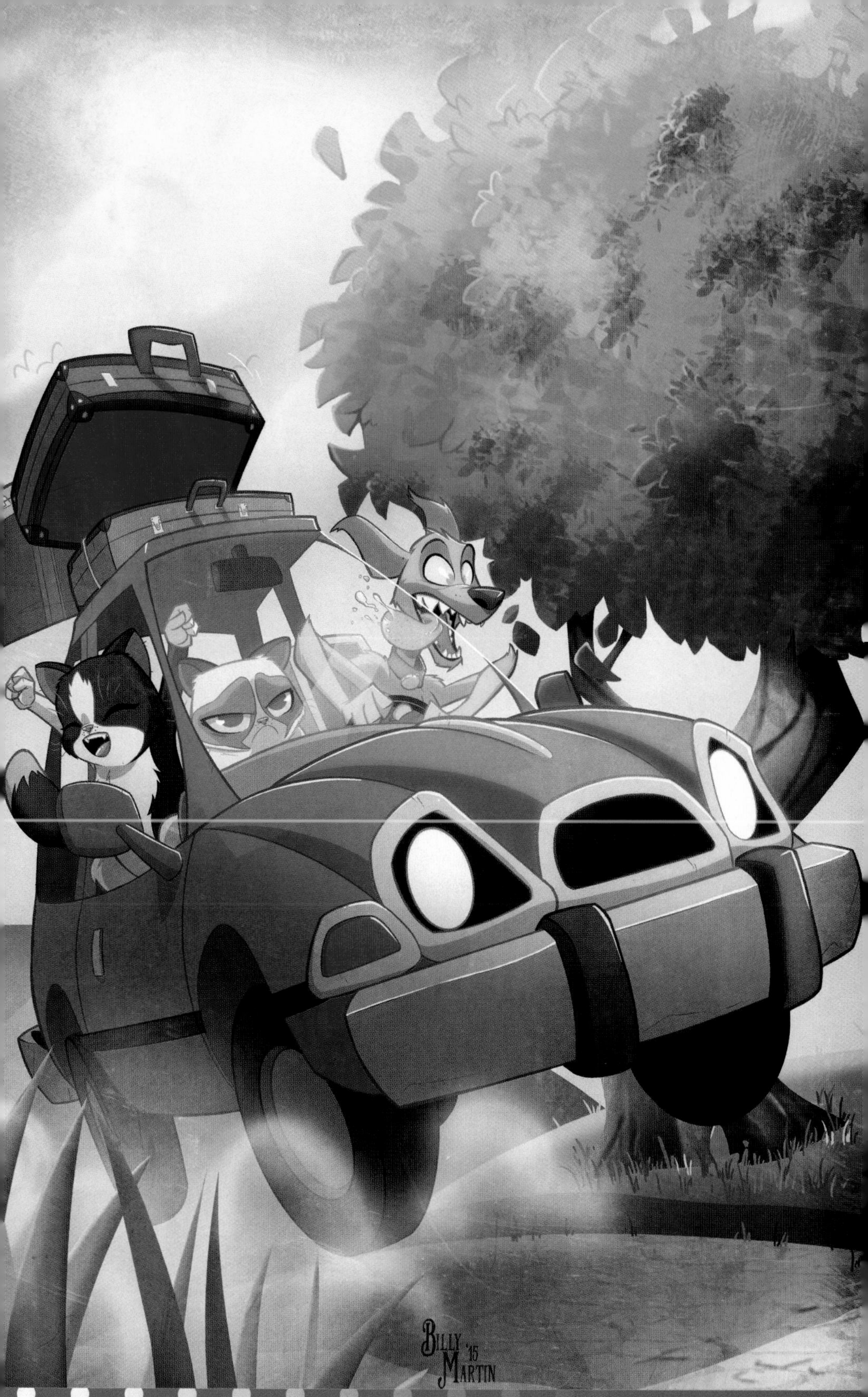
BILLY '15
MARTIN

Issue 3, Cover B By **BILLY MARTIN**

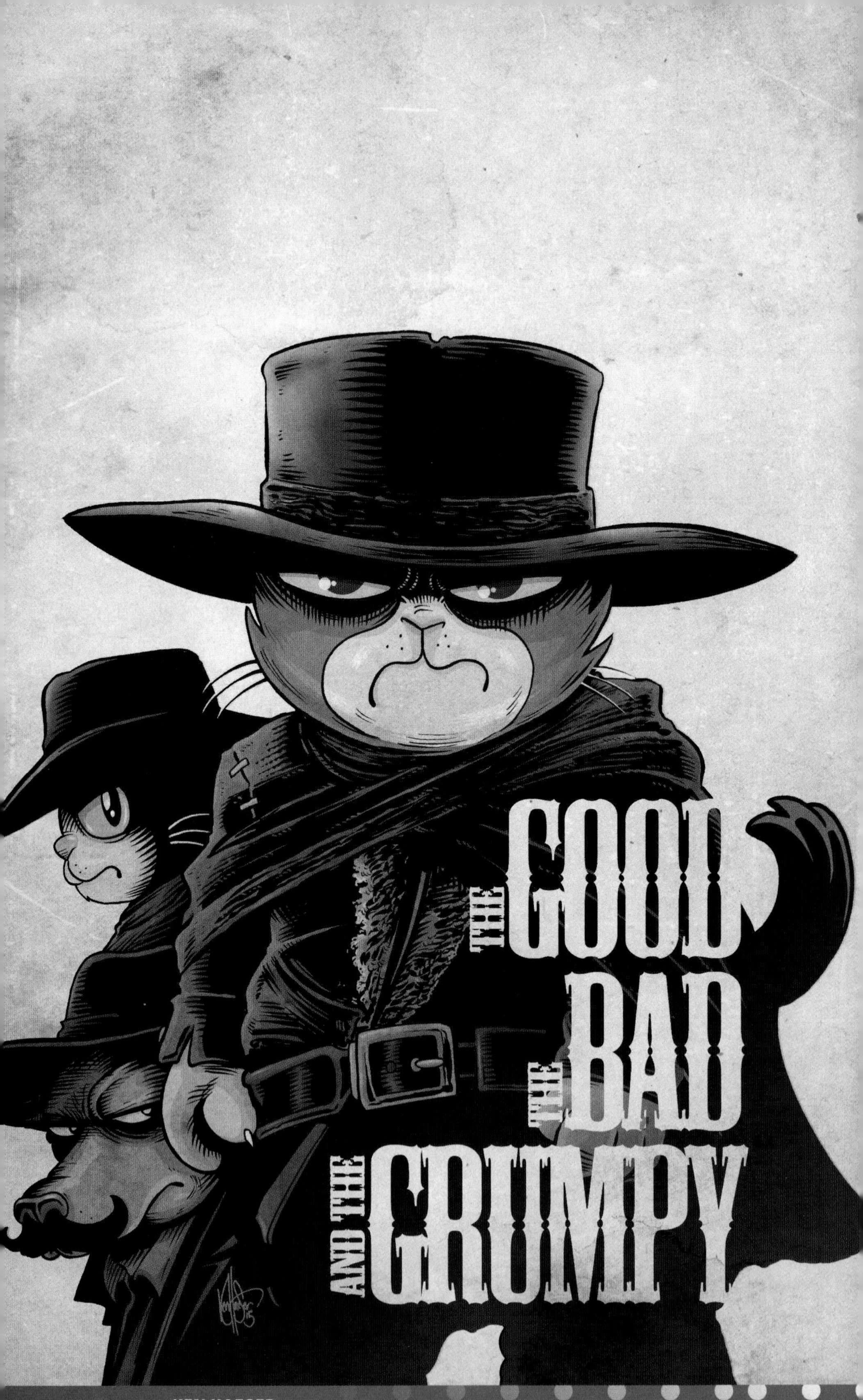
THE GOOD
THE BAD
AND THE GRUMPY

Issue 3, Cover C By **KEN HAESER**

# HANG IN THERE!
Until your enemies are beneath you. Then, aim for their heads.

# The A-MAZE-ING GRUMPY CAT!

CAN GRUMPY CAT FIND HAPPINESS?

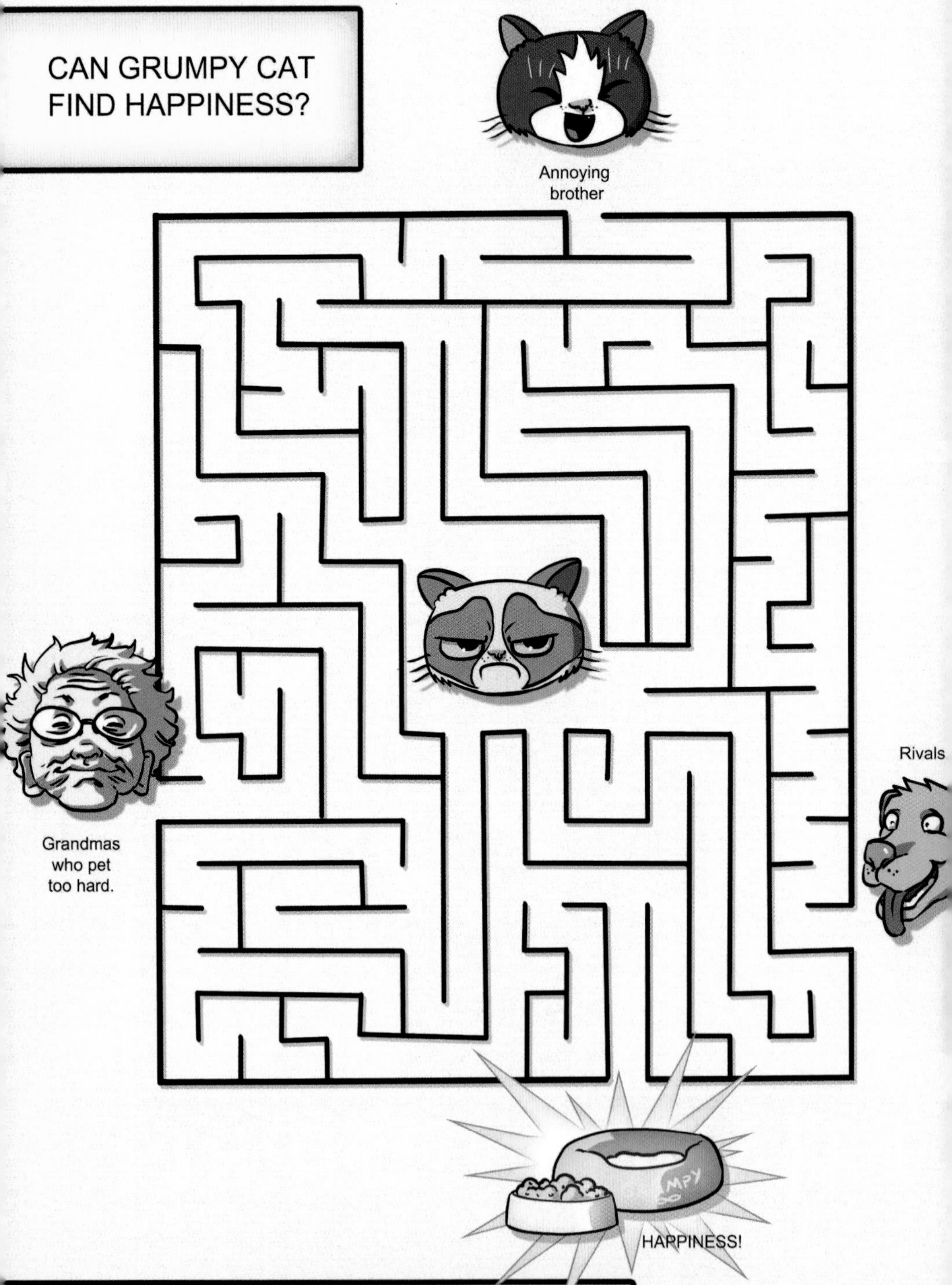

Annoying brother
Grandmas who pet too hard.
Rivals
HAPPINESS!


Grumpy's fate is all in your hands! Don't give up!

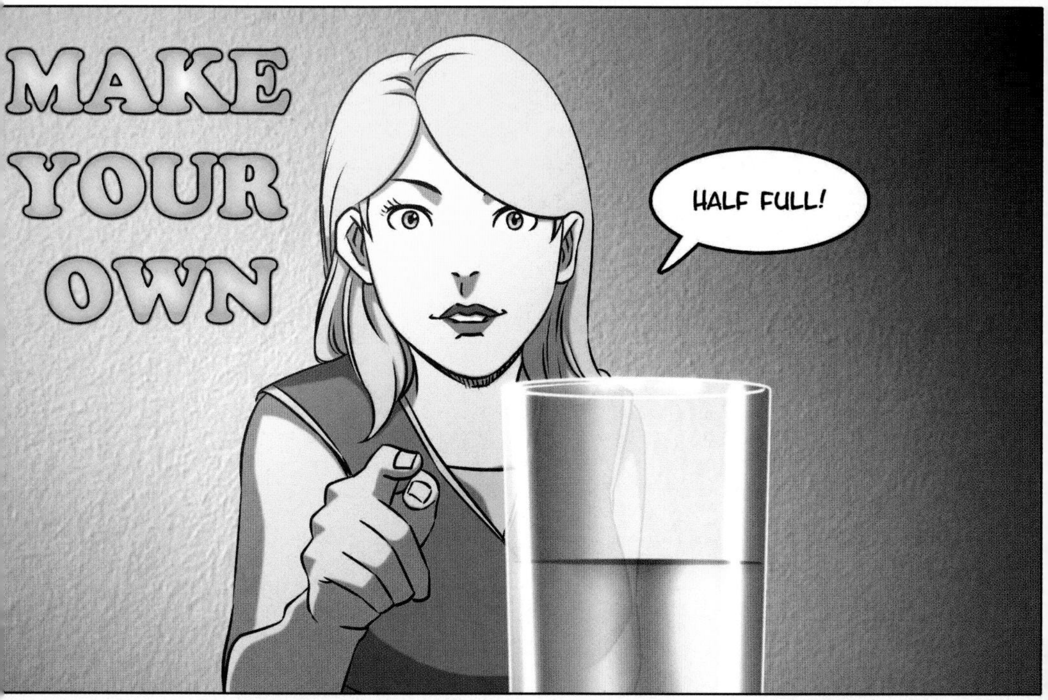
MAKE
YOUR
OWN
HALF FULL!

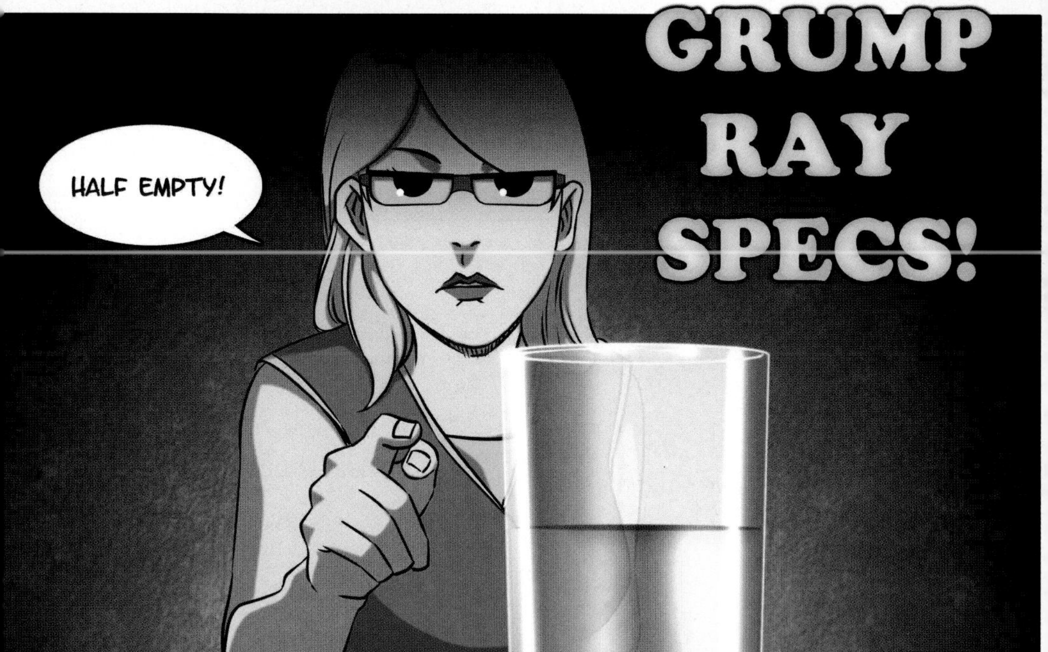
GRUMP
RAY
SPECS!
HALF EMPTY!

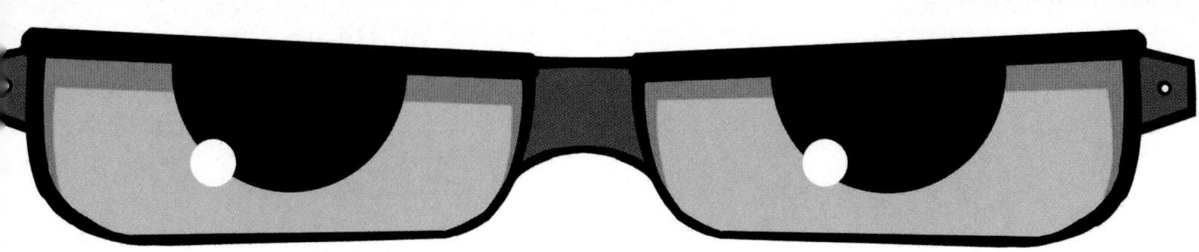

Instructions:

1. Carefully cut out or make a copy of the Grump Ray Specs.
2. Cut a hole in the temple corners.
3. Insert a rubber band or tie a string through the holes.
4. Wrap the Grump Ray Specs around your head and see the world through Grumpy's eyes!

# Dear Grumpy Cat

**Dear Grumpy Cat,**

What is the secret to life?

Signed,
Optimistic About The Future

### DEAR OPTIMISTIC (YOU SHOULD REALLY CHANGE THAT NAME.),

THREE WORDS.
NEVER. START. CARING.

**Dear Grumpy Cat,**

I have so many things I want to ask you I don't know where to start!

A) How can I stop my dog from barking at strangers?
B) What should I get my cat for Christmas?
C) I hate my boss. Should I quit my job?

Signed,
So Many Questions

### DEAR SMQ,

SIGH. SO MANY QUESTIONS SO LITTLE TIME.

A) SEND THE BEAST TO NEW ZEALAND.
B) SEE A. THAT WILL MAKE YOUR CAT HAPPY. TRUST ME.
C) I HAVE NO IDEA WHAT THIS "JOB" THING IS. IF IT INVOLVES A BARKING DOG THEN QUIT. NO BRAINER.

**Dear Grumpy Cat,**

How do you balance work and family?

Signed,
Walking the Tightrope of Life

### DEAR WTTOL,

IT'S A STRUGGLE EACH DAY TO FIND ENOUGH TIME TO TAKE MY CAT NAPS, BUT I MANAGE. THE IMPORTANT PART IS TELLING YOUR FAMILY TO LEAVE YOU ALONE.

PROBLEM SOLVED.

THE EDITORS OF THIS PUBLICATION ASKED IF I WOULD WRITE AN ADVICE COLUMN AND ANSWER QUESTIONS FROM ALL OF MY ADORING READERS. I TOLD THEM NO WAY. SOMEHOW, I'M STILL HERE. SEND ME YOUR TERRIBLE QUESTIONS ON TWITTER (TWITTER.COM/REALGRUMPYCAT) WITH THE HASHTAG #ASKGRUMPYCAT AND I'LL DO MY WORST TO ANSWER EVERY SINGLE ONE. THIS IS GOING TO BE AWFUL.

~GC

**Dear Grumpy Cat,**

I want to get a second dog but don't want my first dog to feel threatened. How do I do this?

Signed,
People Pleaser

## DEAR PP,

NEVER MIND GETTING A DOG. GET A CAT.

IF THE DOG FEELS THREATENED, SEND THE DOG TO NEW ZEALAND. THERE'S ANOTHER DOG WAITING FOR HIM THERE.

THIS ISN'T ROCKET SCIENCE, PEOPLE.

**Dear Grumpy Cat,**

I'm having a hard time saving my money since I spend it all on clothes, toys and eating out. Can you help me make and stick to a budget?

Signed,
Reckless Spender

## DEAR RS,

THE FIRST THING YOU NEED TO DO IS WRITE DOWN A LIST OF YOUR EXPENSES. ON ANOTHER SHEET OF PAPER WRITE DOWN "WANTS" VERSUS "NEEDS" IN TWO COLUMNS. THEN TAKE BOTH SHEETS OF PAPER AND TEAM THEM UP. IT WON'T SOLVE ANYTHING. BUT YOU GET TO TEAR UP PAPER.

**Dear Grumpy Cat,**

My wife is kind of a hoarder and I am more of a neat freak, how do I get her to organize her stuff?

Signed,
Odd Coupled

## DEAR OC,

POKEY HAS THAT SAME PROBLEM. HE HOARDS CAT TOYS. SO TO TEACH HIM A LESSON, I TAKE HIS TOYS AND BURY THEM IN THE BACKYARD. I LIKE TO CALL IT A SCAVENGER HUNT.

# GRUMPY GIFT TAGS

## Just copy, cut, and enjoy!

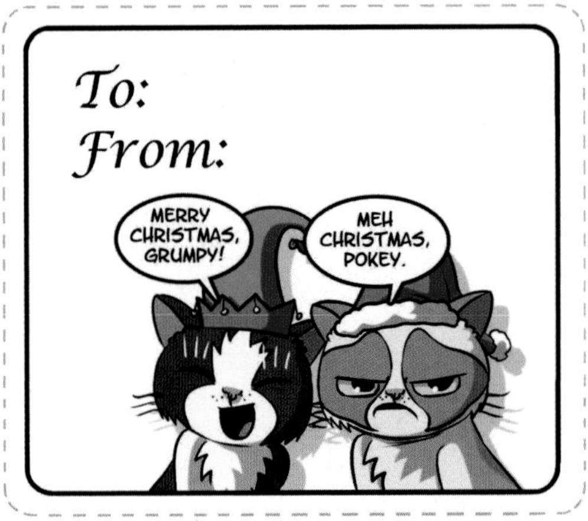
To:
From:
MERRY CHRISTMAS, GRUMPY!
MEH CHRISTMAS, POKEY.

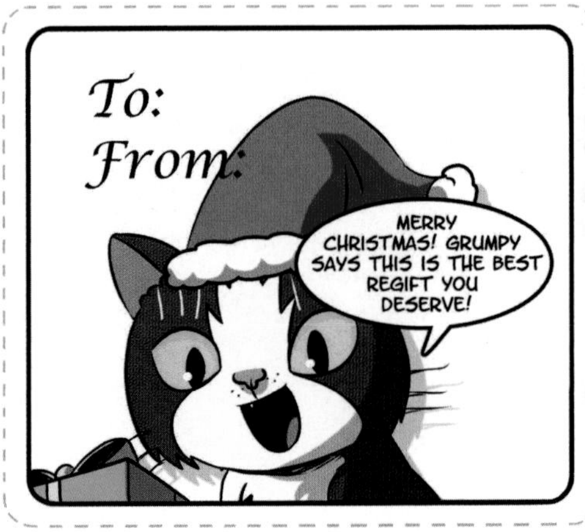
To:
From:
MERRY CHRISTMAS! GRUMPY SAYS THIS IS THE BEST REGIFT YOU DESERVE!

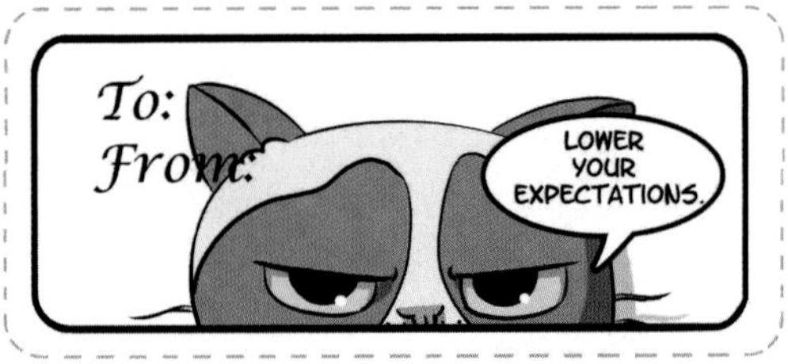
To:
From:
LOWER YOUR EXPECTATIONS.

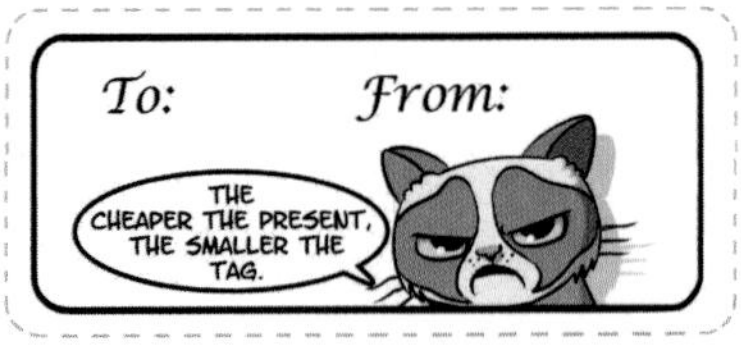
To:
From:
THE CHEAPER THE PRESENT, THE SMALLER THE TAG.

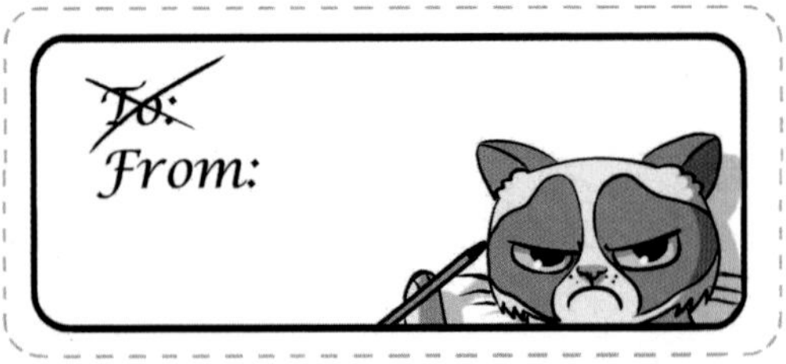
To:
From:

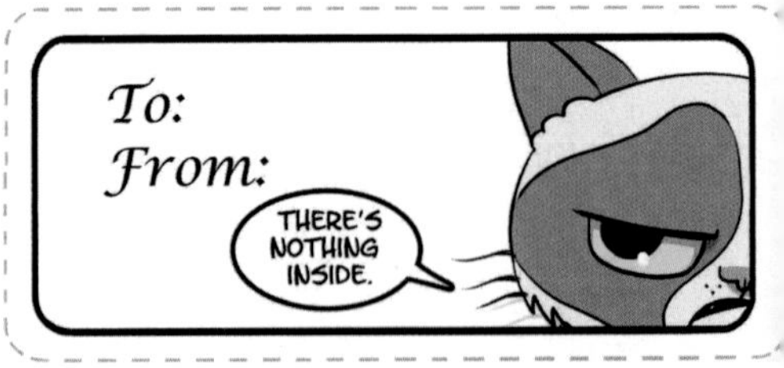
To:
From:
THERE'S NOTHING INSIDE.

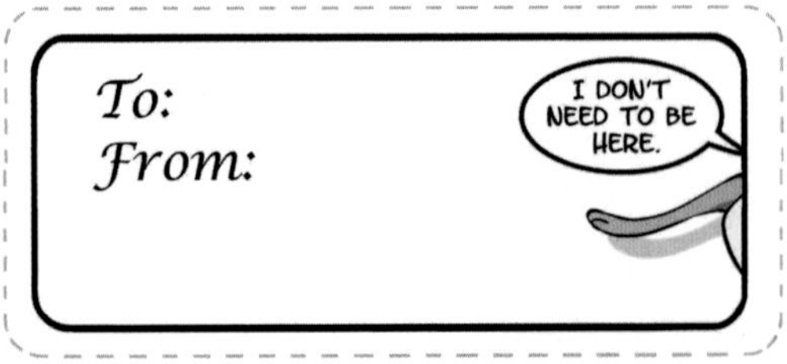
To:
From:
I DON'T NEED TO BE HERE.

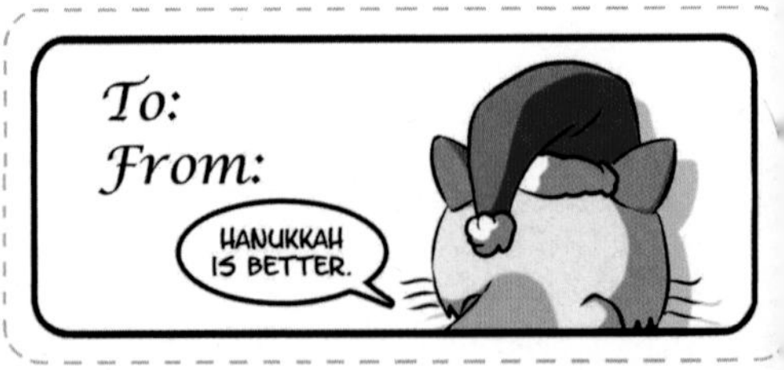
To:
From:
HANUKKAH IS BETTER.

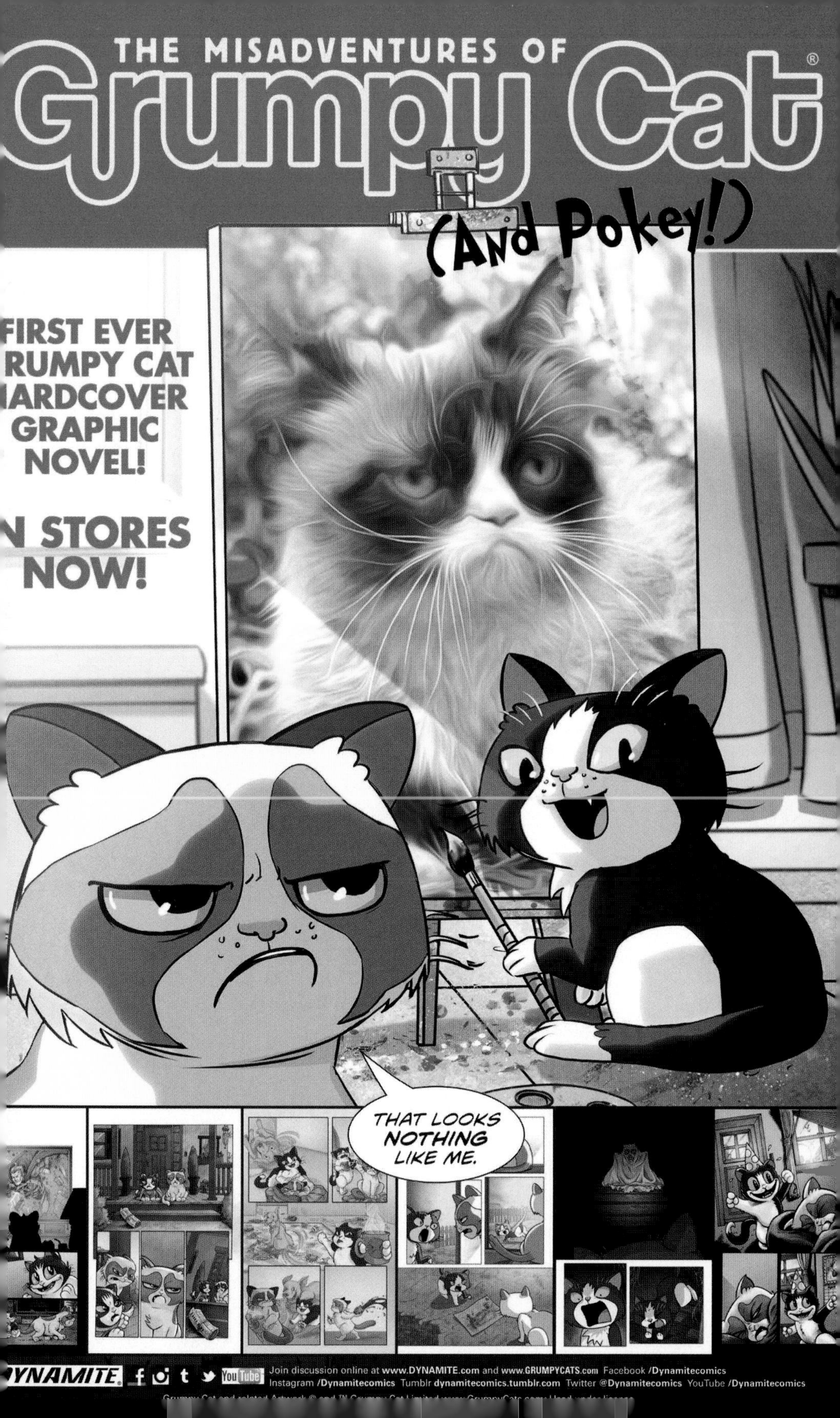
THE MISADVENTURES OF
Grumpy Cat®
(And Pokey!)
FIRST EVER
RUMPY CAT
ARDCOVER
GRAPHIC
NOVEL!
N STORES
NOW!
THAT LOOKS NOTHING LIKE ME.
YNAMITE
Join discussion online at www.DYNAMITE.com and www.GRUMPYCATS.com Facebook /Dynamitecomics
Instagram /Dynamitecomics Tumblr dynamitecomics.tumblr.com Twitter @Dynamitecomics YouTube /Dynamitecomics

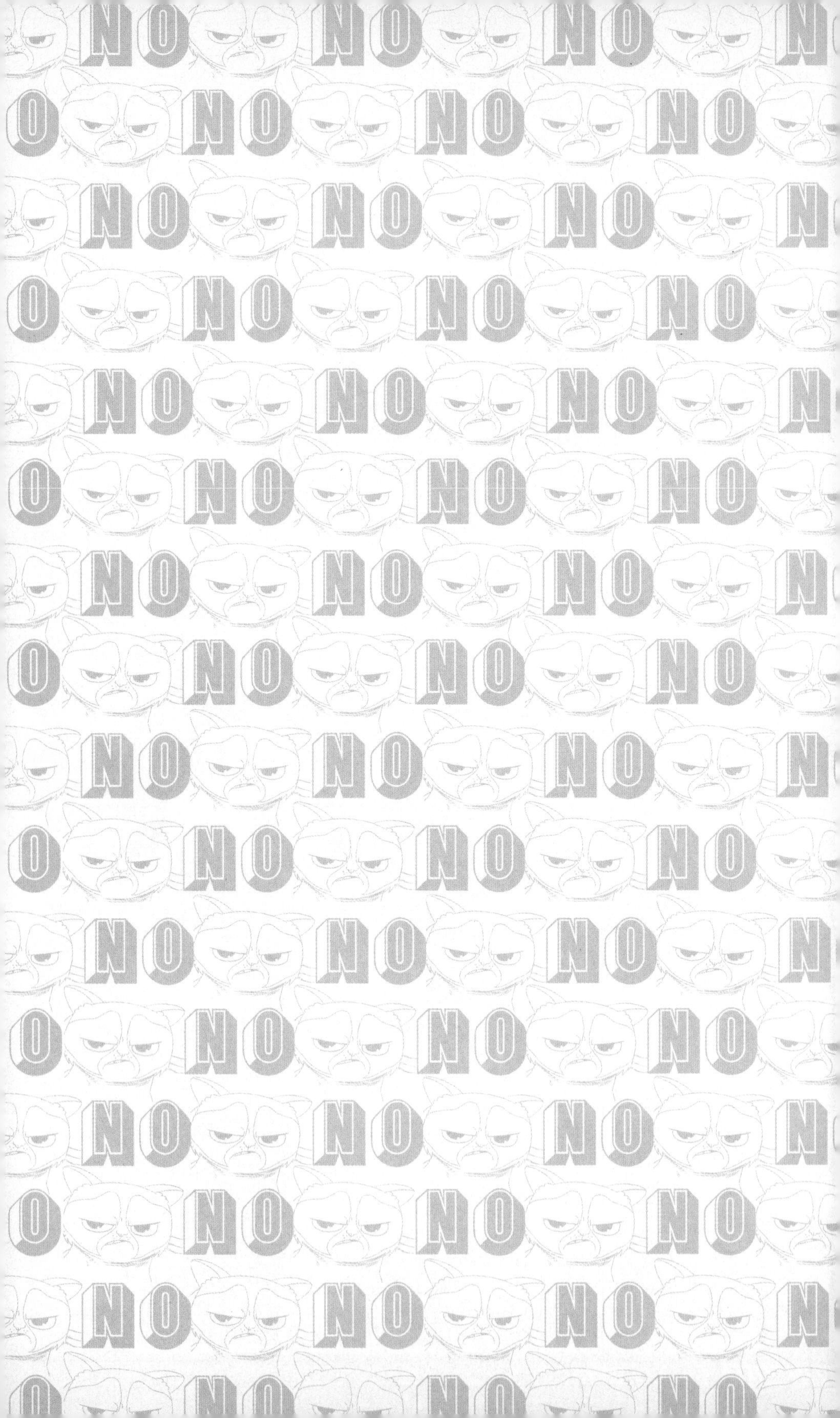
NO